HOW I FOUND YOU

GABRIELLA LEPORE

First published in Great Britain in 2012 by The Book Guild Ltd

This edition published in 2015 by
OF TOMES PUBLISHING
UNITED KINGDOM

Photography by Sasha Alsberg
Book design by Inkstain Interior Book Designing

For all the friends you meet by chance…as if by magic!

HOW I FOUND
YOU

It is foretold, on the day of his end,
so doth life begin
At the stroke of the eleventh hour,
he shall awaken
All will bow before him
All will perish at his mercy
Only one can end the blood spill
She, the girl with the heart of a witch
Before the hour turns to twelfth,
she must grant him her death
Two will take her to him, and all will be spared
Two will turn away, and all will be slaughtered

PROLOGUE

August

MY NAME IS ROSE WINCHESTER.

That's one of the three things I know for sure.

The other two are these:

One—it's raining.

Two—I belong to him.

I raced across the gravel yard, stumbling as I tried to move faster. It was useless. The faster I strove to run, the slower I seemed to move.

A bolt of lightning flashed above me, momentarily lighting my path. It made no difference. I didn't need light. I already knew where I was going.

The rain lashed down on me and the ice-cold wind stung my face. Normally I didn't mind the rain; in fact, I quite liked it. But this wasn't ordinary rain. It was angry and threatening. A sign that something sinister was on its way. Something far worse than a thunderstorm. In retrospect, I should have known that was the case—it certainly explained all the summer storms that had hit Millwood this year.

I quickly glanced back at the manor. My drenched hair whipped across my face. The rain-soaked strands were jet black—a far cry from the usual golden brown I was used to.

Squinting in the darkness, I could just about make out the shape of the unlit house. It was bleak and motionless, as though it had been abandoned long ago. But the fact that it looked deserted didn't exactly fill me with optimism. I knew they were in there. And if they weren't in there, then they were out here—which, I could categorically state, would have been much, much worse.

I was nearing the forest now. The way I saw it, I had two options.

Option one: blindly stagger my way through the maze of evergreens.

Option two: stick to the path, the only clear route leading out of the private estate.

I picked the latter.

Okay, so taking the path seemed like an obvious choice, although perhaps not the best way to stay hidden, but I didn't dare venture into the forest. Put it this way—if they were looking for me, they'd find me whether I was under cover or not.

The road dipped and I fell forward. My hands smacked down onto the waterlogged dirt track. Jagged clumps of mud and rocks dug into my palms; I winced as they pierced the skin.

Let me tell you this: I would never have considered myself to be a quitter, but I wouldn't have branded myself as a fighter, either. As it happened, I was so close to giving up that I didn't even care. Call me a quitter if you want, because after what I'd been through, I honestly didn't see any shame in it. In a way, it would have been a relief to have given up. I could have huddled beneath the evergreens to await my fate. I imagine it would have been quite pleasant. After all, fate's fate, right? Besides, I'd already lost a part of myself and as for the leftover part, I didn't want it.

But, as it turned out, I am a fighter, because—what do you know?—I got back onto my feet and carried on running. I guess that little leftover piece was worth fighting for after all. Or maybe I'm just stubborn.

As I dashed on, I noticed a flash of yellow on the ground. I dived on it, snatching it up and stuffing it into my shoe for safe keeping. This wasn't over yet.

Above the moan of the wind came a new sound. A sound that made my heart stop.

A car engine.

My stomach flipped. *I should have taken the forest,* I realised in hindsight.

Too late. A black Lamborghini shot past me at the speed of a bullet—almost knocking me down, I might add. I hated that car.

It skidded to an abrupt halt, the back wheels sliding across the mud until the nose of the car was facing me, like a panther waiting to pounce. The headlights were off and the windows were tinted, so I couldn't be sure who was behind the wheel. I figured it was one of three.

The car was blocking my path, so there was no going

forward. And backwards, well, that was probably a bad idea. It took several seconds before I realised that I hadn't taken a breath since hearing that engine. That's what mind-numbing fear does to you.

The driver's door opened and I nearly passed out from anticipation. I didn't know who I wanted to see step out of that car. In many ways, they were all equally as bad. But, at a push, I could tell you who I *didn't* want it to be.

"Oscar," I choked out at the sight of him. His raven black hair was damp and tousled. He wore black jeans and a charcoal T-shirt with a black, waxed jacket over top.

I despised how handsome he was. It was one of his best weapons. His ultimate weapon, however, was, quite simply, himself. Yep, I despised him.

"Come with me," Oscar said, his voice taut. The storm had swept strands of wet hair across his brow, and his eyes narrowed as he looked at me.

I was about to speak—to yell at him, in fact—but I felt my eyes sting and my chest tighten. There was no way I was going to let Oscar see me cry. Not because of him, anyway. I wouldn't give him the satisfaction.

"Get in the car," Oscar said through gritted teeth. His sullen, husky tone grew tenser with each word. "You are so… stubborn."

Okay, so that's what I'd said, too. But *he* didn't have the right to pass judgement over me.

I was about to say something. Hopefully something good.

"How could you do this to me?" I managed.

Oscar took an agitated step forward, closing the gap

between us. "I didn't."

"Yes, you did!" My eyes began to sting again.

I could tell Oscar was frustrated because he rubbed his hands over his face. I knew him well enough to know what was coming next. He'd kick something, or stamp his foot.

"Get in the car, Rose," he shouted, kicking the ground.

Part of me wanted to go, but I knew I wouldn't.

"Get in the car," Oscar said again, "or you will be killed." His statement reverberated hauntingly in the night air.

That was about as much as I could take.

I glanced over my shoulder. The manor was no longer in sight. Instead, I only saw the curving path, bounded by the evergreens on either side. I returned my gaze to Oscar. Even in the darkness I was able to make out his eyes; hard, yet pleading at the same time, the russet colour of autumn leaves.

"Trust me," he urged.

I had no voice now, but I didn't need words to show him that I did *not* trust him.

He grimaced. "*Trust* me," he repeated, his hand extended towards me.

"No!" The fury in my voice startled me. And by the look on his face, it startled him too.

Oscar's eyelids lowered. He gave me a look of regret. "Then you will die."

Without another word, he paced back to the car. He flung open the driver's door and slid into the seat, slamming the door shut behind him.

All of a sudden, the car headlights exploded to life. I

raised my hand to shield my eyes from the glare. Before I had time to regain my composure, I heard the hum of the engine, droning like the low growl of a wolf.

Hidden behind the blackened car windows, Oscar plunged his foot down onto the accelerator, causing the car to jolt forward. In the blink of an eye, the black Lamborghini was tearing down the path like a rocket, leaving only deep-set tyre marks in its wake.

I stood alone on the path, tears and rain spilling over my cheeks.

It had begun.

PART ONE

ROSE

CHAPTER ONE

Night Visitors

July 27th

WATCHING THE BUS LUMBER AWAY down the deserted road gave me a strange sense of foreboding. It wasn't as though I was overly fond of the bus—far from it!—but I was sorry to see it leave.

I dropped my suitcase onto the hot pavement and sat on the kerb beside it, leaning against the rusted *Welcome to Millwood* signpost.

The sleepy town of Millwood. My summer home. My aunt and uncle's home, to be more precise.

For as long as I could remember, I'd spent every summer in Millwood. My aunt Mary was my father's sister, and she and her husband, Roger Clements, and their one-year-old son, Zack, lived in a peaceful old manor house set in acres of private forest.

Don't get me wrong, I loved my trips to Millwood, but I could think of other places I'd rather have been. Namely, in my own home with my own parents, especially considering that the rest of my year was spent at boarding school—which was a drag, to say the least. But my parents were both photographers and they went wherever the work took them, which often meant away from me. This time it was Africa. I wasn't complaining, though; like I said, I loved Millwood. And I loved my aunt and uncle.

I closed my eyes and tilted my face towards the sky, letting the late-afternoon sun warm my skin. With a deep breath, I inhaled the fresh air and pleasant scent of pine. I'd been raised and schooled in metropolitan cities, so the countryside always felt like luxury to me. I savoured the brief opportunity to unwind after my tedious bus ride.

Just the thought of it made me yawn.

Although, I must admit, the bus journey wasn't the sole culprit for my lethargy. I hadn't been sleeping well lately. And it was becoming more apparent than ever that the sleepless nights were taking their toll on me. It wasn't that I *couldn't* sleep; it was more that I didn't *want* to. It seemed a little childish to be afraid of nightmares, especially at sixteen, but anyone who could laugh off a nightmare clearly wasn't having the one that I was having.

Uck. It made my stomach knot.

The strident honk of a car horn blasted through the tranquillity.

I jumped at the noise and banged my head on the signpost.

A few metres down the road a powder-blue minivan pulled up onto the kerb. I knew the driver—a cheery woman in her early forties with a round face, broad smile and fluffy, strawberry-blonde hair.

My aunt, Mary.

She waved frantically whilst clambering out of the car.

"Rose!" she exclaimed, hurrying along the pavement towards me.

"Hi, Mary!" I bounced up and greeted her with a hug. "It's so good to see you!" Sometimes when people say that, they're just being polite, but I meant it.

"You, too! You look so beautiful!" Mary took off her oversized sunglasses and gave me a thorough inspection.

I blushed. Beautiful was such a strong word. What made a person beautiful, anyway?

I saw Mary as beautiful. Agreed, she wasn't the stereotypical supermodel or the glamorous Hollywood-type. But I loved her, so she was beautiful to me.

As for myself, I was just *me*. I'd hardly have described myself as extrovert, and my dress was always downplayed; that day I was wearing jeans and a casual purple top. My eyes were dark green and my hair was mousey brown. I supposed that, to most people, I probably looked like any other teenage girl, but not to my aunt. She insisted that I was 'unique'.

I couldn't decide if that was a good thing or a bad thing, but it didn't particularly bother me either way. What bothered me was her saying it in public! The woman was unstoppable! That was Mary, though. She was affectionate, too—especially towards me. She once told me that she thought of me as a daughter, and I quite liked that. Actually, the feeling was reciprocated, though I'd never said it out loud; it seemed too cruel towards my real mother. But I was pretty sure Mary knew.

She gave me another squeeze. "How was your trip?"

"Okay. I had the same driver as last year."

Mary snapped her fingers in recognition. "Mr Show-Tunes! What did he play on the stereo this time?"

"The soundtrack to *Cats*." I raised a cynical eyebrow.

"Six hours, on repeat." The lyrics were still playing on a loop in my mind. It was quite traumatic, actually.

"Ooh, I wonder what you'll get next year." Mary's eyes lit up. "Fingers crossed for *Mamma Mia*."

She chuckled warmly at my dubious expression.

"Come, come," Mary bustled me over to the minivan. "Come and see Zack. He's a lot bigger than when you last saw him."

I peeked into the back of the car. Baby Zack, with his wispy blonde hair and tiny dungarees, sat contentedly in his top-of-the-range car seat.

Mary fussed over him for a while, showing me each and every one of his rattles and accessories. After several Zack-related anecdotes, she threw her hands in the air. "Listen to me, *yap*, *yap*, *yap*!" she chortled. "I'll bet you're desperate to get back to the house and put your feet up."

Yes. "No, I'm fine," I said aloud, brushing off the remark, "whenever you're ready."

"Oh honey, you don't have to be polite for my benefit!"

That was one of my favourite things about Mary—she knew me scarily well.

I smiled.

"Let's get you home," Mary said, grinning.

Of course, 'home' wasn't technically *my* home, but it was as good as.

With one last effort, I hauled my suitcase into the back of the minivan and climbed into the front passenger seat. Mary did a final Zack-check before getting behind the wheel.

As soon as we were belted in, she started the engine and steered the car out onto the main road. We drove along for quite a while, talking comfortably and gazing out at the scenic chain of trees. It wasn't until ten minutes into the journey that Mary slowed down and pulled out onto a smaller access road—the Clements' private road. The journey suddenly became noticeably bumpier and narrower—so narrow, in fact, that the branches of the evergreens brushed up against the windows on either side of the car.

I tried to peer through the trees into the depths of the forest. Somehow it seemed darker than usual, even with the blush of daylight creeping through the branches. I looked up at the evergreens as we passed each one by. They held themselves staunchly, like soldiers standing in a ceremony to welcome me home.

After a minute or two, the narrow road opened onto a gravel driveway and Mary rolled to a stop.

There was the manor.

I couldn't count the number of times I'd seen that house, but it always took my breath away. It was like something straight out of a Jane Austen novel—grand and gothic, and still bearing most of its original features.

My uncle Roger stood at the door, waving just as Mary had done earlier. In my opinion, he looked like the classic archetype for Lord of the Manor: smartly dressed with rectangular glasses and greyish hair parted to the side.

I hopped out of the car and crossed the driveway to greet him, while Mary busied herself untangling Zack from his car seat.

"Hello, dear!" Roger gave me a slightly awkward hug. "You look well. New haircut? It's lovely."

I smiled to myself. *Nope, it's exactly the same haircut as last year.* Long and a little wavy… I wasn't one for change. But I had to hand it to Roger—the poor man had learned the hard way about the repercussions of not noticing Mary's haircuts.

I decided to throw him a bone. "Thanks!" I said, shaking out my hair.

Roger's chest puffed out with pride for his successful observation skills. "Yes, it's very *you*," he elaborated.

"Oh, that's kind of you to say."

"I'll fetch your suitcase," Roger offered.

"No, don't worry, I can get it." I trotted back to the minivan and heaved the suitcase from the boot. It dropped heavily to the gravel, missing my foot by a fraction of a centimetre.

The suitcase had wheels, but sometimes they were more like a burden than an aid. I opted to drag it across the gravel.

Roger took this to mean that I was struggling. He rushed across the yard to my rescue.

I relinquished my grip on the handle and made my way

into the house.

Once inside, the memories of previous years came flooding back to me. The smell of trees and vanilla filled the air; it triggered a wonderful sense of *home.* I couldn't imagine a more stunning place to live. Even the hallway was elegant, with a tall wooden coat rack and varnished oak flooring.

I eyed the wide staircase in front of me. "Can I still have my usual room?" My gaze travelled up the stairs.

Mary appeared behind me, carrying Zack in one arm. "Yes, the attic room is all made up for you. Now, are you sure you don't want to try one of the guest bedrooms on the main floor this year?"

I shook my head adamantly. "No, I love my room."

"I have no idea why," Mary chuckled. "It's so small. It's a shoebox compared to the rest of the house."

I laughed. "You'd be surprised. It's like a Tardis when you actually get inside it."

"It's your special room, isn't it, Rose?" Roger joined in with a good-natured grin. "Old faithful. This girl doesn't like change."

Well said, Roger, I thought. *The man knows his stuff.*

"I'm too set in my ways to learn how to get to any of the other rooms," I added in jest.

"Dear me," Roger teased, "it would be a terrible hassle to move you now. However would you cope!" He lugged the suitcase to the foot of the stairs. "I'll take your bag up and then you can get settled."

"It's okay, I can manage," I said, taking the handle from

Roger and hoisting it up into the air.

The main staircase was fitted with wine-red carpet, and running alongside it was an extravagant, cast iron banister complete with an authentic oak handrail. As I lugged the case upstairs, I could guarantee that my aunt and uncle were wincing every time it crudely bashed against the banister. Oops.

The top of the staircase opened out into a long corridor leading off to seven bedrooms and an enormous family bathroom. To the far right was a second stairway—a smaller one, as though it had been added as an afterthought. I heaved the case to the smaller flight of stairs—my personal staircase—and shuffled upwards. At the tenth step there was an arched, wooden door. I gave it a little nudge and it swung open.

My room.

I sighed gratefully at the sight of it. It was uncomplicated: a neat, rectangular attic with a sloping ceiling and only enough space for the bare essentials. It took a few seconds to reacquaint myself with the layout. At the back of the room stood a low-set single bed with a pine headboard and coffee-coloured bedding. The rest of the furniture was spread out simply: a pine chest of drawers was standing opposite the bed, with a matching pine wardrobe and dressing table at the window.

The window. I smiled. Possibly the best feature of the entire room—the entire *house*, even. It was a long, lead-framed hatch overlooking the grounds from a bird's eye view—the kind of view that made its occupants feel as though they were sitting high up in the tree tops.

Dropping the suitcase on the floor, I flopped down onto my bed and nestled into the soft pillows. With a deep breath, I indulged in the scent of cherry blossoms wafting from the freshly washed linen. I rolled onto my side and gazed over at the dressing table, mentally assessing how I could use the space.

The table top itself was relatively bare, with only a vanity mirror and a toffee-coloured candle. That dusty candle had sat in the same spot for years, awaiting an opportunity to be lit. I suspected that opportunity may never come. Not from me, anyhow. I was nervous of fire. My mother would have labelled it an irrational fear, but I would hardly call it irrational. Um, hello? It was *fire*, for crying out loud! Fears don't get more rational than fire! Anyway, because of my debatable fear, I didn't actually light candles, but I enjoyed looking at them. They were my version of art.

Right, back to the dressing table.

Let me see. What did I bring with me? A jewellery box, wash bag, a book…

My gaze wandered to the window. Beyond the glass, a procession of feathery white clouds floated leisurely by.

The movement must have been lulling because, to my surprise, I felt my eyelids droop. It wasn't long before I surrendered to their weight and let them close completely.

Maybe a little nap wouldn't be such a bad thing…

THE GIRL WALKED STIFFLY THROUGH a forsaken landscape. No plants or life grew. There was nothing but parched ground and a dark, oppressive sky. She walked on, reluctant but unable to stop.

The dull, opaque clouds churned above her, and she could hardly see beyond the grim shadows that lurked before her. But she could see one thing—the only other living entity in the sparse land.

Hunched on the ground was some sort of creature. Its body was arched on the floor, concealed by a black cloak. It remained perfectly still, only taking occasional shallow breaths, causing the form to pulsate slightly.

The girl stopped walking, instinctively fearful.

And then, with a guttural moan, the creature began to convulse. Out from beneath the cloak an ivory claw revealed itself, hooking down into the ground, anchoring itself, pulling its body forward.

The girl tried to cry out, but no sound passed her lips.

Still hunched low to the ground, the creature heaved itself towards her. As it closed in on her, its body began to rear upwards, growing taller and taller until it was twice her size. Shrouded behind the cloak, only two menacing black eyes were visible; the beady eyes of a crow bulging from the ashen skull of a man.

She let out a petrified scream.

I WOKE MYSELF UP, SCREAMING. Simultaneously, a clap of thunder echoed throughout my bedroom.

Oh my God. Oh my God. Oh my God.

Where did all the daylight go?

The attic room was submerged in total darkness and was

literally shaking under the pressure of a violent storm. Outside, the rain hammered fiercely upon the roof and stabbed against the window pane, vigorously rattling the delicate glass.

Scrambling off my bed, I dived for the light switch. Those five seconds during which I stumbled around in blinding darkness—post nightmare, I might add—were the longest five seconds of my life. Somewhere between second number three and second number four, I became convinced that I was having a heart attack. Thank God for second number five, which shall evermore be referred to as 'The Bringer of Light'.

Artificial light flooded the little room. I felt a degree of relief, but my heart was still hammering in my chest.

After a nightmare, I knew, the logical thing to do was remind myself that 'it was just a dream'.

I skipped that stage and went straight to the 'something's in the room with me' rationale. Logical thinking was not my strong point. Besides, when you have the same dream one hundred times over, logic kind of loses its novelty.

"Mary?" I yelled.

When there was no response, I peeked out from my bedroom. At the bottom of my private steps I could see that the upper hallway was empty and the lights were out. Mary and Roger must have been downstairs.

I hurried down the attic steps and crossed the hallway to the main staircase.

I made it down two flights of stairs in record time—navigating a dark manor house always made me move a little faster.

I could hear Mary and Roger talking, and I traced their voices to the kitchen.

Mary greeted me brightly when I appeared in the doorway. "Hi, Rosie! We thought you were asleep. I was just about to come upstairs and wake you."

I stepped into the kitchen. It was warm and spacious, decorated in wholesome shades of apricot. A long breakfast table ran through the centre, with eight stools positioned around it. Mary and Roger were seated on stools opposite each other, sipping at mugs of tea.

I pulled up a stool beside Mary. "Yeah, I must have fallen asleep. I think the thunder woke me up." I didn't bother mentioning the nightmare. It was less embarrassing to blame it on the thunder.

"Funny old day," Mary said as she gazed out of the kitchen window, looking over the unlit garden. "That storm came out of nowhere. It's hard to believe that it was sunny this afternoon."

Roger rubbed his chin thoughtfully. "Yes. What a strange summer it's been. Very unpredictable."

"Hmm," Mary nodded and took a sip of her tea. "Oh, Rose," she said suddenly. "You must be starving. I thought I could make us a late dinner, to celebrate your first night here. Only something light. How does a chicken salad sound? Will that be enough for you?"

"Yes, that sounds perfect. Thanks." Come to think of it, my stomach was feeling hollow. "Can I help with anything?"

"No," Mary gulped down the last of her tea and took

the mug to the sink, "the salad's already made and the dining room table is set." She toddled over to the fridge and took out a clay salad bowl, filled to the brim with leafy greens, croutons and strips of cooked chicken.

Roger and I made our way through the kitchen and into the adjoining dining room.

The furnishings in the dining room were all dark mahogany, even down to the dark wood floors. It was arguably the most stylish room in the house, adorned with a chandelier, high-backed dining chairs, and gold-framed patio doors. The dining table itself was equally elegant. It had been lit up with decorative lanterns and three places had been laid out, all with matching wicker placemats, white china plates and elaborate silverware.

While Roger and I took our seats, Mary surfaced, carrying the salad bowl. She dished out three portions and placed the half-empty bowl in the centre.

Together we sat down to eat, beginning our first family night of the summer. Just the three of us.

"It's really coming down out there," Roger commented, peering over the rim of his glasses.

Mary and I looked to the patio doors.

"I'm glad I got my washing done nice and early," Mary mused. She pierced her fork through a crisp lettuce leaf and popped it into her mouth.

"I wouldn't want to be out on a night like this," Roger added.

As if on cue, the melodic chime of the doorbell rang through the hallway.

Mary looked at Roger in utter bewilderment. "Who would be calling round at this time? In this weather?"

Roger pushed his glasses up on the bridge of his nose. "I don't have the foggiest." He patted his mouth with a napkin and folded it neatly on the table. "Let's see who this is," he muttered, excusing himself to answer the door.

Mary and I stayed quiet, listening for the exchange that was about to take place. We heard Roger's footsteps click along the wooden floor, and then the sound of him unhooking the front door latch.

"Oh," he said, clearly surprised. "Hello there. What can I do for you?"

Mary and I frowned at one another.

Then came the first unfamiliar voice. A male, polite and well spoken.

"Hello, sir. My name is Caicus Valero. This is my brother, Oscar. We're terribly sorry to call upon you at such a late hour, but we're having some car trouble."

"Oh dear," Roger replied. "What seems to be the problem?"

Now the second voice spoke, this one smooth like dripping honey. "We can't be certain," he replied to Roger's question vaguely and with a touch of disinterest. "You know cars."

"Oh dear. Well, you'll never get a mechanic at this time of night…" Roger trailed off.

"No, I'm afraid not," agreed Caicus. "That's why we were thinking it would be best if we stayed the night here."

There was a brief pause, and then Roger spoke again.

"Absolutely. Do come in."

At this point, Mary and I gawped at one another.

"Uncle Roger can't just let strangers sleep in the house!" I spluttered.

"No, he most certainly cannot!" Mary dropped her fork onto the table, ready to charge out and *un*invite the uninvited guests. But before she had even risen from her seat, in walked Roger, followed by two boys, both aged around eighteen.

The first boy was blonde and, although dampened by rain, his hair fell in immaculate waves that curved flawlessly across his brow. His eyes were ice blue and he wore smart beige trousers, a white shirt and a denim jacket. He flashed Mary a dazzling smile, then fleetingly glanced at me.

"Ladies. My name is Caicus Valero." He offered his hand to Mary. She shook it, visibly stunned.

The second boy stepped forward. This one had raven black hair and copper-coloured eyes. He wore black jeans and a charcoal grey T-shirt, with a black waxed jacket on top.

Let me just say that if ever I had any doubts about the definition of the word 'beautiful', then they were eradicated at that moment.

He was beautiful.

In fact, both boys were extraordinarily handsome, but in appearance they looked nothing alike. Polar opposites, even. Their only comparable feature was the same arrogant smirk that occasionally flickered over their lips.

"I do apologise for such an impromptu visit," Caicus said, addressing Mary as though they were old friends. "My brother and I have found ourselves in quite a pickle. You understand, though."

Presumptuous! I thought, in disbelief.

"Of course," Mary answered the blonde boy. "Car trouble, is it?"

He feigned an overly saddened expression. "Oh yes. Terrible car trouble. And on such a stormy night. My poor brother has found the entire thing very distressing. His nerves are shot to pieces, God love him."

The dark-haired boy seemed to be battling to suppress a grin. "I'm of a nervous disposition as it is," he chimed in, though his remark was highly unconvincing.

Were these guys for real?

"Oh, my apologies," Caicus slapped his hand to his head. "I have not properly introduced my dear brother, Oscar." He gestured to his companion.

Oscar gave Mary a striking smile. "Oscar Valero."

"Oh. Pleasure to meet you both," Mary told them. "I'm Mary Clements. You've met my husband, Roger. And this is our niece, Rose. She's staying with us over the summer."

Caicus fixed his cool blue eyes on me. "Oh, how nice," he said in a sickly sweet voice.

Yuck. I grimaced. *Insufferable!*

Regardless of my inward dislike, I forced a smile. They may have been good looking, but they definitely weren't good people. They oozed falseness and superiority. I didn't like them and I most certainly didn't trust them.

Caicus continued, "I think it's best if we stay here tonight," he stated, specifically to Mary. "Wouldn't you agree?"

I stared at him, incredulously. I watched as his unnerving eyes seemed to bore into Mary.

Whoa.

It seemed totally implausible, but I was almost sure that Caicus's eyes had changed colour. A second before they'd been blue, but at the moment he focused upon Mary, they gleamed like white diamonds. Even in the dimly-lit dining room, his eyes shimmered like glaciers. And if that transformation alone hadn't been bizarre enough, something even more peculiar happened. To my sheer astonishment, Mary nodded her head in concurrence.

"Yes, you must stay here," she insisted. "You can sleep in one of the guest bedrooms. The twin room at the far end will be perfect."

"Aunt Mary!" I exclaimed. "Perhaps the boys would be better off in a hotel."

Caicus and Oscar seemed taken aback, almost as though they were shocked by my disinclination.

"No," Caicus rejected my suggestion. He cast his crystal eyes onto me now. "It's best for us to stay here," he repeated assertively.

Suddenly I felt dizzy and exposed.

"I think that's very inappropriate," I countered, trying to maintain a cool head.

Now the boys looked only at one another. Caicus's eyebrows knotted together, and for a second it seemed as though they were communicating silently. After a moment of hesitation, Caicus returned his attention to Mary.

"So, the guest bedroom?" he prompted, evidently choosing to ignore me.

With Caicus's eyes cast away from me, I felt normal again.

Mary, however, was acting far from normal. She blinked as though someone had shone a bright torch directly at her. "Yes, I'll show you the way."

The newcomers gave their first genuine smiles of the evening.

"Wait!" I made one last attempt to talk some sense into my aunt and uncle. But as I leapt up from my chair, Oscar whirled around to face me. For the first time that evening, I really saw him.

The intensity of the connection stopped me in my tracks. But not in the same way that Caicus's stare had unsettled me. Quite the opposite. Where Caicus's eyes had felt intrusive, Oscar's gave me a sense of recognition—almost to the point where I would have staked my life that I knew him, or knew those eyes at least. And, judging by his agitated expression, it was as though he recognised me, too.

But I *didn't* know him. How could I?

His lips parted as though he were short of breath.

I *did* know him.

"I know you," I murmured.

Oscar pressed his lips together and swiftly tore his gaze from me. Without a word, he stalked out of the dining room. No one else seemed to notice the unusual reaction, because Mary and Roger continued to chat casually with Caicus as they escorted him into the hallway.

I found myself frozen to the spot, staring after them, numb.

An eerie chill ran down my spine.

Whoever the Valero brothers were, it became apparent to me at that moment that they were here to stay.

CHAPTER TWO

Intuition

THE NEXT MORNING I AWOKE before sunrise. I squeezed my eyes shut in the hope of drifting back to sleep. But my attempts were in vain and I soon abandoned that wishful thinking.

Kicking off my quilt, I rolled out of bed. I went through the motions of rummaging around for my wash bag and plodding down the attic steps. All of these things I did with my eyes closed. It was far too early to use my eyes.

Unsurprisingly, the rest of the house was still asleep – it was Saturday, after all. I borrowed a clean towel from the airing cupboard and crept into the family bathroom.

Okay. Time to turn on a light.

I tugged the cord.

Tentatively, I opened one eye. And then the other. All around me, the sparkling ivory floor tiles glistened. In the centre of the room stood a grand, mother-of-pearl bathtub with gold taps and four gold clawed feet. A shower cubicle stood separately, matching the bath in its impressive elegance.

I draped my peach bath towel over the radiator and brushed my teeth at the corner sink. Once that was out of the way, I moved on to the shower, twisting the gold taps until a light stream poured from above. I hovered around while the water built up a gentle steam and then stepped under the flow.

It only took a few minutes before I started to unwind. The warm water from the shower poured over me, and if I hadn't been so fond of dry land, I probably would have been tempted to stay under there forever.

But my respite was short lived.

There was a bash against the bathroom door. It was as though something, or some*one*, had fallen against it.

I held my breath, listening carefully for any noise. But all I could hear was the patter of water as it splashed against the base of the cubicle.

"Hello?" I called.

There was no response.

I fumbled to turn off the taps. The final drips fell from above as I hopped out onto the cold floor tiles.

Wrapping my towel securely around myself, I edged across the bathroom and pressed my ear to the door.

I quickly pulled the bolt across and flung the door open.

Nobody there.

The hallway was deserted, just as I had left it. Not that I was unfairly accusing anyone, but I glanced over to the guest bedroom at end of the corridor.

Caicus and Oscar's room.

Their door was closed.

It was feasible that I'd imagined the whole thing. Old houses like this one were full of creaks and groans. Or maybe it was a mouse. A *giant* mouse.

Alone in a dim, empty corridor, I wasn't particularly keen to dwell on the incident, so I bundled my clothes together and made for my bedroom.

Given that I hadn't finished unpacking, I was able to occupy myself with that for a while. Finding space for my clothes proved to be the most challenging task. I hadn't brought much with me, but the only storage space was the small pine chest of drawers and the narrow wardrobe. I did my best to cram my clothes into the three shallow drawers, keeping aside a pair of jeans and a beige top to wear that day.

Outside the sun was still quite low, meaning that the others would probably still be sleeping. Having done everything I could think of to pass the time—including dressing and blow-drying my hair—I decided to head downstairs.

It was hard to cross that house without disturbing anyone – like I said, creaks and moans – but I successfully accomplished it. I tiptoed all the way to the ground floor and ducked through the first door I came across.

That door happened to lead into the conservatory – a quaint, airy room with floor-to-ceiling windows overlooking the forest, a mahogany bookcase, and a coffee table encircled by salmon-pink armchairs.

I strolled over to the bookcase and skimmed the selection. There was every genre imaginable, ranging from classic literature to romance novels and political biographies. Admittedly, I'd already read most of them at least once over the past few years, including the cringe-worthy trashy novel, *Amour in Paris*, as well as the brick-sized *Biography of Winston Churchill*, which, ironically, was rather exciting—though I would never divulge that secret out loud.

With some deliberation I eased out a leather-bound copy of *The Complete Works of William Shakespeare.* It seemed like a safe bet.

Book in hand, I retreated to one of the armchairs and tucked my legs up on the soft pink cushion. Once I was sufficiently comfortable, I began leafing through the dog-eared pages. I doubted that I would actually read it, not cover to cover anyway, but it was something to do all the same.

As it happened, my initial cynicism was proved wrong and I found myself engrossed in a chapter entitled *Sonnets.* I was about halfway through the chapter when a voice behind me made me jump out of my skin.

"Ah," breathed Oscar Valero in his smooth, sultry tone. He peered over my shoulder and read aloud from the open page. His warm breath brushed against my neck as he recited, "All days are nights to see till I see thee, and nights bright days when dreams do show thee me." He reached over my shoulder and tapped the page. "Significant, wouldn't you agree?"

I was stunned. So stunned that I didn't even hear what he had said. The words themselves were lost on me; all I took from them was the breath that brushed my ear.

I slammed the book shut. "I didn't hear you come in." My speech sounded stammered.

Oscar meandered around the coffee table and took a seat in one of the vacant armchairs. He stretched his arms up over his head and yawned loudly.

I watched him from across the table. "Can I help you?" I asked curtly.

"No, thank you." He smiled.

"I didn't hear you come in," I said again, fortunately more in control of my voice this time.

After adjusting to the initial shock of his materialisation, I realised that what baffled me most of all was the fact that I hadn't heard the door open, nor had I felt the breath on the back of my neck until he had spoken.

"Okay."

"Okay, *what*?" I stared at him, mystified.

"Okay, you didn't hear me come in," he replied casually.

My eyes narrowed. "How long were you standing behind me?"

Oscar shrugged. "I've forgotten. It was a while ago now." He sat perfectly still, his arms resting on either side of the chair. He wore a black shirt that was open over a deep red T-shirt, and the same jeans that he had been wearing the night before. His dark hair fell with effortless style and he seemed to be smirking, though his mouth was indifferent.

Much to my irritation, I realised that I was blushing. I was ashamed to admit it, but I was blushing because he was so attractive.

But, good looks aside, there was something else that

drew my focus back to him. As odd as it might have sounded, I simply couldn't shake the feeling that I *knew* him. It was uncanny. I felt like I knew everything about him—every thought and feeling he'd ever had, the good, the bad, I knew it all. And yet, I'd never met him before in my life.

He returned my gaze with his warm, russet eyes. Eyes that were animated with a lifetime of secrets and mystery. They were utterly disarming.

Trying to maintain my last shred of composure, I looked away, returning my attention to *The Complete Works of William Shakespeare*.

"How's the book?" Oscar enquired lightly, now exhibiting a much more obvious smirk.

"Fine." I refrained from looking up, pretending to be absorbed in a randomly selected page.

"Which is your favourite?"

"Which is my favourite *what*?"

"Sonnet. Which is your favourite sonnet?"

I sighed. "I don't know. I like them all."

That wasn't true. I had favourites.

Oscar bent forward, resting his chin on his knuckles. A few strands of ebony hair fell in front of his eyes. "Recite one for me. Please," he added as an afterthought.

Now my cheeks reddened even further. "No." I turned the page, bluntly illustrating the fact that I was reading. Well, pretending to read.

"Then I'll recite one to you." He reached across the coffee table.

"No!" I clutched the book to my chest, out of his reach.

"Hmm." Oscar sat back down in his seat. "Possessive."

"I'm not possessive. I'm…" I fumbled for a feasible defence. "Reading!" I finished.

"Oh. Would you rather I let you read in peace?"

"Yes, please."

We were silent for a minute or two. Oscar sat, pensively looking out at the garden while I pretended to read.

Then he spoke again. "This is boring."

I exhaled loudly. "Not my problem. Where's your brother?" My voice had a cold edge to it. "Shouldn't it be *his* job to entertain you?"

"Caicus is sleeping. Otherwise he *would* be entertaining me. But instead, I've got you. Or you've got me, if you prefer."

I laughed in spite of myself. "I don't really prefer either."

Oscar shot me a playful grin. "You're hurting my feelings."

"I'm sure you'll get over it," I replied, wryly.

He reclined in his seat with a contented sigh. "Yes. I can't imagine it'll be hard."

I went back to ignoring him and gazed out of one of the windows. It was light out now, so I could clearly see the meadow garden leading down to the evergreen forest. A few wood pigeons fluttered around the tree tops, rustling the leaves as they flapped their wings.

"What are you looking at?" Oscar demanded, following my line of vision. I was beginning to get used to his unpredictable manner of speaking—his tone would constantly switch between blunt and smooth. It was hard to tell which would be next.

"The birds," I told him.

He craned his neck to get a better view. "Pigeons?" He made a noise of revulsion. "Pigeons aren't birds. They're rats with wings." Blunt.

"I like pigeons," I said.

"No. There's nothing to them." Smooth.

"I didn't say *you* had to like them. I said *I* liked them." It was hard to be diplomatic with Oscar; he made you want to argue.

"Well, you *shouldn't* like them." Blunt. "They're just... *there*. Now, an eagle on the other hand, *that's* a bird. A true predator." Smooth.

"Just because they're a bird of prey, doesn't make them better."

Oh God, he's sucked me in. I'm arguing about birds!

"I'm afraid you're wrong," Oscar told me. "Predators aren't just better, they're the *best*. Every species needs one. Without hunters, the world would be bedlam. Total chaos. And sure as hell they get the better deal. The thrill of the hunt is..." he searched for an apt description. "Well, it's exhilarating."

I frowned. "You sound like you're speaking from experience."

"Nope," Oscar answered simply. "I'm just an excellent spokesman for the eagle." He pushed up the sleeves of his shirt, revealing toned, muscular forearms. "Do you play?" he asked suddenly, nodding down at the coffee table.

Imprinted onto the varnished mahogany surface was a decorative chess board.

"No," I admitted.

"Do you want to play?" Oscar rephrased his question.

I shook my head. "No."

"I'll teach you," Oscar decided.

"I said I didn't want to play!"

He stood up and walked over to the bookcase. Without even searching, he took a small leather box from the top shelf and brought it back to his seat. Opening the lid, he emptied the contents onto the coffee table: thirty-two carved wood chess pieces.

Okay. That was weird. He'd only arrived at the house last night, and yet he already knew the whereabouts of the chess pieces? Even *I* didn't know the whereabouts of the chess pieces!

My eyes narrowed. "How did you know where to find them?"

Oscar kept his concentration on the board, which he began preparing for the game. "I'm intuitive. It's a gift."

I stared at him. "*Intuitive*?" I echoed.

"Yes." He looked up at me, a glint of sunlight catching in his russet eyes. "Intuitive. When it comes to the important things."

"Chess pieces?"

"Yes." Oscar resumed the board arrangement. "Chess is important to me."

"So important that you were able to guess where the pieces were?"

"Yep." He spun a rook between his first two fingers and then placed it on the board.

"Well, if you ask me, you're either massively deluded or a bad liar."

Oscar leaned back in his chair with a conceited sneer. "Maybe I'm both."

"You probably are," I muttered under my breath.

"Right then." He rubbed his hands together eagerly. "Are you ready?"

"No," I grumbled.

Oscar's delighted smile could have lit up the room.

"Let the lesson begin." All of a sudden his expression grew serious. "Now, please try to keep up. There are a lot of rules in chess—"

"Sounds like fun," I remarked.

Oscar glared at me. "There are a lot of rules in chess," he repeated, "but personally I like to play by two in particular. Rule number one," he held up an index finger, "don't let your king get into checkmate."

"How do I do that?"

"By playing well."

"Sounds like hard work."

"Rule number two," Oscar went on, "protect the queen."

I made a half-hearted attempt to examine the assortment of pieces. "Which one is the queen?"

"You can work that out for yourself," Oscar scoffed.

I wrinkled my nose. "They all kind of look like they could be the queen. Except the little ones in the front—" I prodded at the front row.

"The pawns." Oscar swiped my hand away. He didn't like me touching the board.

"And I suppose that one's a horse—"

"Knight," he corrected wearily.

"Ah-ha!" I isolated one of the larger centre pieces and lifted it up for closer inspection. "Found her." I held the queen-shaped piece high and made her dance in the air.

"Okay. You can put it back now. It's not a toy."

I dropped it back down onto the board, deliberately nudging the two pieces on either side of it. I imagined that would be the most fun I'd have all game.

He grimaced.

I smiled. "So, protect the queen—"

"Because she's your best player."

"And don't let the king get into checkmate."

"No."

I hesitated. "And why is that important?"

Oscar's mouth twitched in irritation. "Because once you're in checkmate, you lose."

"I see. So, how can I avoid that?"

"Always watch your back," he elaborated. "If your opponent is on the attack, make sure you have an escape route. Don't get caged in from all angles. That's checkmate."

From across the room, the conservatory door rattled open.

How did I not notice that when Oscar came in?

I swivelled around to see my aunt standing in the open doorway, wearing a lavender dressing gown and carrying a green watering can. Her short, strawberry blonde hair was pinned up in rollers.

"Good morning!" Mary sang out.

"Morning," I replied. I sat up straighter in my chair as if I'd been caught misbehaving.

"Good morning," said Oscar in a strained voice.

"Oh, you're playing chess," Mary observed. She wandered around the room, watering her collection of house plants. "Who's winning?"

"I am," Oscar answered immediately. He gave me an enigmatic smile.

"Actually," I shot back, "the game hasn't started yet."

Oscar seemed impressed by my response, because his smile broadened. "I don't need to play to know I'm going to win," he retorted in a low whisper, quiet enough to go unheard by Mary.

Instinctively I drew back from him. What was that supposed to mean?

Mary finished with her plants and wiped her damp hands on her dressing gown. "Who wants breakfast? I'm making eggs Benedict," she cajoled.

Oscar clasped his hands together and made an exaggerated show of enthusiasm.

The falseness of his sentiment was clearly lost on Mary, because she toddled off towards the kitchen with a jolly smile on her lips.

But it wasn't lost on me. And it really, *really* riled me.

I stood up and glowered at him. "That was rude."

"What?" He blinked up at me with doe-eyed innocence.

"Don't play dumb! You know exactly what I'm talking about."

Oscar cocked his head to one side. "What?"

"You're obnoxious and rude!"

"And?" he said, challenging me. "I can't change who I am just to please you, *Rose*," he spat out my name with contempt.

I folded my arms. "I don't know why you're here, but I think you should leave. Get your brother and go."

All of a sudden, Oscar's eyes blazed. "That's not your decision to make. It's not *your* house."

"You may have fooled my aunt and uncle, but you won't fool me. You're bad news, I can feel it."

Oscar rose to his feet and side-stepped around the coffee table until there were just inches between us.

He stood over me, his lips pressed together tightly. The intoxicating scent of his skin contaminated the air that I breathed.

I didn't flinch.

"You're right," he murmured darkly, "I am bad news."

His presence didn't scare me. It should have, but it didn't.

"I'm going to get you out of here if it's the last thing I do," I warned him.

He smirked back at me. "Interesting choice of words."

A shiver moved over my skin. "What's that supposed to mean?"

The unexpected sound of someone clearing their throat cut through the icy atmosphere.

Caicus hovered in the doorway, his pale eyes fixed on Oscar. "Breakfast is ready," he said in a silken voice.

Oscar backed away from me and the boys locked eyes with each other for a long, bated moment.

At last, Oscar broke the silence. "Breakfast, of course. I'll be right there." He smiled pleasantly.

Once Caicus had disappeared back into the hallway, Oscar picked up *The Complete Works of William Shakespeare* and returned it to the bookcase.

"Do you want to know *my* favourite sonnet?" he asked, his voice gentle, as though the altercation had never happened.

When I didn't respond, he glanced over his shoulder at me. "Well, do you?" he pressed.

I swallowed. My throat felt as dry as sandpaper. "Not really. But I've got a feeling you're going to tell me anyway."

Oscar slipped the book back without glimpsing at its pages. He touched the hard spine as he spoke, "When to the sessions of sweet silent thought, I summon up remembrance of things past, I sigh the lack of many a thing I sought, And with old woes new wail my dear time's waste."

CHAPTER THREE

Hutton Ridge

After breakfast, Roger departed for his habitual golf day and Mary formulated a plan to take me shopping. Millwood wasn't much in the way of retail therapy—unless you were after a pint of milk or half a dozen eggs—so we decided to drive to the next town over, Hutton Ridge.

"Make sure you're wearing comfy shoes," Mary joked. "We're going to shop till we drop!"

I forced a weak smile. Shopping wasn't exactly number one on my list of favourite things to do. I had an incredibly low threshold when it came to the much-dreaded shopper's fatigue, and I guessed that I would be dropping a lot more than I would be shopping.

However, for Mary, the opportunity to recruit a spending-spree companion was grabbed with both hands. She beamed joyously as she cleared away the breakfast remnants and piled the plates into the sink.

"I'm going to treat you to something today, Rose," Mary declared. "Something special."

"Thanks. That's kind of you." I wiped the breakfast table with a cloth, deliberating whether to brush crumbs at Caicus and Oscar, who remained seated, having excused themselves from cleaning duties.

"Well, if I can't spoil my niece, who can I spoil?" Mary chuckled. She untied her apron and hung it on a kitchen hook. "Boys, if we're going to Hutton Ridge today, you can come along and speak to the mechanic. He's seen to my car in the past. He's good and he's very reasonable."

Caicus and Oscar shared an ambiguous look.

"I don't feel like going to Hutton Ridge," Caicus declined in an offhanded manner.

"Me, neither," Oscar concurred.

Mary gave them a puzzled frown. "Oh. Okay. Do you want me to get the mechanic's phone number? Perhaps he could come to the house."

The boys looked at one another again, conferring silently.

"No," Caicus said slowly, twiddling his thumbs like a small child.

"No?" Mary repeated.

Caicus brought his blue eyes up to her. This time I was absolutely certain that they lightened, just as they had done the night before. It was as though his eyes were frosting over somehow.

"We think we should stay here a little while longer," he purred.

I spluttered at the audacity.

But Mary simply reached over and patted Caicus's hands warmly. "If you think that's best, dear."

Caicus nodded his head earnestly. "Yes, I do. Thank you, Mary."

I stared at him, wide eyed. *How is he doing this?*

Unlike me, Mary didn't seem bothered in the slightest. She trotted away to get baby Zack ready for his trip to Hutton Ridge. Only Oscar, Caicus and myself remained in the kitchen.

"How did you do that?" I demanded.

Caicus and Oscar turned their perfect poker faces upon me.

"Do what?" Caicus asked.

"You know what!" I slammed my palm against the wooden breakfast table. "Trick my aunt into letting you stay."

The boys made an over-the-top show of appearing affronted by my remark.

"*Trick* her?" Caicus gasped. "I would never."

"Your comments are quite vicious, Rose," Oscar chimed in. "We are merely two down-on-their-luck boys who are in need of a friendly neighbour."

I placed my hands on my hips. "Yeah, right," I hissed. "Come to think of it, I don't believe there's anything wrong with your car at all."

"Are you accusing of us lying?" Caicus exclaimed.

"Yes. Give me your car keys and I'll prove it."

The boys laughed whimsically.

"No, thank you," Oscar replied to me. "We don't do that."

"Do what?" I snapped. My temper was really rising.

"We don't let other people touch our car," Caicus clarified.

"Especially not girls," Oscar added with a wicked grin.

I knew I had to get out of the kitchen before I smashed Aunt Mary's crockery over their pretty little heads.

I held my tongue and stormed out. The truth was that I'd be fighting a losing battle, trying to contend with both of them at once.

"Don't forget your coat," I heard Oscar call after me. "It's going to rain."

In the hallway, Mary was zipping Zack into his woolly fleece. "Ready, dear?"

I mumbled 'yes' as I took my tan jacket from the coat rack. For the record, that was *not* because Oscar had told me to. I was going to do it anyway.

I followed my aunt outside and waited patiently while she settled Zack into his car seat. Before we climbed into the car ourselves, I glanced over at the black Lamborghini parked on the gravel a few metres away. It looked immaculate, apart from a splatter of mud that had dried on the chrome hubcaps.

"I wonder what's wrong with their car," I mused. "Looks all right to me." Planting the seeds of doubt. Good idea.

"You never can tell with cars," Mary said with a shrug.

"Funny how they managed to get it right up to the front door," I added pointedly.

"Yes. They were lucky." Mary took her seat behind the steering wheel and checked Zack in the rear-view mirror. Her hair was out of the rollers now and fell in curls around her full cheeks.

I pulled my seatbelt across. "It's strange though, don't you think?"

Mary looked over at me, not quite following my train of thought. "What's that, dear?"

"The boys. Don't you think there's something *off* about them?" I coaxed.

"I think they seem like nice enough boys. Could be a bit of company for you, anyway. Aren't you glad to have some other teenagers around the house?"

She started the engine and steered the minivan onto the access road. The gravel crunched loudly beneath the weight of the tyres.

I kept silent. Was I judging the Valeros too quickly? And if that was the case, had I fabricated reasons to justify disliking them? It was a possibility that my aunt and uncle were genuinely being neighbourly, and that *I* was the one out of line. I didn't like that theory, though. But I had to admit, it made a lot more sense than my theory of Caicus hypnotising them.

As we drove along the narrow, snaking road, I found myself thinking of only one thing.

Oscar Valero.

Who was he? And what could he possibly want in Millwood?

AFTER A LENGTHY AND MONOTONOUS drive through Millwood, the minivan finally crossed the border into Hutton Ridge. Mary found a parking spot on the main high street and cut the engine.

Hutton Ridge wasn't exactly thriving. The town centre was made up of a few cobbled streets, scattered with run-of-the-mill shops and the occasional upmarket boutique.

"I have an idea," Mary announced as she fumbled to unfolded Zack's pushchair. "How about we go to Amara's and buy you a new dress?"

Amara's was one of the most chic clothing stores in Hutton Ridge; everything was designer and everything was overpriced.

I lingered at the car door. *A dress?* I looked down at my jeans with a sentimental sigh.

Mary chortled. "Good heavens, Rose! You're acting like I've asked you to hand over a puppy or something," she teased. "It's just a dress. Lots of girls wear them."

"I suppose..." I pondered it. "It's just, I don't really wear dresses that often."

"That's because you don't own any."

"Yes, and there's a reason for that."

"Oh, come on," Mary tried to entice me. "What's the worst that can happen?"

"Um, somebody might see me wearing it."

Mary guffawed. She shook her head and set off down the high street, her leather handbag swinging from the handlebars of Zack's pushchair.

We hadn't walked far before Mary came to an abrupt halt. She stood outside a small boutique with the word 'Amara's' written above the store in curvy, pink lettering. The two shop windows arched outwards and each displayed a mannequin sporting the latest in designer fashion.

"Shall we?" Mary asked. Without waiting for a response, she pushed open the door and hoisted the buggy through it.

I followed behind her.

The store was relatively small, with glistening beige floors and neatly arranged racks of high-quality clothes. The faint sound of classical music drifted out from a speaker at the back of the shop.

Wasting no time, Mary began sifting through dresses. When she came across ones that met her approval, she snatched them from the rail and thrust them into my arms.

"This one," she muttered to herself. "Oh, *this* one would look gorgeous on you..." She paused and pinched my waist.

"Ouch!"

"Yes, this'll fit you," Mary decided. "You might have to suck in your breath, though." She dumped another three dresses into my now overflowing arms.

"No more," I beseeched her, peeking over the top of the mountain of fabric and hangers.

Mary gave me a little shove towards the fitting rooms. "Try those on. I'll keep looking."

"Oh, I'm begging you, no," I exclaimed. "Don't keep looking!"

She shooed me off into the curtained room at the back of the store.

With a dramatic eye roll, I pulled the red velvet curtain across. The truth was, I didn't *hate* these outing with Mary. It was fun, in a female-bonding sort of way. My own mother wasn't the shopping type, and it was kind of nice to get to dip into that lifestyle once in a while.

I offloaded the heap of clothes onto the dressing-room stool.

Only once in a while, though.

This was going to be a long day.

Already critical of the selection, I took the first dress from the pile. It was vibrant orange and knee length, with a net skirt and puffy sleeves. I grappled with the hanger for a while and then changed into the dress.

Yeesh.

I screwed up my nose at the sight of my reflection in the full-length mirror.

"How's it going?" Mary hollered from the other side of the curtain.

"Awfully," I called back.

"Why?" my aunt's voice returned to me.

"Because I look like Mr McGregor's prize pumpkin."

There was a brief silence.

"Is that the peach one?"

I snorted. "It's not peach—it's pumpkin orange! I'm trying on the next one."

"You're not going to let me see you in the peach one?" Mary sounded distinctly wounded.

"No! I'm humiliated enough just seeing myself in it." I untangled myself from the first monstrosity.

The second dress was no better. A canary yellow satin number with plastic beads along the neckline.

"How's it going in there?" Mary yelled again, her voice

drifting from a different location each time.

"It's getting worse," I shouted back.

"Which one are you in?"

"I'm a lemon meringue pie."

Mary tut-tutted. "Rose, you're not giving them a fair chance."

"I am!" I wailed. "I'm in them, aren't I?" I patted down the inflated skirt.

"You've got to let me see some of them," Mary urged.

I scuffled into the next dress. Halfway through squeezing into it, the dressing room curtain flew open.

Obviously, I shrieked.

In one swift motion, Mary spun me around and yanked up the zipper at the back.

"Oh, that is... That is *fantastic*. That's the one," she breathed.

Dazed, I turned to face my reflection in the mirror.

Mary had been right: the dress itself was stunning. It was a rich mulberry colour, fitted, with a box neckline, and the hem skimming the floor. It was spectacular. But it almost felt too sophisticated for me. I was a first-time wearer, and I was in something that belonged to the pros.

"We're getting this one," Mary stated. She promptly spun me around and unzipped the back, then marched out of the dressing room, closing the curtain behind her.

As I changed back into my own clothes, I allowed myself to briefly indulge in thoughts that I had so desperately been trying to suppress. Something that, there and then, I promised myself I would allow only once, and then block from my mind forever.

I thought of Oscar.

Or, more importantly, I wondered what Oscar would think of the dress. Silly, I know. But I couldn't help it.

I caught a glimpse of myself in the mirror and noticed that I was smiling. Not a smile I'd ever seen before, either. A dopey smile.

Oscar made me smile.

Oh, no.

I stopped that insanity at once.

Oscar is a conniving fraud, I reminded myself. *Oscar is up to something devious and will probably trample you in the process. He is a volatile con artist and you cannot trust him. Ever.*

Much to my dismay, I felt a painful tug in my heart.

Traitorous heart.

I tucked my jacket under my arm and bundled the dresses together. Outside the fitting room, a shop assistant was waiting to take the unwanted items—which, incidentally, there were many of.

Mary scooped up the one successful candidate and toddled off to the cashier's desk. "We're going to take this one," she told the brunette woman at the cash register.

I rushed to catch up with her. "Mary, I don't know about this," I babbled. "I'm not sure if I can pull off a dress like that."

"What are you talking about?" Mary laughed in delight. "It was perfect."

The overly made-up cashier held the dress between her

manicured fingernails. "Are you taking this?"

"Yes," Mary answered firmly.

From the corner of my eye, I glimpsed the price tag.

My jaw dropped.

"Have you seen the price?" I exclaimed. "It's daylight robbery!"

Mary shushed me.

"Do you know how much it is?" I spluttered in an adequately hushed voice.

"Yes, I know," Mary whispered. "Everything in this store is around that price mark. Don't you worry about the cost."

I leaned against the counter in shock as the cashier rang up the bill.

"Thanks, Aunt Mary," I said meekly.

"My pleasure," she replied, beaming.

The cashier placed the dress into a little pink bag and sprinkled some scented beads over the top. She handed the bag to me and told us to have a nice day.

Manoeuvring Zack's pushchair through the store, Mary led the way back out onto the high street.

"We were lucky to find your dress in the first shop we went into," she said to me.

"Yeah. Now we can go look for something for you."

Mary smiled broadly. "Oh Rose, you don't want to be dragged around to all of my shops. Here's an idea..."

Uh oh. Alarm bells went off in my head.

Mary went on, "I think there's a youth club about halfway down Birch Street."

Youth club? I winced.

"Why don't you pop down there and have a look around? It'll be good for you to meet some people your own age."

No, I wailed silently. I couldn't believe she was sending me off on a friend hunt. *Not without a fight...*

"I don't mind staying with you," I began my counter-argument. "I can help you do your shopping—"

"Rose," Mary cut me off, "it's a long summer in Millwood without any company."

"I've got company," I disputed. "I've got you, Uncle Roger and Zack."

"I meant company your own age."

"Caicus and Oscar are company my own age," I pointed out.

"I meant company you actually *like*. A girl, perhaps. You can show her your new dress."

My jaw dropped.

Mary ruffled my hair. "Meet back at the car in, say," she glanced at her watch, "an hour?" She peeked into the pushchair. "Zackie, say goodbye to Rosie," she cooed to her son.

I scoffed. "If Zack could talk, he would never let this happen. Go on, Zack," I said to the plump face nestled in the pushchair, "tell her."

Zack gurgled and drooled a little.

"My thoughts exactly," I told him.

Mary chortled. "Have fun!" she said cheerfully before trundling off down the street.

Wearily I set off in the opposite direction from my aunt. Of course, I had no intention of going to the youth club—I was a non-mover on that. Instead, I ducked onto a side street, which, I quickly found out, sloped down to a huge old church. The building was clearly no longer in use, but it was in good condition all the same. It was typically ostentatious, with elaborate arched doors, stained glass windows, and sculpted gargoyles jutting out from the stone walls. Surrounding the church was a neglected graveyard, and behind that was the beginning of a woodland.

I wandered into the graveyard. The yellowed grass was hugely overgrown and some of the gravestones had been upturned—I was guessing as a result of storm damage. There was a vague path leading out to the wood, so I followed the trail, venturing into the trees.

At least fifteen minutes passed before I even considered stopping, and by then I was deep inside the woodland. It was strangely comforting to be so immersed in nature. I was completely alone, apart from a solo squirrel who scuffled around amongst the undergrowth.

I kept walking, leaving my squirrel friend behind.

When I finally stopped, it was more out of necessity than choice. The trees parted and I found myself on the top of a projection.

I peered over the edge. The woodland below was easily a one-hundred-foot drop.

I had some time to kill, so I sat on the edge of the projection, looking down over the world below. It was a spectacular view, treetops as far as the eye could see. Placing my shopping bag beside me, I lay my jacket down over the grass and reclined back onto it. I closed my eyes and listened to the birdsong. A light wind dusted over my bare arms and swept a few strands of hair over my face.

But just when I felt myself drifting into a blissful state of relaxation, a stomach-churning image flashed through my subconscious. The vision of a decomposing skull teeming with maggots. The decayed face was long dead, but its menacing black eyes were very much alive. And they were staring right at me.

I gasped and sat bolt upright.

All of a sudden, the woodland didn't seem so peaceful anymore. In fact, it felt utterly sinister. Even the sky had taken a dark turn; it was now congested with bulging grey rain clouds.

I sprang to my feet, searching for the path back to town. But there was no path, and every direction looked the same.

My heart began to race. As I stood alone in the clearing, I was overcome by the sinking feeling that I was being watched.

And I knew that I was right.

CHAPTER FOUR

The Impossible

BLINDLY I STUMBLED THROUGH THE dense woodland. I tried to calm myself, but my heart was pounding.

The first heavy drops of rain plummeted from the sky and splashed onto my arms, and the deeper I walked into the woodland, the more unfamiliar things became. Perhaps it was the fear of being lost, or perhaps it was a gut instinct, but I was scared. Really scared.

To make things worse, I was plagued by that instinctual feeling that eyes were upon me. Threatening eyes. Crow-like eyes, which had previously only manifested through my nightmares, but that now appeared to be taking up roots in reality, too. I could feel them burning a hole in the back of my head.

As the rain pattered down, indistinct sounds echoed throughout the woodland. Drops landed like footsteps all around me. I glanced over my shoulder, but could see nothing except the slight movement of leaves. Each new sound sent a fresh wave of panic coursing through my veins.

I broke into a run. I scrambled through the trees, heading in whichever direction fate took me. Although I probably should have been looking where fate was taking me, because without warning, my foot slipped out from underneath me.

I had tripped over a fallen branch and was tumbling face first onto the muddy ground.

I braced myself for the impact.

But before I hit the forest floor, a strong hand grabbed my arm and effortlessly propped me back upright.

It took me a few seconds to register that there were vice-like fingers clasped around my elbow.

A scream caught in my throat.

I jerked my arm free and stumbled backwards.

"Careful!" said a light-hearted voice.

Oscar.

"What are you doing here?" I cried. My voice was quite a few octaves higher than usual.

Oscar shook the raindrops from his dark hair. "I helped you," he said with a shrug.

"What are you doing here?" I choked again.

"Helping."

"What-are-you-doing-here?" I drew out the words breathlessly. "Why are you in Hutton Ridge? In the woods?"

"Oh," Oscar hesitated, mulling over his impending response. "I'm…walking. I'm taking a walk. Nice day for it." He smirked as a raindrop dribbled over the bridge of his nose.

"You're taking a walk?" I stammered. "Here?"

"Yes. This is where I come for my..." he trailed off, almost as though he'd lost his train of thought. Or simply lost interest in the sentence.

"Walks?" I finished for him.

"Yes, my walks."

"In Hutton Ridge?"

"I said so, didn't I?"

"How did you get here?" I demanded. "I thought your car was broken." For a moment I thought I'd done it. Caught him in a lie. Put him in checkmate, so to speak.

But Oscar was distinctly unruffled. "I walked. I walk."

"All the way here? It's a half-hour car journey. It would have taken you *hours* to walk."

"Okay then, I ran."

My mind whirled with questions. Could he really have run there? And how could he possibly have known where to find me? Surely this couldn't be a coincidence?

"You're lying," I accused.

Oscar pushed back wet strands of hair from his brow. "No, I'm not."

I narrowed my eyes.

Oscar's gaze began to flicker between me and the trees. He cleared his throat. "Shall we go?" he said at last. He extended his hand to me, but I didn't take it.

Instead I folded my arms. "Go?" I echoed. "With you?"

He raised an eyebrow. "What, you'd rather stay out here on your own?"

We both looked up to the towering treetops and grey

rainclouds skulking through the sky.

Great, I thought sourly. I was torn. I didn't want to go with him, but I didn't want to stay out there alone, either.

"Just point me in the right direction," I said with a grimace.

Oscar laughed.

I frowned at him. "Fine then, don't. I'll find my own way back."

"Oh right! Because that's worked out well for you so far," he drawled.

In fairness, he was right—I had had absolutely no idea where I was going. But I didn't want Oscar to know that. Oh, he'd have lapped that up.

I marched into the thick of trees.

I could hear him muttering irritably to himself as he strode to catch up with me.

"Not that way," he shouted.

I hesitated and glanced back at him. "I don't need your help," I scoffed. "I don't even know you!"

For a split second he actually looked hurt. But it might as well have been a mirage, because in the next instant his expression was stony.

"Suit yourself," he said coolly. "I don't know why I bothered anyway. Die out here for all I care."

Our eyes met through the misted rain.

I sighed. Okay, I *did* need his help, but I really didn't want to admit that.

"Would you just..." Oscar raked his hands through his damp hair, "just trust me?" He shifted his weight restlessly from one foot to the next. "Just for today?"

I wiped the rainwater from my eyes. "How can I trust you? All you do is lie to me."

He stopped fidgeting and fixed his russet gaze on me. When he answered, he spoke slowly, earnestly. "It's not safe for you to be out here by yourself. That's the truth."

Without waiting for a response, Oscar took hold of my wrist and guided me into the trees. His grasp was light and yet unmovable at the same time.

I dug my heels into the mud. "Let go!"

Oscar stopped walking. "If I let you go, will you promise to walk with me?"

Go willingly? I knew I had to make that judgement there and then. "Do you promise that you're not taking me off to," I lowered my voice, "kill me?"

Oscar chuckled in amusement. "Oh, you've caught me," he teased. "Listen, if I was going to kill you, girl, don't you think I would have done it by now? I mean, it's raining."

Good point. Not a practical time to linger.

"Come on," Oscar urged. "Let's just go, eh?"

"I—"

"That's the spirit," he cheered. "Now, I'm going to let go of your wrist and you're going to be a good girl and follow me." He cautiously released his iron clasp and took a few watchful steps forward.

As it turned out, my legs moved faster than my brain, because sure enough, I followed him. But I wasn't entirely happy about it. In fact, I seriously doubted that we were even heading in the right direction.

"This is the wrong way," I told him, adamantly.

"No, it isn't."

I snorted. "Admit it, you're lost."

Oscar laughed loudly. "I'm never lost. This is the way." He cast me a sideways glance. "I am certain."

"How?" I shot back. "Every direction looks the same." I waved my hand at the tall pines surrounding us.

"Not to me." Oscar tapped his temple with his index finger. "Intuitive," he said, with a sanctimonious smirk.

"Give me a break."

"Or perhaps I've laid out a trail of breadcrumbs," he joked. "One hundred and fifty invisible breadcrumbs."

The rain fell more heavily now, drenching our clothes and hair. I must have shivered, because Oscar shrugged out of his black jacket and tossed it to me.

I caught it. It was heavy and felt warm and dry on the inside. Even at arm's length, I could smell Oscar on the material.

"I told you to bring a coat," he reproached.

All of a sudden, my stomach lurched. "My jacket," I groaned. "And my dress. I left them on the ridge!"

"You're not going back for them," my surly companion rebuffed before the idea was even suggested.

"I have to!" I thrust his jacket back into his hands. "Mary bought me that dress today. I can't just leave it in the woods."

Oscar's eyebrows drew together. "You're going to have to," he snapped. He made a half-hearted attempt to shelter us both with his jacket, lifting it above our heads like an umbrella.

Without thinking, I turned and ran away from him, retracing my steps back to the ridge.

"Hey!" Oscar yelled. "Where do you think you're going!" I heard the crunch of the undergrowth as he jogged after me. "If you go back to the ridge," he shouted, "don't expect me to follow you!"

I broke into a sprint.

"I mean it!" Oscar bellowed.

But I kept running. I ran as fast as I could over bracken and debris until I burst through the trees and emerged into the clearing. The first thing I saw was my tan jacket, crumpled on the grass, soaked and muddy. To my dismay, I saw no sign of the pink shopping bag.

"Oh no!" I panted. "Where is it?" I lifted my jacket from the grass and scanned the glade.

Oscar stood some distance away, scowling, his hands stuffed in his jeans pockets. He leaned against a tree trunk, watching the rain form pools on the ground.

Where was it? I'd definitely had it when I reached the ridge. An awful thought dawned on me. I stepped closer to the verge and peered over the edge. My heart sank. "It's fallen over the edge," I cried. "I can see the bag at the foot of the cliff!"

Oscar broke into a grin.

I glowered at him. "It's not funny."

"Isn't it?"

"No!" I wailed. "I'll never be able to get that bag. It's too far down."

"Oh well."

"What am I going to do?" I realised that I was appealing to Oscar in utter despair, as though somehow he would be able to give me an answer.

Oscar exhaled loudly. "I'm getting soaked," he grumbled.

"It's gone," I said quietly, turning to face him.

Oscar opened his mouth and began catching raindrops on his tongue. "So, we're done here?" he asked.

I felt sick. How could I have been so careless?

Oscar frowned at my expression. "Get over it. It's just a dress."

"It was expensive. It meant so much to Mary, and I just…" *Uh oh.* My voice caught in my throat. I quickly pressed my fingers to my eyelids.

Oscar marched across the glade and stood before me. He pulled my hands away from my eyes.

"You've got to be kidding me?" he exclaimed. "You're not crying, are you?"

"No—" my voice cracked. *Abort sentence!*

"Come on, crying? *Crying?* I didn't sign up for this!" He clumsily patted me on the back. "There, there," he said stiffly.

I pursed my lips and wiped away a tear from the corner of my eye. "I can't help it," I mumbled. "I have overactive tear ducts."

He threw me a dubious look.

"It's a thing," I insisted.

"Look, let's cut to the chase, crybaby," Oscar moved on. "I'm no good with waterworks." He pressed his palms together. "What's the protocol here? You feed me the lines and I'll say them. Don't make me work for this."

"There's nothing you can say," I sighed softly. "The dress is gone and there's no way I can get it back. We might as well go."

Oscar gave me an approving smile. "Yes. Good."

We began walking back into the woodland. I kept my head bowed, in my own private funeral march. I sniffled a little bit.

"Are you still crying?" Oscar asked, unable to disguise the exasperation in his tone.

"I'm upset."

He kicked the ground. "This is annoying."

I glared at him. "If I'm so annoying, then maybe you should do us both a favour and leave me alone."

"No, I didn't mean that *you're* annoying," he rectified hastily, holding up his hands in submission. "I meant the *situation*. The thing is, there is one way that I can help you. But I really shouldn't do it."

I frowned. "What do you mean?"

His nose twitched. "There is a way to get the dress back," he confessed, "but only in an extreme emergency. I *really* shouldn't do it."

My eyes widened a fraction. "This is an extreme emergency," I pointed out.

Oscar stopped walking. For a long while we were silent. Then at last, he said, "I can't. I'm sorry, but I can't. Forget I said anything."

My shoulders sagged.

Oscar changed tack. "Is there any other way to shut you

up?" He must have noticed my insulted expression, because he swiftly re-worded. "I mean, is there any other way to *cheer* you up?"

I smiled in spite of myself.

Oscar's copper-coloured eyes softened for a moment. "You didn't lose the dress on purpose," he reassured me in a gentle voice. "Your aunt will understand. It was an accident."

"I know that. It's just..." I gazed at the interlacing branched around us. "It meant a lot to Mary." I paused, then added, "It meant a lot to me."

Oscar lowered his eyelids and exhaled tautly. "Okay," he said through gritted teeth, "if I could get the dress back, would the crying stop?"

I blotted my tears with the back of my hand. "Well, yes. But it's impossible. It must be a one-hundred-foot drop, and there's no way down. Unless you know a way down?"

His mouth curved up at the corner. "Do you want the dress?"

I swallowed a lump in my throat. "Yes, please."

Oscar flashed me a puckish grin. "Then I know a way down." He rubbed his hands together. "Right. I'm going to get that damn dress back, on one condition."

"Go on," I urged.

"That you walk over to those trees," he pointed to a cluster of oaks on the other side of the clearing, "and close your eyes."

"What? Why?"

Oscar held up his hands. "Those are my terms. Do you accept or not?"

How could I not accept? I was in no position to argue. I nodded my head in concurrence.

"Good girl." He gave me a little shove in the direction of the oaks. "Go. And don't open your eyes. Remember, a verbal contract is binding in the town of Hutton Ridge." He winked.

Confused but compliant, I walked to the shelter of the trees and reluctantly followed orders. Standing around in the rain with my eyes closed seemed well and truly absurd.

"This had better not be some dumb practical joke," I yelled into the breeze.

"Are your eyes closed?" Oscar called to me.

"Yes," I replied.

In the next second, I heard the pounding of feet on the muddy ground, as though Oscar were racing to the edge of the precipice.

Of course, my eyes instinctively shot open. And it was a good thing they did, because I was just in time to see Oscar hurtle off the ridge.

"No!" I screamed, clutching my heart. I raced across the clearing, severely dreading what I was about to see on the ground below.

I braced myself for the sight of Oscar lying motionless, broken and bleeding. I felt as though I was a heartbeat away from seeing something that I would never recover from.

What happened over the next few seconds, though, would forever be one of the most significant moments of my lifetime. I could honestly say that imagining Oscar dead changed my life forever. It was surreal, as though I had floated out of my body and was watching myself run to the ridge. For a brief instant, everything became clear. For the good and the bad, I couldn't live without Oscar. It wasn't a romantic Romeo and Juliet-esque proclamation, it was simply a cold, hard fact. I mean, it wasn't as though I knew Oscar, or even particularly *cared* to get to know him for that matter. But I knew that, somehow, on some bizarre level, losing him would lose me.

But as I peered over the edge of the ridge, I came crashing back down to reality.

Oscar stood staunchly at the foot of the cliff, completely unaffected by the jump.

"You absolute, brazen liar!" he shouted up at me. "You swore you wouldn't open your eyes!"

"You jumped off a cliff!"

Oscar raked his hands through his rain-soaked black hair. He cursed under his breath.

"Are you hurt?" I yelled down to him. "And also, are you crazy?"

"No," he snapped. "You shouldn't have opened your eyes. Now I'll never trust you again." He spat out the words with disdain.

I shrugged my shoulders. "You're not exactly the most trustworthy person yourself, Oscar."

He looked up at me with what I vaguely made out to be a sarcastic smile. "*I* haven't done anything to merit untrustworthiness," he stated. "*You*, however, have. You duped me, Rose."

I crossed my arms. "I'd hardly call it *duping* you," I

called down to him. "It was a shock. It's not every day that someone leaps off a cliff." I paused. "You did jump, didn't you? I didn't imagine it?"

"Yes, you imagined it," he replied.

"No, I didn't. You jumped!" My gaze travelled down the sheer rock face. He really jumped! "How are you going to get back up?"

"I'm not coming back up." He folded his arms stubbornly. "Not now, anyway."

"Why not?"

"Because I can't trust you not to watch," he sulked.

"Well, obviously I'm going to watch. You just performed a death-defying stunt. You can't expect me to look away while you perform the next one."

"Exactly. That's why I'm staying down here."

"Why can't I watch?" I pressed, frankly confused by the whole situation.

"Because it's none of your business." He dug his foot into the ground, agitated.

I sighed. "Okay. If it's really that important to you, then I'll close my eyes." *Maybe.*

He looked up at me, rightly suspicious. "That's what you said last time."

"Well, last time you didn't warn me that you'd be jumping off a cliff," I reasoned.

He puckered his lips, uncertain whether to believe me or not. "Do you swear?"

"Okay."

"That's not very convincing."

I sighed again. "I swear," I said, and I think I actually meant it that time.

After a brief mental deliberation, Oscar called back to me, "You'd better not be lying again."

I watched while he picked up the pink shopping bag and stuffed it into the back pocket of his jeans. Then I returned to the oaks and reluctantly closed my eyes.

I began to count.

One, two, three…

"You can open them now," Oscar whispered into my ear.

I gasped at the sound of his voice. It had scarcely been a few seconds since I'd seen him standing at the foot of the cliff.

"Oscar?" I choked.

He held up his hand to cut me off. "No questions." With a nod towards the woodland, he strode off into the trees, apparently confident that I would follow him.

And I did.

"By the way," he added, "don't mention this to your aunt. Or to anyone." There was a faint trace of anxiety in his tone.

"Okay," I agreed uncertainly.

"Not just about the cliff. I mean *all* of it. I'll make sure you get out of the woods, but then I'm out of here. Don't tell anyone that you saw me."

I chewed on my thumbnail. The idea of lying to Mary didn't sit well with me.

"Can't I tell my aunt that you're here? Don't you want a lift home?" I attempted to entice him with a free ride.

Surely he wouldn't choose to walk all the way back to Millwood in the rain?

"No, you cannot tell your aunt!" Oscar spluttered. "You've landed me in enough trouble as it is."

"How?" I furrowed my brow.

Oscar didn't reply.

"Okay," I exhaled heavily. "I won't tell anyone."

"Good." Oscar stalked ahead of me. Then, without taking his eyes from the path ahead, he yanked the pink bag from his back pocket and tossed it over his shoulder.

I caught it and peeked inside at the mulberry-coloured dress.

"Reunited," Oscar remarked, glancing back at me with a reluctant smile.

Somehow I knew that he wasn't referring to the dress.

PART TWO
OSCAR

CHAPTER FIVE

See No Evil, Hear No Evil

IF THERE WAS ONE THING that I regretted, it was letting Rose see me jump off the cliff. If Caicus had ever found out about that, he would have absolutely flayed me. Ha! At least she didn't see my vertical sprint to get back up to the crest. That would have taken some explaining. Dumb girl. She should have watched.

Anyway, after that colossal slip-up, the next few days passed by reasonably uneventfully. Caicus and I made ourselves at home; we even managed to slot ourselves in as part of the family. No questions asked.

Caicus hung around in the kitchen a lot, making weird dough-based concoctions with Mary. Personally I couldn't have thought of anything worse. I tended to linger wherever Rose was. It worked for me.

We did all right, pitching in with odd jobs here and there. Although I always drew the line at cleaning duties. Cleaning wasn't for me.

Apart from that, things were running relatively smoothly. I'd noticed a few signs that something was coming, particularly as the weather had been so grim. And, of course, that meant that we'd been penned in for the past week like a flock of clucking battery hens. Believe me, I was sick of the sight of every single one of them. The lone consolation was that Roger worked during the weekdays. I couldn't have stomached him, too.

As it happened, our first dry day came on a Tuesday, a week and a half after our arrival.

Outside, the sun shone brilliantly—a typical August afternoon. During a walk around the grounds, Caicus and I stumbled upon a truly inspired idea. But to pull it off, we would need to gather the necessary implements without rousing questions. As a general rule, the fewer questions asked, the less chance there was of being exposed. Anyway, we improvised some cock-and-bull story about how we'd love to do some gardening for Mary – calling it our way of thanking her for her kind hospitality.

It was hard to keep a straight face when reeling off that one.

So, whistling as we went, we trundled off to the garden shed. I especially liked the fact that we wore our matching navy polo shirts that day - it really made me feel in uniform.

I unbolted the wooden shed door and switched on the light. A solitary bulb swung from the ceiling, providing a spotlight of colour in the windowless, dingy room. We selected a few grubby tools and took them to the garden. Neither of us spoke. There was no need to.

Mary's garden was a patch of land at the back of the house. It was okay. A couple of flower beds and rose bushes. It was a garden; what more could be said?

I watched as Caicus jammed his pitchfork into the soil and rested his foot upon it.

A pitchfork? I thought irritably. *Right. 'Cause that doesn't look suspicious at all. We're not farming crops, idiot.*

"Snapdragons!" Caicus remarked brightly. "Isn't that nice?" His powder-blue eyes and fair hair made him seem almost angelic under the glow of the sunlight; it must have been an extreme contrast to my darker attributes. I guessed I was the fallen angel.

I looked down upon the snapdragons, some of which had wilted in the mid-summer climate. I flipped my spade into the air and caught it by the handle. "Is anyone watching?"

Caicus subtly glanced over to the house. "No one's in the kitchen," he confirmed. "Or the dining room."

"Good. You keep lookout."

I stabbed my spade into the ground and began unearthing the sprigs of snapdragons. Damn, it was fun. Authorised destruction. That was only one step below my personal favourite—*un*authorised destruction.

With complete reckless abandon, I uprooted the flowers and handed them to Caicus, who began methodically plucking off the snout-shaped petals.

"That ought to do it," Caicus said, giving me a little nudge with the toe of his boot.

"Sure?" I asked.

"I don't know." He opened out his fist to show me the

contents. "What do you think? Is that enough?"

I pushed his hand away. "How am I supposed to know?"

"Well, *I* don't know. What do you *think*?" He waved the snapdragon petals at me again.

I contemplated it for a while. "Eh, whatever," I said at last. "It'll do. And if it doesn't work, it doesn't work. Isn't it enough that we had the idea at all?"

Caicus nodded his head enthusiastically. "It was a good idea," he reflected. "We should give ourselves more credit. We're really good at..." he paused. I could tell he was trying to think of something profound to say. "Ideas," he finished.

Oh. Well, good enough.

I hopped to my feet and brushed the soil from my hands. "Yes, we are," I agreed matter-of-factly. "And we're always so underappreciated."

"True," Caicus agreed with a sombre sigh.

We had no modesty. It wasn't a trait that applied to us.

"I wish the others could see us now." Caicus licked his lips in excitement. "The look on their faces when they found out that *we* were the chosen two!"

I grinned. "That was a great day. If only I'd had my camera."

"To think they ever doubted us. *Us*," Caicus boasted. "I mean, *they* didn't find her, did they?" he went on, feeding our egos. "No. *We* did. All that time wasted searching, and we're the ones to find her!"

I laughed under my breath. "It must make them sick."

"Sick!" Caicus echoed.

"Speaking of sick, I don't know how much more of my

pleasant attitude I can stomach," I grumbled. "Or yours, for that matter."

"The feeling's mutual," Caicus jeered. His face contorted in distaste. "I'll be glad when this is all over."

I felt the familiar lurch of foreboding.

"Yeah," I grimaced.

I looked up to the sky, squinting in the bright light. All of a sudden I was overcome by what could only be described as extreme irritation. I stabbed my spade into the soil, relishing the sensation of the blade plunging into the ground.

Caicus cocked his head to the side. "Something bothering you, brother dearest?" he asked. I could sense a touch of misgiving in his tone.

"No."

"Hmm." He raised a cynical eyebrow. "Far be it for me to say, but I hope you're not getting too comfortable."

I laughed bitterly. "I am far from comfortable, my friend. In fact, I am categorically *un*comfortable." My gaze drifted up to Rose's attic window. There was no sign of movement from inside the room. I didn't like that. I liked to know where she was at all times. It made things easier.

"I can't figure her out," Caicus mused, joining my line of vision. "She infuriates me. My powers are useless on her. It's as though she knows who we are. I mean, that's the only logical theory I've come up with; she's found out our secret and is now immunised from our powers." He let out a howl of impatience.

I tapped my index finger to my mouth. "No," I muttered. "There must be some other way. She has no idea who we are."

For a while I thought she did. I thought she'd recognised me. But she didn't. She didn't know who I was. And she didn't know who *we* were.

Witches.

Valero Witches, to be precise.

I went on, "I don't know. She's…" I paused. What was she? "Special." As soon as the word had left my mouth, I knew I'd put my foot in it.

Special? What was I thinking?

Caicus looked at me bizarrely. "What? You're calling her *special* now?" He looked away again. "Anyone would think you're fond of her."

"Hardly!"

"Oh? What would you call it, then?"

More than fond, I thought.

Instead I said, "Work. It's my job to keep a close eye on her. We don't want you-know-who finding her now, do we? Not when we've come this far."

Caicus responded with a cat-like smile. "Eyes on the prize."

"Precisely."

"Well, this should help to keep her hidden," he said. He handed over the petals, and I stuffed them into my jeans pocket.

There was an old trick where the shape of snapdragons would catch the eyes and ears of unwanted seekers—straight into the dragon's jaws, so to speak. Ancient witch tribes would surround their camps with the flower so as to conceal their whereabouts from enemies. Normally I wasn't one for tricks and illusions, but desperate times call for desperate measures.

An abrupt shout from the manor startled us both.

It was Mary.

"Hello out there!" she called, waving at us from the kitchen window. "We're making sandwiches if you're hungry."

We exchanged a quick glance.

"The show must go on," Caicus muttered under his breath. He raised his voice to reply. "Thank you, Mary!" he gushed. "That would be lovely!"

"Oh yes," I harmonised in my most repulsive tenor. "Thank you!"

We dumped our gardening tools on the ground and crossed the lawn towards the house. Caicus led the way through the dining room entrance and we strolled into the adjoining kitchen.

Mary and Rose were already seated at the breakfast table, preparing sandwiches for lunch. The baby sat in his highchair beside them.

I couldn't resist sneaking a glance at Rose. She wore white linen trousers and a cookie-coloured summer top. Her autumn-brown hair tumbled loosely over her shoulders.

I scowled. She was beautiful. No, scratch that—she was *way* beyond beautiful. That was the most annoying thing about her.

Whatever. Game face on.

I decided not to look directly at her; that was becoming a fairly practised way of keeping my focus. Instead I looked at the breakfast table. Fascinating.

On the other side of the table, Mary buttered bread whilst Caicus engaged her in harmless conversation. As she chattered back effervescently, Caicus slipped his mind onto a different frequency, speaking only through thought and reaching only my ears. We'd learnt to communicate this way from a very young age, it certainly came in handy.

Oscar, Caicus signalled to me silently, *now's the time. I'll keep them distracted.*

I acknowledged his words whilst simultaneously remaining blasé to anyone beyond the private conversation.

Alright, I replied to Caicus. *I need an exit strategy. We don't want them getting suspicious.*

He winked at me. *There's only one strategy you need: charm. Now be a good boy and show me that pretty little smile of yours.*

Ha! I'll show you my pretty little fist in a minute. Jackass.

He sniggered under his breath. *Yeah, yeah. Are you going or not?*

I'm going. Make sure that you warn me if they leave the kitchen, I added. Then out loud, I oh-so-politely said, "Excuse me, Mary, may I use the shower?" Gag.

She nodded her head, sending her strawberry blonde curls bouncing around her cheeks. "Of course, dear. There are clean towels in the airing cupboard."

I flashed her an impossibly charming smile. "Thank you, Mary."

I excused myself and sauntered out of the kitchen. I could feel Rose's eyes on my back as I meandered to the staircase.

Once I was out of sight, I picked up my speed and, in

the blink of an eye, I was in the upstairs hallway.

I went through the motions of collecting a towel from the airing cupboard and hanging it on a hook in the bathroom. After that, I twisted the shower taps until the water cascaded down, pattering against the pearl white base. In the background, the hum of the water heater droned loudly. A nice touch.

I caught a glimpse of myself in the mirror and smirked at my reflection.

Hello, me.

Now for the fun part. Noiselessly, I strode out of the bathroom, closing the door behind me with a click.

After a sly check that the coast was clear, I swiftly ascended the second flight of stairs—the stairs leading to Rose's bedroom. And when I say swiftly, I mean my feet barely touched the floor. Add to that my exceptional lightness, which allowed me to strategically dodge all of the creaking floorboards.

Yawn. Give me a challenge.

I opened the bedroom door.

Damn... Maybe I spoke too soon.

If I was looking for a challenge, I got one when I stepped into Rose's room. This was the first time I'd actually been in the attic, so I was momentarily stunned by the undiluted scent of Rose. Everything from her clothes to her books—it was all *her.*

I recoiled. It was far too potent for my sensitive nose. I liked it a little too much.

Keen to get out of there ASAP, I stepped over to the bed

and lifted the mattress. I dug through my pockets and scattered the snapdragons along the frame of the bed. They were a little squashed, but still comparatively snout-shaped.

Eh, that'll do. I thought.

Satisfied with my work, I dropped the mattress back down and made for the door.

On my way out, I paused at the dressing table. There was a candle. It smelt sweet, like toffee. This was peculiar to me. In my experience, candles are used as tools, not as scented ornaments.

What does she use this for? I wondered.

I lifted it up for closer inspection and rotated it with interest. The wick was intact. It had never been lit.

My curiosity was interrupted by the sound of Caicus's raised voice travelling up from the ground floor.

"Rose!" I heard Caicus shout from downstairs. "Where are you going?"

I froze. She was on her way upstairs.

"To my room," Rose replied.

"Why?" Caicus demanded.

"Because I want to," Rose answered with an edge of impertinence. Her gentle footsteps echoed as she crossed the wooden floor towards the main staircase.

Oscar, Caicus wailed silently. *Get out! Get out now!*

Rose reached the first-floor hallway and headed for her bedroom staircase. However, as she passed the family bathroom, her footsteps stopped.

I listened to Caicus and Rose's conversation.

"So," Caicus began prattling away frantically, "this is

some cuckoo weather we're having, eh? Can you believe it? One day it's raining, the next day it's—"

Rose cut him off. "Oscar said he was going for a shower, right?"

"Uh, no. No, he didn't." Caicus laughed nervously. "No, wait, I mean, *yes*. Of course! Who else would be in the shower? It's not going to run itself, now is it? That would be ridiculous! Have you ever seen the view from my bedroom? It's fabulous. Come and have a look," he urged.

Jeeze, Caicus.

For the record, I would have dealt with the situation so much better.

Thanks to my razor-sharp hearing, I detected the delicate sound of Rose resting her fingertips on the bathroom door handle.

"He's not in there," she murmured.

Time to spring in to action. This is how the big boys do it.

Before Rose could make her move, I made mine. I shut off the shower and abruptly flung open the bathroom door.

Oh, did I not mention that I'd made it back to the bathroom? I could be *very* fast when I needed to be.

The best thing about this little stunt was Caicus's face. It was a picture! He was as white as a ghost. Sure, I could have told him that I was in there, but why waste a perfectly good opportunity to make him look like a jabbering buffoon?

I stood in the open doorway, my hair and body dripping with water and a pale yellow towel wrapped around my waist.

Just to rub it in, I feigned surprise at the sight of my

evident company.

Rose blushed and cast her eyes down to the floor.

Behind her back, Caicus's body language relaxed. He bit his lip in barely suppressed glee.

That was cutting it a bit close, he remarked to me, silently.

Nope. Easy, I responded. *No thanks to you! What was with the spiel about the weather? Have you no imagination?*

I panicked, Caicus protested. *You could have told me you were in there!*

I grinned wickedly.

"I-I'm sorry," Rose stammered. "I didn't mean to… I mean, I wasn't standing out here to, um, see you. I was just, um… I was just passing."

Caicus's face lit up in amusement and Rose hurried off to her bedroom.

Once we were certain that she was safely in the attic, we made our way to our own room.

It was a spacious twin bedroom, decorated to Mary's taste. There were a few oddly matched pieces of carved furniture and two single beds, both sporting daisy-patterned bedspreads—which incidentally matched the daisy-print curtains. No comment.

"Well?" Caicus pressed as we closed the door behind us.

"I lay the snapdragons under her mattress," I told him. "That should keep her inconspicuous for the time being." Sure, the snapdragon trick was a myth, but we'd been brought up to believe in myths. Living the life we'd led, I believed just about everything. Oh, with the exception of Mary's interior design taste. That was unbelievable.

Caicus flopped back onto his bed while I got changed into clean clothes.

I quickly threw on a black T-shirt and jeans and collapsed onto my own bed. Restless, I pulled the pillow from under my head and frowned at it.

"Urgh." I grimaced. "Was it really necessary to get the daisy pillowcases too? That woman is seriously unhinged."

Caicus ignored me.

"Cai, Look at this," I grumbled. "Doesn't it make you want to revolt? I'm genuinely concerned. There are daisies *every*where."

He didn't respond.

"Caicus," I snapped. I hated it when he ignored me. "*Caicus*, listen to me."

"I heard you, Oscar," he grunted. His eyes were closed.

"It's degrading. I feel… dirty." I lobbed my pillow at Caicus, who caught it and tossed it to the side.

"Forget the daisies," he griped, opening his eyes for the sole purpose of glaring at me. "Let me see the book, would you?" He stretched out his arm but made no attempt to prop himself upright.

"No. Get it yourself."

Bickering was something we did a lot.

"Come on, Oscar," he whined. "Just get it for me. I'm really tired."

I closed my eyes. "So am I."

That was a lie. I wasn't tired at all.

Caicus laughed like a naughty child—which always made me laugh, too. Perhaps because it reminded me of when we actually *were* naughty children.

"Please? Just do it!" he shouted, kicking his legs on the mattress.

This was how we had our fun, by the way—winding each other up, usually until it came to blows. Oh, then we were sorry. Or, he was, anyhow. At least that's the way I'd tell it.

Anyway, I decided to let him win one, so, with a very deliberate sigh, I reached under my bed and heaved out a worn brown trunk. Hanging precariously over the edge of my mattress, I coded in the lock combination and opened the lid.

It took a bit of rummaging, but buried beneath a mound of clothes was a heavy, leather-bound book. The antique cover was faded gold, and the yellowed pages were thicker and coarser than ordinary paper. Midway through, a page had been marked with a piece of string.

I flipped the book open to the marked page and handed it to Caicus.

For a moment he stared intently at the words imprinted on the aged paper. He didn't need to read them out to me—I knew them off by heart. I wouldn't have been surprised if he did, too.

THE PROPHECY OF LATHIAUS

It is foretold, on the day of his end,
so doth life begin
At the stroke of the eleventh hour,
he shall awaken
All will bow before him

All will perish at his mercy
Only one can end the blood spill
She, the girl with the heart of a witch
Before the hour turns to twelfth,
she must grant him her death
Two will take her to him, and all will be spared
Two will turn away, and all will be slaughtered
Our fate awaits.

"Lathiaus," Caicus spoke the name aloud.

"Lathiaus," I repeated. "It'll be a cold day in hell before I bow to him," I scoffed.

Yes, that was resentment in my voice. What could I say? I don't bow.

Caicus snorted. "I'm banking on it not coming to that."

I said nothing.

He carried on, "Let's just make sure this goes smoothly, okay? I have no intention of going head to head with Lathiaus. I don't want to be turned into kibble and bits."

"'Perish at his mercy'?" I jeered. "I bet he's all talk."

Caicus guffawed. "Wanna bet your life on that? People have been talking about this prophecy for centuries. 'Lathiaus's resurrection from the dead'," he mimicked our elders. "'The end to all witches, blah blah blah'. I think they were taking it pretty seriously, Oscar."

"Yeah, well…"

"And they're counting on *us* to pull this off," he added.

Pull this off?

He meant hand Rose over. She was the girl in the prophecy, after all. The girl with the heart of a witch. And when it was time for old Lathiaus's big comeback, it was going to boil down to this: us or her. If we handed her over to Lathiaus, we'd spare the lives of an entire race of witches. If we let her go, it'd be nuclear bye-bye for our kind. That's why everyone had been searching for the prophecy girl—she was our ticket out of extinction. And all Caicus and I had to do was take away her life force at exactly the right time.

Yep, that was the plan. No doubts at all. None whatsoever.

I rolled back onto my bed and gazed up at the white ceiling.

"Caicus, what if we…" *How shall I put it?* "What if we, say, don't do it?"

"We will do it."

"But what if we don't?"

"Then Lathiaus will end the line of witches. Everybody goes kaput. You, me, everybody."

"Right."

"But you already knew that," Caicus pointed out astutely. "You needed a bit of a reminder, eh?"

He wasn't stupid. He knew where my thoughts were heading.

"Would you really sacrifice all of our lives for some girl?" he asked bluntly.

I sighed. "No, of course not."

He was right. I shouldn't even have entertained such ludicrous thoughts. *Argh! She's ruining everything. I need to focus. Focus, focus, focus.*

"Anyway, I wasn't talking about *her*," I backtracked. "I'm not some sort of renegade. I was merely expressing a momentary concern. What I meant was, what if something goes wrong?"

Caicus clicked his tongue on the roof of his mouth. "It's all doom and gloom with you sometimes. Look, we've found the girl. We're guarding her until the day of reckoning. When it's time for Lathiaus's return, all we have to do is hand her over. Even a prize fool like you can't mess this one up."

I fanned my arms out across the ugly bedspread. "All the same, I'd rather that it wasn't our responsibility. It's such a drag. And you know how I get under pressure." I yawned apathetically.

"It's not all bad," Caicus said as he stared beyond the window. "Just think of the aftermath… I don't know about you, but I'm already choreographing the steps to my victory dance. We'll be legends, Oscar!"

He had a point.

"I wouldn't mind being a legend," I muttered.

"It makes the endurance of our overt manners that much more bearable."

"I suppose. But I don't know how much longer I can keep this up for."

"Well, you'd better pace yourself, because it could be weeks to go yet."

The truth was, no one could be sure of exactly when Lathiaus would return. We knew it would be on the anniversary of his death. But that wasn't much help, because he'd been vanquished hundreds of years ago, and the precise calendar date remained unclear. We'd taken a vague stab at guessing and decided that it would be some time in August.

All we could do was wait and hope that Lathiaus didn't somehow get to her first. Or, in my case, hope that I didn't have too much time to talk myself out of it.

Oh hell, I was the wrong person for this job.

I punched my fist into the mattress. "Curse my dreams!" After all, my dreams were what had landed us there in the first place. More specifically, I'd been having *visions.* Visions of Rose.

"No. The dreams were fine," Caicus piped up. "The dreams were the key to unveiling the prophecy girl. What I curse is our friendship. And the damn fact that you requested me as your companion. Swine!"

I sat upright and grinned broadly. "Who else would I choose? You're my best friend, not to mention the only Valero witch that I can tolerate being in the company of for more than five minutes."

"True. Although, don't forget, that's our family you're slandering, Oscar."

"Not by blood," I contradicted him. "We're just a coven of witches with only our powers in common. That does not a family make."

"They're the closest thing we've got to family," Caicus pointed out. "Besides, I'm not bound to you by blood, but am I not your brother?"

He had me there.

"Yes," I relented, grudgingly. "You're my brother. But I actually like you—that's the difference."

I smiled like butter wouldn't melt in my mouth. I could hold my hands up to the fact that I wasn't the easiest person in the world to live with, but Valero witches—excluding myself and Caicus, that is—were, without a doubt, the most insufferable people who ever existed. And I lived with all of them.

"Believe me, I'm not keen on them either," Caicus drawled. "They're a bunch of pompous, conceited know-it-alls, but they *are* our family. And you can't choose your family."

"If I could, I'd choose this one." I glanced around the room, my eyes landing on a framed photograph of Roger and Mary on their wedding day.

"Liar!" Caicus accused. "The woman aggravates you, I can tell."

"Well, obviously." I looked at him as though he were a complete imbecile. "But at least she's not a know-it-all. In fact, she's a know-nothing. I like the simplicity of her inane brain."

Caicus smirked.

"And as for the man," I went on, "he's rarely here. And when he is here, he doesn't speak all that much. I like that in a person. The less you hear their voice, the easier it is to forget the sound of it."

Caicus was markedly entertained by my analysis. "What about the kid?" he pushed.

"The baby? He's no trouble. He *can't* speak. That's even better."

"And the girl?" Caicus goaded.

I hoped he didn't notice the sudden tenderness in my expression. "Rose? She is... tolerable."

"*Rose*," Caicus mocked me. "I'm sorry, Oscar, I didn't realise we were calling her by her name now."

"Shut up, Caicus."

I made a mental note to work on better comebacks.

"You shut up, Oscar," Caicus retaliated.

Now we were just getting lazy.

"Personally," he added, "I can't be bothered to learn her name." He yawned like a lion, his golden blonde waves curling around his brow. "What's the point? She'll be dead soon, anyway."

As if it had been timed to fit Caicus's chilling words, we heard the sound of a piercing scream.

Rose's scream.

CHAPTER FIVE

Pocket Full of Tricks

THE SOUND OF ROSE'S SCREAM made my stomach knot. I sat bolt upright.

It had come from the bathroom.

I stared wide eyed at Caicus. Words seemed unnecessary, because there was no doubt that we were thinking the same thing. We sprung from our beds and pelted to the bathroom.

The door was closed and the bolt had been pulled across. But Rose was definitely in there. I could sense her.

I clasped the handle and rattled the locked door.

Damn.

My head spun. I had to get to her.

With a quick glance, I double checked that Caicus and I were alone, and then, with impeccable accuracy, I ploughed my fist through the solid door and my hand burst through the metal bolt, sending it clattering onto the bathroom floor tiles.

"Oh, good one, Oscar," Caicus grumbled, giving me a

hefty clip around the ear. "Like they're not going to notice a hole in the door. Oaf."

I didn't care. I shoved Caicus aside and raced to Rose, who lay unmoving beneath the sink. A trickle of ruby red blood dripped from her temple, blemishing the pristine, ivory tiles.

My mouth went dry. She looked so serene. *Too* serene.

I pushed back her golden brown hair and checked her pulse, pressing my fingers to her throat. Okay. There it was, the gentle rhythm of her heartbeat.

She was alive. I could breathe again.

I knelt beside her and lightly tapped her face. "Rose."

Caicus stood over us, peering down hesitantly.

"Do you think it was...*him*?" he asked in a hushed voice.

I examined the wound on Rose's head. It looked as though it might have been caused by a fall. "It doesn't seem like an attack..." I glanced to the bathroom window, which was latched shut. "No sign of an intruder."

Caicus crouched down and prodded Rose as though she were toxic. "So, what happened? Just an accident?"

"Looks that way. Maybe she slipped or something."

"Well, then, that's not our domain," Caicus stated frankly. "Let's get out of here before we're placed at the scene of the crime."

"Hand me that towel." I nodded towards the heated towel rack.

With a huff, Caicus snatched a white hand towel and tossed it over to me.

"This is a waste of time," he griped. "She just slipped.

Why are we still hanging around?"

I nursed Rose's head in my lap, dabbing at the broken skin with the towel. I didn't mind doing it, either.

"She's bleeding," I told Caicus—as if he couldn't see that for himself. "She'll probably have concussion."

Caicus threw his hands in the air, exasperated. "So?" he demanded. "That's not our problem."

"We can't leave her if she has concussion."

"Oh jeeze, Oscar," Caicus muttered under his breath. He pressed his knuckle to his mouth and waited until he was calmer before he spoke again. "Come on now, bro. Remember what I said, eh? Don't get too attached. Keep your eyes on the prize. Remember?"

I glowered at him. "Of course I remember," I snapped. "I know what I'm doing." I slid my arms under Rose's body and lifted her, cradling her close to my chest. She felt weightless. Perhaps because I was used to carrying heavier things. Or perhaps because my strength was, let's just say, above average. But not just that, it felt as though she belonged in my arms.

"Oscar," Caicus pleaded with me.

"I need to take her to her bed."

"Put her back!" Caicus hissed. "Put her back on the floor where you found her. She's fine."

"No." I waltzed out of the bathroom, carrying Rose in my arms. Her face was nuzzled into my shoulder. That was another thing that I didn't mind. Definitely didn't mind.

Caicus, however, shook his head with unmasked disapproval.

"Anyway," I added, glancing over my shoulder at him. "If I lay her in bed, the snapdragons will conceal her from Lathiaus. That's forward thinking." I didn't wait for Caicus's response–mostly because I didn't care. Instead, I cheerfully ascended the attic staircase and let myself into Rose's room.

I was starting to like it in there.

Very carefully, I placed Rose onto her bed, fluffing the pillows for her. Once she was settled, I took a tissue from the box on her nightstand and began swabbing at the wound on her temple. It had more or less stopped bleeding, but I kept at it for a little while longer. I realised that I was looking at her with absolute, out-and-out devotion.

"I'll take care of you," I told her.

A combination of the disturbance from my action and the sound of my voice gradually stirred Rose from her slumbering state. Her eyes opened hazily.

I perched at her bedside. "Hello."

She blinked up at me. "Hi," she mumbled, disorientated.

I reached out for one last tissue dab.

"What are you doing?" Rose mumbled blearily. She tried to sit upright.

"Bad idea," I said, easing her back down onto the bed. "You shouldn't move too quickly. You might have concussion."

Her eyes searched mine as she began to blearily piece the events together. "The bathroom…" she murmured. "I slipped…"

She sat up now.

"*You*," she hissed. "Get away from me!"

"Me?" My eyes widened. "What did I do?"

"You know what you did!"

"Clearly I do not," I answered thinly. "You're delirious." I began overly enunciating my words, as though she may have been hard of hearing. "You hit your head." I was aware that my comment was extremely patronising. I couldn't help myself. It was just my way.

"I know I hit my head," she shouted. "Get away from me!"

I folded my arms. "Talk about ungrateful. I just saved your life, Rose. Your *life*. You could have bled to death on the bathroom floor." Yes, it was a slight exaggeration, but it illustrated my point nicely. "Is that what you wanted? Such an unseemly demise? To die beside a toilet?"

Rose tentatively touched the scrape on her head. She winced.

I winced for her.

"You didn't save me! You're up to something..."

Here she goes, I thought fondly, *throwing accusations around again. She's so cute when she does that.*

"Voodoo or something!" she finished.

I laughed loudly. "Oh really? Voodoo?"

"Or something!"

"Yes, if that *something* is saving you." I was still waiting for my hero's welcome, by the way.

"You're always around," Rose rambled on. "And I know I've met you before..."

A surge of excitement rushed through my veins.

Go on, I willed.

"The eyes..." she said.

Yes, I urged silently. *You recognise my eyes. You know me.*

But the conversation didn't progress in the way that I'd hoped it would. They weren't *my* eyes that Rose was referring to after all.

"Those crow eyes," she went on, "and all of the weird stuff that happens when you're around..."

She doesn't remember me.

"Coincidence," I replied, with about as much lustre as an old boot.

"And the bizarre things in your pockets."

I stiffened. *Wait, what? My pockets?* That didn't sound good.

She gauged my expression. "Yes, I know about all the creepy voodoo."

"What creepy voodoo?"

Damn, damn, damn. She's bluffing.

"The sage, the knife, the coin," Rose reeled them off one by one.

She's not bluffing. How does she know about those? Damn, my clothes! After the shower I'd left my clothes in the bathroom. *Idiot!*

She must have gone through my pockets. I racked my brain, trying to recall what she had said she'd found. My cluster of sage, my ceremonial knife, my talisman coin...

Rose began to tremble. "You're some kind of... something."

I licked my lips, struggling to retain a blasé façade. "I'm sorry, but I don't have the faintest idea what you're talking about. You bumped your head, remember?" I leaned over her, talking slowly and carefully. "My name is *Oscar.*"

She took a swipe at me. "I don't have amnesia! I know exactly who you are."

"Hmm. Well, you seem to be talking nonsense."

She staggered unsteadily to her feet. She stumbled and unthinkingly grasped my shoulder for support, then immediately yanked her hand away as though she'd been burned by me.

"You can hold on to me if you want," I said with a vague, satirical smile.

"No, I don't want," Rose shot back. She began stumbling across her room.

Uh oh. "Where are you going?" I stood from her bed.

"I'm going to expose you for the psycho you are." She stormed for the staircase.

Caicus, I called silently. *Go to the bathroom and empty my jeans pockets. Quickly!*

"I'm going to prove that you're lying," Rose insisted, stomping down the attic steps. "And then Mary will see you for who you really are. *What* you really are," she corrected herself.

I jogged behind her, my heart racing.

Rose charged along the corridor and into the bathroom. Heaped on the floor beside the shower were my discarded clothes. Rose riffled through the pile until she found my black jeans.

I hovered in the doorway, holding my breath.

Please be empty, please be empty, please be empty…

Empty!

Hallelujah.

"I-I don't understand," Rose stammered. She dropped the jeans onto the tiled floor. "You," she turned to face me. "You must have emptied the pockets."

I shrugged my shoulders. "Sorry. I don't follow. I have absolutely no idea what you're talking about."

Rose's emerald eyes turned frosty. "Just leave me alone," she hissed. "And leave my family alone." She stormed out of the bathroom, deliberately shoving past me as she went.

I watched as she thundered up the attic staircase and slammed her bedroom door behind her.

I let out a breath. Another disaster averted.

Hastily, I bundled my clothes together and returned to my own bedroom.

Caicus was sprawled out on his bed. The contents of my jeans were scattered over the daisy-print duvet in front of him.

"Close call," he commented.

"Why didn't you reply when I told you to clear out the pockets?" I scolded him. "I didn't think you'd done it in time. My little black heart was practically beating right out of my chest." I paused to glower at him. "You're lucky I didn't die from heart failure."

Caicus smirked. "Payback for earlier. Now you know how it felt to be standing outside the bathroom with her about to burst in on *nobody* in the shower."

I grinned.

He grinned back.

"It was close, though," he said, his tone dropping to a serious note. "I only just made it back to our room before she came down the stairs like a whirlwind. You must have really riled her this time."

"I can't believe that sneak went through my pockets." I slapped my head in disbelief.

"Sneaky shrew! We'll have to be more careful in future. And no using our powers around her."

I sat down on my own bed. I still hadn't told Caicus about my little cliff-jumping show the week before. And I intended to keep it that way.

"So," Caicus went on, thankfully changing the subject, "turns out you weren't quite her knight in shining armour, eh?"

I smiled complacently. "It's too difficult being the hero. I think I'll just go back to being me."

"Oh good. You know I have a weak stomach for heroic gestures. It was upsetting to see you being so…" he grimaced, "considerate."

"Sorry about that. Minor error in judgement. Happens to us all from time to time."

Caicus puffed out his chest. "Not me. You'll never catch *me* being considerate. Not out of choice, at any rate."

"Okay, okay." I rolled my eyes. "I get it. You're faultless and can do no wrong." He was so smug it made me want to clock him. "Anyway, if I hadn't taken her up to her room, we never would have had a chance to clear out my pockets before she showed the contents to Mary, Mary, Quite Contrary."

"True," Caicus agreed. "How did you explain it?"

"I told her she'd imagined it."

Caicus doubled over with laughter. "Don't tell me she actually bought that?"

"Maybe. A knock on the head can make you go all kinds of crazy. But she also mentioned something else. Something about eyes. Crow eyes."

"Crow eyes?" Caicus repeated, his eyebrows pulling together. "What's that about?"

"I think it's Lathiaus."

He tensed. "She's seen him?"

I contemplated it for a moment. "Only in her sleep. In her dreams she must be close enough to see his eyes now." The thought made my heart wrench.

"Then it's almost time."

"Yes," I said quietly.

"We're nowhere near prepared," Caicus grumbled. "It could have been today, you know. Right there, in the bathroom. And we'd have missed the whole thing."

"It's not today," I told him.

"It could be today," he argued. "We're not ready. We need to prepare the brew, we need to get the others out of the house—"

"It's not today," I snapped.

"What makes you so sure?" he challenged.

"It's just not, okay? There have been no signs. The weather's glorious, no tremors or storms, nothing."

"What about your visions? Are they getting any clearer?"

I felt my shoulders tauten at the mention of my visions.

Or my dreams, if you will. Well, not *my* dreams exactly. Rose's dreams.

For the past few months, our dreams had somehow fused together. Almost as though I had slipped through a crack in between dimensions and ended up in her unconscious mind. I was a spectator, watching her nightmares play out like a Hitchcock horror. And that was how I was able to track her to Millwood.

It was strange, but I'd developed a bond with her through our subconscious meetings. Every time she had a nightmare, I was there too. Yes, I always stood out of sight, skulking through the shadows like a creature of darkness, but I saw it all. I saw Rose walk mechanically towards the demon Lathiaus, and each time I wanted to call out to her—to stop her. At first he was just a mound, hunched beneath a black cloak. But with every dream he grew a little stronger, forewarning of his imminent awakening. Now he stood tall before her, gigantic and intimidating.

The nightmares were terrifying—even for me, who kept to the sidelines. But I saw her, and I learnt so much about her from those unearthly encounters. I felt as though I knew her better than I knew myself. It was because of this connection that I was able to find her. That was my power—I could find anything I wanted, as long as it had a place in my heart. And she did.

"It's not time yet," I said to Caicus. That was all he needed to know.

"I wonder if she knows," Caicus muttered to himself. "Maybe she knows about Lathiaus."

"No. She doesn't know. She blames everything inexplicable on me." I looked over at the former contents of my jeans, which were sprawled on Caicus's bed. My cluster of cleansing sage, tied together with a piece of red string, and my ceremonial dagger, the handle engraved with our coven symbol—basically just an elaborate 'V' for Valero. How imaginative.

"Great," Caicus grumbled. "If she's suspicious, then it's only a matter of time before she finds us out."

"So what? What's the worst that can happen? She exposes us and your powers of persuasion no longer work on her? Guess what, numbskull, your powers already don't work on her."

"No, *numbskull*," he echoed back. "The worst that can happen is that she blabs to Mary and we're booted out of the family home. Things will be a little less straightforward if we're exiled. You know full well we can't stick around if we're not invited. Not to mention the fact that the prophecy girl's not going to be so willing to guzzle down a potion brew handed to her by two witches."

"She doesn't know anything," I repeated. "And you've got Mary eating out of the palm of your hand, so you've got nothing to worry about there."

Caicus grinned and cast his pale blue eyes upon me. Fooling around, he blinked his irises into an icy white. Of course, it had no bearing on me because I was a witch. But to a human it was mesmerising, like a blinding flash dazzling them into believing and agreeing with everything Caicus said. That was Caicus's power. The one loophole to this was that if the victim exposed him to be a witch, then his power would be weightless. All bets would be off.

Rose was the exception. It was odd. We couldn't be sure how exactly she was immune to Caicus. She certainly didn't seem to know that we were witches. Our only explanation was that she herself was a witch—or part witch, anyway. After all, the prophecy did refer to her as 'the girl with the heart of a witch'.

I clasped my hands together and rested them in my lap. "I don't sense her to be a witch," I said absentmindedly.

"Neither do I."

"I wonder why the prophecy forecasts her? Her, and only her." It was a question I'd asked myself often.

Caicus shrugged. "Perhaps she's the only one of her kind—the only known entity with the heart of a witch but the body of a human. Like a rare jewel."

"What do you think will happen…you know, when we hand her over?"

Caicus let out a heavy sigh. "I don't know, Oscar. But I imagine it'll be quick."

My chest tightened. I nodded my head.

"Then it'll all be over," he added. "And things can go back to normal."

"Yeah."

"Anyway," said Caicus, his tone lightening, "you should put these away." He tossed the contents of my pockets over to me. "And find a better hiding place this time, dimwit."

My sage, my dagger…

Wait.

Something was missing.

"Oh hell!" I shouted.

Caicus jumped at my outburst. "What? What is it?"

I leapt to my feet and began flinging up his bed sheets. He shuffled back until he was sitting on his pillow.

"What?" he demanded.

"My talisman. Did you get it from my pocket?"

Caicus's eyes widened a fraction, but he said nothing.

"Have you seen it?" I barked.

"No!" he yelled back. "It wasn't in your pocket."

"It's *always* in my pocket."

"Well, obviously it's not, because I emptied your pockets and it wasn't there," he fired back. "So don't blame me."

"Argh!" I pounded my foot on the floor. "*She's* got it."

"Damn it, Oscar! The talismans are inscribed. If she finds out we're witches, we can kiss the plan goodbye. It's over. We're out of here, and Lathiaus will kill us all."

I kicked my bed in temper. I must have kicked it a little too hard, though, because it skidded across the room and crashed against the wall.

"Oscar!" Caicus hissed. He threw a pillow at me.

I took a deep breath. Okay. This wasn't irrevocable yet.

"I'll get it back," I told Caicus. Before he could reply, I was out of the room.

Slow down, I reminded myself.

I inhaled deeply, tasting the air. Rose wasn't in her bedroom. That was handy.

I closed my eyes. *Talisman*, I willed. That was how my

power worked. I pictured what I wanted to the finest detail: the thin, cold brass, the faded tawny colour, the words imprinted on the surface... I felt it in my heart and envisioned it with the deepest love.

Got it.

I was able to see it clearly in my mind's eye, tucked safely into a secret compartment of Rose's jewellery box.

Nice try. I smirked.

In a heartbeat I was in her room and rummaging through her jewellery box. Bracelets, rings, blah blah blah... talisman!

"Hello, love," I said, kissing the brass coin.

And then I heard the attic door open.

Busted.

PART THREE

ROSE

CHAPTER SEVEN

Words

I SAT ON MY BED WITH the covers bunched around me.

Maybe Oscar had been right. Maybe I really was imagining things. Perhaps that was a symptom of concussion? Come to think of it, I was feeling a little light headed. Although I presumed that was fairly common after being bombarded with a serious overload of unexplained events.

I touched the bump on my temple. It was sore. Of course it was—I'd clipped it on the porcelain sink. Ouch. Even the memory hurt.

I leaned back against my pillow, gazing out of the window at the cloudless blue sky. It was nice to see a clear day for a change. I'd spent the past week watching the rain fall, working my way through Mary and Roger's literature collection, and playing chess with Oscar. Conveniently, Oscar always seemed to show up whenever I was alone. It was strange. I still didn't exactly trust him, but I hadn't come any closer to uncovering his agenda. If there was even an agenda to uncover.

Of course, I still had reason to be suspicious. The Valero boys seemed to be magnets for baffling things. One good example was their weightless footsteps. It was virtually impossible to hear them cross the corridor, even with the extremely creaky floorboards hindering their path. In fact, compared to the rest of the occupants of the house, Caicus and Oscar's footing was beyond light—it was almost illusory.

But the incident that stood out above all was what had happened in Hutton Ridge. Despite the amount of time Oscar and I had spent together, we had never spoken of our encounter that day—mostly because Oscar refused to. Having had over a week to dissect it, I somehow convinced myself that Oscar's perilous jump was not entirely unfeasible. After all, I'd never jumped off a cliff, so how could I be sure if it was possible or not?

On more than one occasion I had contemplated talking to my aunt about it, but something held me back. It was as though I felt a loyalty towards Oscar that I simply couldn't betray.

I sighed.

Gazing out at the distant tree tops, I watched the leaves sway gently in the breeze. And then, in front of the window, something else caught my eye. The candle on my dressing table.

Something was different.

I hopped up from my bed and walked over to the table. Carefully I picked up the candle and examined it, trailing my index finger along the smooth wax surface.

Now, that candle had sat in the same spot for the past God-only-knew-how-many years. Subsequently, I could practically picture every detail just from memory alone. Most noticeably, there was a distinctive stripe of ochre trailing from the wick to the base. From my bed I'd always been able to see that marking, and yet that day, somehow, the stripe was facing out to the window.

The candle had been moved.

What? Why would someone come into my room and move my candle? Mary and Roger never went up there, and baby Zack couldn't walk, let alone climb two flights of stairs and rearrange my room. I knew I hadn't moved it. That left two people…

So much for giving the Valeros the benefit of the doubt. They'd been in my room! But *why*?

My mind was jumbled. I needed to think clearly.

Okay, retrace my steps, I decided.

After bumping into Oscar post-shower, I'd gone up to my room. When I came back down I passed the bathroom and noticed Oscar's clothes dumped on the floor. I wasn't usually one for snooping, but I counted that to be extenuating circumstances. I ducked into the bathroom and locked the door behind me. Before I could stop myself, I was rummaging through his pockets. I wasn't sure what I expected to find. In fact, I didn't really expect to find anything.

But that had been wishful thinking.

In actual fact, I found a whole lot more than I bargained

for.

There were three objects in total: a small dagger with some kind of marking engraved on the handle; a cluster of sage bound together by a worn piece of string; and a brass coin inscribed with unfamiliar words.

I didn't imagine it. The memory was too vivid.

I felt sick just thinking about it. Suddenly everything started to feel a little too real. Why would he carry those things around in his pocket? I mean, a dagger, for crying out loud! Obviously, to me, a non-dagger-carrying citizen, that stuff seemed psychotic.

But it's Oscar. I found myself saying that phrase an awful lot these days.

In all honesty, when my fingers first touched the cold blade of the dagger, I wanted so badly for it to be the final straw. And it should have been. I wanted to hate him, but instead I began making excuses. *Maybe he's been using it for gardening.* Yes, that was fairly believable. *Maybe it's for opening boxes.* Shaky, but still not completely unreasonable.

And then my rational side kicked in. *He carries a dagger.*

That was enough. I didn't want to see it any more. Any of it. I just wanted to get out of that bathroom. Moving hastily, I returned the items to his pocket and made my getaway.

There was one slight catch, though. I must have slipped on the wet floor tiles, because I remembered falling forward towards the sink. I must have knocked myself out cold, because the next thing I knew, Oscar was sitting at my bedside, dabbing my head with a tissue. Then, of course, we argued, and I stormed off to show him what I had found in his pockets. But when I looked through his jeans again, the contents had vanished.

Or had they?

Wait. Backtrack. Before I'd left the bathroom, I'd put everything back…hadn't I?

My hands began to tremble. Maybe I hadn't put *everything* back. Even in my state of avoidance, I hadn't been able to let go of the one thing that might have given me some answers. *Genuine* answers.

I quickly dug through my own pocket and drew out the brass coin.

There. Whatever it was, whatever it meant, it was real. I saw it, plain as day, before my very eyes. I had been right all along. And Oscar had lied to me—again.

There was an inscription on the coin. The print was minute and written in an unfamiliar language.

I grabbed a notebook from my dressing table and jotted down the words onto a blank page.

Bellator Tenebris. Mortifer Veneficus

I tore out the sheet of paper and folded it into a small square. Something about those words sent chills down my spine. This was my chance to finally piece together a part of the Valero jigsaw, and I wasn't going to waste it. For the good or the bad, I needed to know the truth.

I scanned the table for a safe place to keep the coin—somewhere Oscar wouldn't look. My eyes fell on my white leather jewellery box. Inside it there were a couple of secret compartments which would go unnoticed by anyone who didn't know much about jewellery boxes—which I was guessing Oscar didn't. Anyway, it seemed as good a hiding place as any, so I tucked the brass coin into one of the compartments, beneath a heap of assorted rings and bracelets.

Once the coin was hidden, I left the attic and snuck downstairs, all the while with my fingers crossed. If ever there was a good time *not* to bump into the boys, it was then.

I made it to the ground floor undetected and found Mary in the conservatory.

"Hi," I said, hovering in the doorway. Uh oh. I'd almost forgotten about the huge bump on my head. If Mary saw it, she'd probably insist on my going to hospital to get it checked out. I was not loving that idea. Quick thinking time. I shook my hair forward to conceal the shiner. *If she asks, I'm experimenting with the grunge look*, I decided.

But she didn't ask. She was lounging in one of the pink armchairs, reading a romance novel and sipping tea from a dainty china cup.

"Hello, dear," she said, peering up over her reading glasses. "Everything okay?"

"Yep," I smiled. "Everything's fine."

In the far corner of the room, Zack played with a plastic train, making an occasional choo-choo noise.

"Are you bored, honey?" Mary asked, placing her book down on the coffee table. "Where are the boys?"

"The boys are upstairs," I said, struggling to keep my tone indifferent. "I'm not bored. I was wondering—"

Mary cut me off. "Why don't the three of you go on a day trip or something? You can borrow the minivan. I'm sure Caicus would be able to drive it."

The thought of getting into a car with Caicus Valero was positively nauseating.

"No, thanks," I replied. "Actually, I was wondering, do you have an internet connection here?"

"Umm..." Mary mulled it over. I knew technology wasn't her forte. "Yes, I believe Roger has the interweb."

The interweb? Okay, technology *really* wasn't her forte.

She went on, "It's on his laptop, though. Is that any good?"

"Yes," I nodded my head eagerly, now using my palm to conceal the bump in an I'm-so-laid-back-I-can't-even-hold-my-own-head-up kind of way. "Could I use it for a minute?"

"Sure, honey. It's in the study. I could show you where, but don't ask me how it works. I'm hopeless with computers!"

"No problem," I smiled. "I should be able to figure it out."

Mary picked up her book from the coffee table. "I'll leave you to it then, shall I?"

"Yes. Enjoy your book." I gave her a quick wave and then closed the conservatory door.

Right then. I was off to Roger's study. It was a room at the back of the house—one of the ones I rarely went into; I'd never had much reason to in the past.

Rather tentatively, I twisted the door handle and peeked inside. The walls were mahogany panelled and the carpet was a rich brown. There was only one small window, which didn't appear to allow much light in, so the room seemed drab. In fact, I suspected that the study was pretty much a forgotten room. Roger was inclined to do the majority of his work at the office of his accountancy firm, and the chunky black laptop sitting atop the desk was coated with a fine layer of dust. One potted dracaena plant stood tall in the corner, its leaves drooping ever so slightly. I made a mental note to come back and water it when I had more time.

Pushing the thought aside for the time being, I approached the desk and brushed the dust from the laptop. The internet connection cable was already hooked into the port, so all I needed to do was switch it on at the mains. After that, things were relatively straightforward. There was a fast connection, too, which almost seemed wasted on people who didn't use it—especially since my connection at home was so poor that it was hardly worth the bother.

While the search engine loaded, I took a seat in Roger's office chair.

It was only when I started typing that I noticed my palms were clammy. Apparently, what I was about to do was affecting me far more than I cared to admit. The truth was that whatever secret I unearthed, it would change things forever. Would change *Oscar* forever. There would be no turning back.

Swallowing nervously, I tapped my index finger on the keys.

Translations.

I clicked 'Search' and watched as a long list of results appeared on the screen. I scrolled down until I found what looked like a good link and clicked on it. As the webpage materialised before me, I unfolded the notebook paper and re-read the scrawled words.

"Bellator Tenebris. Mortifer Veneficus," I spoke them quietly before typing them into the translation box.

Below the text box were the final two steps required for the translation process.

'Choose language to translate from' and 'Choose language to translate to'.

The latter option was simple, so I began with that first. I highlighted 'English' on the selection of language choices.

The top option, 'Choose language to translate from,' was much trickier to complete.

I wasn't familiar with any of the words on the coin, so that narrowed my search down to *not English.*

What language is it likely to be? my brain churned. Well, Valero sounded Italian. I started with that.

I highlighted 'Italian' and clicked on 'Translate.'

It took a few seconds, but the results were inconclusive. Annoyingly, the text box was wiped clear.

Okay, so it was not Italian. I retyped the words into the space provided.

Think logically. I stared at the lettering. It seemed sort of symbolic. Maybe from one of those old world places. I drummed my fingers on the desk. *Ancient Greece?*

I highlighted 'Greek' and waited for the results. Again the text box came back empty.

This was ridiculous. Why hadn't I learned more languages when I had the chance? I tried to remember the language classes available at school: Spanish, French, German, Latin…

"Latin," I murmured as I retyped the words into the box.

I scrolled through the language options and selected 'Latin' then clicked 'Translate'.

And this time, the text returned to me. Translated.

Oh… my… God.

I felt the colour drain from my face.

Breathe, I reminded myself. I knew things were bad if I had to remind myself to breathe. And yet I still wasn't doing it.

I let out a puff of air.

Moving on autopilot, I shut down the laptop. Before leaving, I crumpled the notebook paper into a ball and stuffed it into my pocket. And then I ran. I ran all the way along the corridor and up both flights of stairs.

At the top of the attic staircase, I burst through the door to my bedroom.

What the…?

Oscar was standing at the window. The contents of my jewellery box were scattered across my dressing table. One guess what he was holding in his hand.

The brass coin.

He spun around to face me.

Okay. I had two options. One, confront him with what I knew, all guns blazing. Or two, play it his way.

"What are you doing?" I asked calmly—as if I didn't know.

It took several seconds before he replied.

"I'm looking for something," he said.

Several seconds and *that* was the best he could come up with?

"What are you looking for?" I pushed.

"Safety pins," he improvised.

"Oh. Why?" This was good. Very quick-fire.

"Because I have things to be… pinned."

"What?"

"Socks."

"Socks?" I echoed. "You want to safety pin your socks?"

"Yes." He didn't blink.

"Right." I folded my arms. "And you thought you'd find safety pins in my jewellery box?"

"Yes."

Now, if I hadn't been so aware of what was in his left hand, I probably would have missed this. The speed of it was quite astounding, really. Here's what happened: with remarkable slight of hand, Oscar slipped the coin under his belt whilst making it appear as though he was just resting his thumb in the belt loop.

"So, you weren't looking for the coin?" I asked simply.

Unsurprisingly, he played dumb. "Huh?"

I laughed. "Don't tell me you're going to deny it."

"Deny what?" He smiled mockingly. "That bump on the head must have—"

I abruptly cut him off. "I know about the coin."

"What coin?"

"The one you just tucked under your belt."

A glimmer of anxiety flashed across his handsome face, then disappeared as quickly as it had come. He unbuckled his black leather belt and pulled it from his jeans. It slid through the coarse material seamlessly. Gripping it in his fist, he held it out proudly and it swung from his hand like a restrained snake. Nothing had dropped onto the floor. The coin was nowhere in sight.

"See?" he said. "No coin." He strode up to me and grazed his fingers over the bump on my head. "Get some rest. You need it."

I let him pass me. But before he could leave the room, I took the crumpled notebook paper from my pocket.

"Bellator Tenebris," I read aloud. "Mortifer Veneficus."

Oscar froze.

I carried on, "Bellator Tenebris. The Dark Warrior."

His hands balled into fists.

I kept going, "Mortifer Veneficus." My throat went dry. "The Deadly Witch."

Deadly Witch.

CHAPTER EIGHT

The Fiery Truth

OSCAR STOOD MOTIONLESS IN THE attic doorway. He kept his back to me.

I read from the notebook paper again. "Mortifer Veneficus. The Deadly Witch."

He whirled around and snatched the paper out of my hand.

"Why do you keep saying that?" he asked, attempting to sound detached.

"I'm sure this isn't the first time you've heard it." I found myself standing uncomfortably close to him. His rasps of breath brushed against my cheek.

"Oh? Doesn't ring a bell."

"Well, it was written on your coin."

Backed into a corner, Oscar changed tactics. "Oh, that little thing. I don't even know what that is. It's one of those novelty gimmicks. I don't know why I still keep it. Funny how people get attached to inanimate objects."

"Very funny," I replied. "At least you know what I'm

talking about now. Your memory must be coming back."

"Must be," he agreed, matching my dry sarcasm.

"I know you took it from my jewellery box." I wasn't playing anymore.

Neither was he.

He promptly dug into his pocket and produced the coin, then shoved it into my hand.

"You see?" he said. "Just a useless piece of brass."

I stepped away from him and walked to the window. I noticed that his eyes were transfixed on me, intently watching my every move.

"Is it important to you?" I asked.

"Nope."

"So, can I have it?" I ventured.

"Sure." His eyes were locked to my hand.

Yeah, right; I could 'have' it until he stole it back later that day.

"If it's so trivial to you, then let me..." I glanced to the candle on my dressing table, "melt it."

Oscar clenched his jaw. "What would be the point of that?"

"Does it matter?"

"Nope. Go ahead," he spoke in a taut voice. His focus didn't move from the coin.

Okay, Oscar, time to call your bluff.

Mary kept a mini box of matches in the top drawer of my dressing table, just in case I ever wanted to light that old toffee candle. But of course, with my fire phobia, that would have been about as likely as pigs flying. Come to think of it,

I'd never even struck a match before. Talk about facing your fears.

I set the coin down on top of the candle, nestling it beside the wick.

Oscar shifted his weight from left to right. He looked as though he were about to implode.

As I opened the box of matches, my stomach did flips.

Oh God.

I selected a matchstick and pinched it between my thumb and forefinger, preparing to strike it against the rough side of the box.

Oh God. There's going to be fire. It's going to be in my hands...

I raised the match.

Oh God! What if the fire spreads to my arm and I burst into flames? What if the whole house burns down?

I gulped.

I give up. I can't do this.

He won.

But just as I was about to throw in the towel, Oscar beat me to it.

It all happened so fast that I could scarcely believe my eyes. In a fraction of a second, Oscar was upon me. He gripped my wrist and pinned my hand to the window, causing the glass to rattle and the box of matches to drop to the floor. The spilt matchsticks scattered across the carpet like the fatalities of our own private war.

Our eyes met.

"Thought so," I whispered. I yanked my hand free.

He didn't speak.

I reached over to the candle and retrieved the coin. Without dispute, I handed it back to him. After all, I didn't want it. All I wanted was the truth.

He nodded a vague 'thank you' and returned it to his pocket.

"It is important to you," I noted.

"It's lucky."

"Like a charm?"

"A talisman," he corrected.

It was fair to guess that his answers were going to be basic, one-word, hope-she-stops-asking kind of answers.

"You're a witch, aren't you?" I got straight to the point, looking into his troubled russet eyes as I spoke.

His lips pressed together obstinately.

As I searched his eyes, it dawned on me that he was vulnerable. Needless to say, this came as a shock. Until that point, 'vulnerable' would certainly not have been a word I would have used to describe Oscar Valero. The fact of the matter was, it hadn't occurred to me that he might have been hiding his secret because he *couldn't* tell me. I had naturally assumed that his lies came from a callous and devious place.

But I had been wrong.

With my gaze fused to his, I stood perfectly still. I couldn't look away, and I knew he couldn't either. We were stuck there, like magnets trapped by an invisible force. And what we shared in that moment was… well, it was incredible. I can truly say that the simple act of looking at Oscar was the greatest consciousness I'd ever experienced. I saw him so intimately, almost as though I were glimpsing directly into his soul.

"Tell me," I pleaded.

He didn't budge.

"You can tell me," I assured him. "Oscar, I've seen what you can do. You're *different...*"

He spoke now, but in a voice so weak that it was barely audible. "I'm not evil."

"I know," I responded without thinking—though I meant what I said. He wasn't evil. He was just *Oscar.* "I don't care what you are." I meant that, too. "But I need to know. I need to hear you say it."

I explored his eyes again. It was frightening how much I saw in just one look: sorrow, regret, secrecy… and fear.

"You can trust me," I vowed, hand on heart. "Remember when you jumped off the ridge and you asked me to close my eyes—"

"Yes," he interrupted, smiling wryly, "but you opened them."

"Well, yeah, because you jumped off a cliff," I justified. "But the second time, when you asked me to close my eyes, I did it."

He seemed hesitant.

"I'll do it again," I offered. "I'll close my eyes." And I did.

We stayed silent for what felt like a lifetime. Without my sight, I listened to the sound of his breathing. It was a nice sound.

Out of nowhere, I felt Oscar's hand entwine with mine.

"Forgive me," he requested quietly.

"I already have."

"Open your eyes," he murmured.

I did as he asked.

He took a deep breath. "I..."

Trust me, I urged silently.

"I am a witch."

The words tumbled from his lips like a surge of water rupturing through a dam.

Even though I already knew it, it still came as a shock to hear it confirmed. There was a small part of me that wanted to flail my arms around and scream "Witch!", but there was a much larger part that quite simply didn't care. He was Oscar. That was all that mattered to me.

I wanted to tell him those things. I wanted to tell him how much I cared for him.

Instead I said "Thanks". It was all that I could muster.

He let out a laugh. I could sense that he allowed himself to feel relieved. Relieved that I knew who he was. The repercussions, I was sure, he would worry about later.

I too allowed myself to bask in a blissfully serene state. For the next few seconds, everything would be perfect. We were who we were, and we wouldn't have to be anything other than us. The two of us. Together.

I closed my eyes again, vainly wishing that the moment would never end. I laced my fingers through Oscar's and he tightened his grip. At that moment, we needed each other.

But, gradually, reality began to creep back into my

awareness. This wasn't over yet. There was something else I had to know.

"Why are you here?" I asked.

His grasp grew ever tighter, although I don't think he was aware of it.

"Don't ask me that," he muttered. "Believe me, it's better if you don't know."

"No. Tell me," I insisted.

He drew in another deep breath and released it in a slow puff. A few ebony strands of hair fell forward onto his brow.

"You've been having dreams," he said.

I flinched.

"Nightmares," he corrected himself. "About a man… well, a demon."

The picture of that haunting skull face flashed through my mind. The decayed bone and the threatening black eyes…

"Yes," I choked. "How do you…"

"They call him Lathiaus." Oscar's own eyes darkened at the mention of the name.

I must have looked queasy, because Oscar led me to the bed and sat me down. He crouched on the floor in front of me, holding both of my hands.

"He has a name?" I stuttered.

"Yes."

"You know him?"

"I know *of* him. And I suppose I've seen him." He paused. "I've seen him in your dreams."

"In my dreams? You've been in my dreams?" My head

spun. "This isn't… this can't be real."

"You and I, we're connected in some way. I've been having visions—or, actually, *you*'ve been having visions—and I've been watching them."

All of a sudden I was short of breath. "How? Why? Why am I having the nightmares? And..." I trailed off.

Oscar gazed up at me with sympathetic eyes. "There's a prophecy," he explained gently. "Lathiaus is to return from the dead—"

"From the dead?"

"Yes. You see, a long time ago, Lathiaus was very powerful. But his power was dark—as dark as dark power comes. Anyway, he was killed. I'm guessing it was by witches, because whadda y'know, he's really got it in for us." Oscar chuckled tensely. "Legend has it he'll return one day to bring about the end to all witches. Talk about holding a grudge, eh?"

I stared at him, stunned and utterly dumbfounded.

He went on, "But there is one loophole."

I blinked.

"You," he elaborated.

"Me?"

"Yes. You can stop him."

"Stop him?"

I was aware that I had resorted to simply echoing everything he said, but that was about as much as my brain could manage.

Oscar winced. "Yes. The prophecy foretells of you stopping Lathiaus. But it's with…"

"With?"

"With your life. Or, your death, I should say."

"Muh…"

I couldn't even repeat things now.

"Are you okay?" he asked anxiously.

I shook my head no. Unequivocally no.

Oscar seemed tortured by my response. His expression was wrought with guilt.

"There is another way…" he began to ramble incoherently. "I'm not sure… I need to think…" He bit his lip and then gave me a look of conviction. "I'm going to do my best to stop this. Do you understand?"

I nodded my head. Actually, I didn't understand. I didn't understand any of it. I believed him, though.

Oscar smiled tenderly. "You're taking this very well," he commended. "You were harder to console when you lost your dress."

I smiled back, although it was probably a rather sad smile.

"Why me?" I asked.

"I don't know." He trailed his thumb in circles on the palm of my hand. "The prophecy says you've got the heart of a witch. You're special. Not quite human or witch."

Um, say what now?

"I'm not human?" My chest tightened.

"No, no." He cringed at his blunder. "You *are* a human. But you're a special *kind* of human."

Okay, this was all way too much for me. I had long overdone my daily quota for life-changing bombshells.

"Stop, Oscar," I implored. "Please stop."

"I'm sorry."

"I can't take any more. I want to go back to… to before. Before, when my biggest problem was *you.*" It had been a whole lot easier when I'd thought his confession would end at 'I'm a witch'. Oh, those were the good old days.

"We *can* go back," he assured me, with a tad more enthusiasm than necessary. "I can still be your biggest problem."

I kind of smiled.

"Perhaps I should make you some tea," Oscar offered. "People always turn to tea at times like this."

"Do you get a lot of times like this?" I asked in a fragile voice.

He shrugged. "This is my first."

"Mine, too."

His mouth curved up at the corner. "Tea it is, then."

"Okay." I gazed off to the azure sky beyond the window. "When will it be?"

"Well, I'll have to boil the kettle…" He moved to stand up.

"No, when will this prophecy thing happen?"

"Oh." He crouched back down in front of me. "We don't know exactly," he admitted. I noticed that his head bowed slightly.

"Soon?"

"I would imagine so."

I looked at him, desperately and with a faint glimmer of hope. "But you're going to help me? You'll stop him?" I didn't care about the 'how'; all I needed was a 'yes'.

He seemed to be choosing his words carefully.

"Yes," he said at last. "We'll stop Lathiaus."

CHAPTER NINE

Swan Song

IT WAS AROUND EIGHT O'CLOCK at night before I stopped spiralling.

Up until then, I had been cross-legged on my bed in a stunned silence, watching the sun set beyond the window. Oscar sat patiently on the floor, leaning back against the door with his eyes closed. When the daylight slipped away, neither of us commented on the fact that we were now sitting in total darkness.

I didn't care. To be honest, I barely noticed. I was too busy mentally processing the grenade that had just exploded over my simple little world.

Firstly, Oscar was a witch. What that meant, I wasn't entirely sure.

Secondly, I was a witch, too. Or, at least, I was some sort of witch-human hybrid disaster.

Thirdly, the crescendo, my imminent death had been foretold. I was to die at the hands of a demon—Ol' Crow

Eyes, as I affectionately called him.

Fabulous.

Although it may seem somewhat judicious to list those...*pitfalls*, shall we say, in such a calm, matter-of-fact way, to get to this charmingly Zen-like state I had to go through five hysterical stages first.

First was denial. Deny, deny, deny. Oscar had made the whole thing up, undoubtedly because he's a devious prankster, and I'd been stupid enough to fall for it.

Second was anger. Blame, blame, blame. I blamed Oscar.

Third, bargaining. Offer someone else in my place. Say, Oscar, for example.

Fourth, depression. Self-pity. I grieved for the things I'd not yet done, like putting Oscar in a chokehold and beating him with my curling iron.

And lastly, acceptance. I accepted my fate. But I swore, there and then, that I wouldn't go down without a fight. And I knew I could count on one person to help me: Oscar.

"Oscar," I said. He hadn't moved in a while. I could just about make out his silhouette in the gloom of my bedroom.

He turned his head towards me. "Yes?"

"It's dark," I commented.

"I know."

We fell silent again.

"I want to get out of the house," I decided at last.

"Okay. Where do you want to go?"

I answered impulsively, "My tree house."

"Your tree house?" he repeated, sounding confused.

Actually, I was confused too. I'd built a tree house in

the forest when I was younger, but I hadn't been to it in years. I hadn't even *thought* about it in years. I don't know why I wanted to go there now. I guessed it was my 'safe' place.

"It's in the forest," I told Oscar.

"And you want to go now?"

"Yes. Are you coming?"

In the shadows I saw him stir. "Of course I'm coming. I'll get Caicus—"

"No," I interrupted, "I don't want to see anyone. I'm not ready to face the others."

He paused. "Fair enough. Though I'll need to pass by my room first. If Caicus is there, then I should give him some sort of explanation. I'm sure he'll be wondering where I've been for the past few hours." He rose to his feet and grasped the door handle. "Meet me at the front of the house."

When Oscar opened the door, a fracture of light crept in from the hallway. I recoiled from it like a scorched vampire, and was relieved when the closing door returned the attic to its dark equilibrium once more.

Moving on autopilot, I crawled off my bed and shook out my stiff arms and legs. Then I tiptoed out of my room and down to the hallway.

I could hear the hum of voices floating up from downstairs. The conversation was light and there seemed to be a chorus of laughter. It sounded as though the chatter was coming from the conservatory. Now this was awkward, because if the conservatory door was open—which, judging by the clarity of the voices, it was—then they would see, or hear, me coming down the main staircase. I definitely didn't want that.

I snuck to the top of the stairs and peered over the cast iron banister.

The door to the conservatory was open and the faint smell of brandy lingered in the air. I could hear Caicus entertaining my aunt and uncle with a sickeningly witty anecdote.

Since they appeared to be preoccupied, I took the opportunity to descend the staircase.

Every time I edged forward, the old structure creaked loudly under the strain of my weight. I paused at the halfway point, certain that I had been detected by the conservatory inhabitants. But their conversation continued to flow, undisturbed.

Surely there was an easier way than this?

And then it struck me.

Hello, banister.

I hopped up onto the oak handrail. Okay, sliding down a banister wasn't quite as graceful as I had imagined. Not when *I* was doing it, anyway. It was possibly the most undignified and ungainly task I'd ever attempted. Even down to my graceless landing, where I slid off the end and cannon-balled onto the carpet.

Well, at least no one saw me.

Or so I'd thought until I looked up and noticed Oscar standing at the top of the staircase, smirking and silently clapping his hands.

He strolled down the staircase—noiselessly, of course—and joined me at the bottom. Maintaining stealth mode, I unlocked the front door and stepped outside.

The sting of cold night air hit me like a salvo of angry wasps.

Before I knew it, Oscar was at my side, holding up his black jacket for me to get into.

"No, I'm fine," I declined the offer.

"Don't be stubborn," he said, his breath misting the air. "It's cold tonight."

"You're in a T-shirt!" I pointed out. Talk about double standards.

"I don't feel the cold," he said, winking mischievously.

"Is that some kind of witch thing?" I asked.

"No. It's some kind of me thing."

With a reluctant sigh, I shrugged into the jacket. The sleeves were far too long for me, but it was warm and snug, and it smelt like Oscar—which I liked. A lot.

"Thank you." He shot me a satisfied smile.

"Thank you, too," I returned. When I sensed that I was blushing, I hastily changed subject. "You weren't able to speak to Caicus," I guessed.

"No. Probably for the best."

I could tell that he didn't wholeheartedly mean that.

"Right, are we going?" he said, evidently not wishing to discuss it further.

I hugged the sleeves of his jacket around me for extra warmth. "We're going."

"Lead on, then."

So I did. I paced across the gravel yard towards the forest of evergreens. Oscar followed closely behind.

The moon shone above, full and lustrous. Around it was an endless scattering of stars, like fireflies hovering in the night sky. It was the sort of evening that made me wonder why I didn't stop and appreciate the world more often. I was glad to be sharing it with Oscar.

Venturing into the forest, we wove in and out of the trees in a comfortable silence. Occasionally I glanced at Oscar, and he smiled but said nothing.

After several minutes of walking, we reached our destination.

"It's around here somewhere." I strained my eyes to see through the obscurity of dark, towering trees. "Over there!" I pointed excitedly to a tall oak standing separately from the evergreens.

There it was. My little wooden tree house, shoddily assembled amidst the thicker branches.

"Hmm. Dilapidated," Oscar remarked.

I skipped to the oak and tugged at the rope step ladder that hung from the tree house. It seemed sturdy enough, so I tested my foot on the first step and precariously worked my way up.

I felt a rush of exhilaration as I climbed inside the den. It was just as I remembered it. Even down to the pungent, rotten wood smell.

"I love this place," I gushed.

"Uh... seriously?" Oscar raised a sceptical eyebrow as he climbed in through the entryway. He spent the next few minutes restlessly trying to get comfortable in the cramped space.

I, on the other hand, was immediately at ease. I huddled in a corner and fumbled around until I found my old torch, which had rolled underneath a beanbag. I flipped the switch and was pleasantly surprised when it actually worked. A weak orange spotlight lit the floor.

I brought the light up to Oscar and he grinned.

"So, this is home," he said. "I like what you've done with the place. Or, *not* done, I should say."

"Hey," I scolded in good humour, "I'll have you know that this property is high end."

"High end? If this is high end, I'd hate to see low end." He smirked slightly. Then he looked at me with a nod of sincerity. "Thanks for inviting me."

"You're welcome." I dipped the torch back down to the plywood floor. "I'm glad you came."

"Wild horses couldn't have kept me away." He nudged my leg with his foot. I guessed that was his way of saying he meant it.

I laughed. "Thanks. But I'm sure there are other places that you'd rather be."

"Such as?"

"The cosy, heated house?" I offered flippantly.

"Pah! I scoff at modern conveniences," Oscar declared. "Besides, I only like the house when you're in it."

My heart fluttered. "Oh."

With the torch cast down to the floor, I couldn't see his face, which made what I was about to say a little easier.

"I have to ask you something," I blurted out.

"Okay."

"What are the chances that I'll survive?"

He paused. "Right now, one hundred per cent."

I didn't really understand that, but it filled me with tremendous confidence. "Really? You think we can stop the prophecy?"

"No. We can't stop the prophecy," he answered truthfully. "It's a divination. Out of our hands. But it's possible to save you."

"And it's possible to save you, too—the witches, I mean."

"Yes."

"So, it is possible?"

"Yes. Anything's possible."

Good enough.

I definitely liked the sound of those one hundred per cent odds.

"I don't want to die," I told him. After I'd said it, the words rattled around in my head as though they had come from someone else's mouth. Not surprising, really. I certainly didn't expect to be having this conversation at sixteen. Whilst sitting in a damp tree house. With a witch.

"I don't want you to die, either," said Oscar quietly.

"Why does it have to be me? What have I got to do with this Lathiaus guy—or demon thing, or whatever?" The word demon wasn't a regular in my everyday vocabulary. It wasn't a favourite, either.

Oscar inhaled deeply. "Hard to say. Maybe you're linked to him in some way. Nobody really knows why it has to be you. It's just the way it is, and has been since before you were even born. You were destined to be the only one of your kind."

My kind. I hated that I was a 'kind'.

"You mean the half-witch thing?" I clarified grimly.

"Yes, the half-witch thing," he affectionately mocked my choice of phrasing.

"Is that why I have the visions?" I asked. "Are they a power?"

Oscar stifled a laugh. "No. Visions are mostly identified as a human attribute. Dreams are intuitive messages from the unconscious mind."

"So, if I'm half witch, then why don't I have any powers?"

"I don't know. And you're not really half witch. You just have a witch's heart. A good heart," he added.

"Well, I don't want it."

"Why do you denounce it as bad?" he mused. "Who you are is exceptional."

"It's terminal."

"It's *you*," he corrected. "It's who you've always been. Who you were born to be. Nothing's changed."

"Everything's changed!" I spluttered. "I'm on a demon's most wanted list."

"Eh. Take it as a compliment."

I shone the torch at myself to illuminate my unimpressed scowl.

Oscar grinned. "It's not a disease, Rose. It's just *you*." He persisted to stress that as though it made everything acceptable. "Your blood is so extraordinary that it can overpower a demon's reign."

"Gross."

"Everybody wanted to find you," he went on. "Everybody. For hundreds of years witches have searched, and no one has ever come close."

"Until you."

"Until me."

"How did you manage it?" I wondered aloud.

"I found you because I—" he stopped midstream, faltering on his words. "You're in my heart," he finished.

"What does that mean?" I whispered, gripping the torch a little tighter and letting the beam dip back down towards the plywood.

Oscar rested his hand in the spotlight on the floor. He said nothing.

He didn't have to say anything. I already knew how he felt because I felt the same. He was in my heart, too.

I brought my hand into the spotlight and touched my fingertips to Oscar's.

We stayed silent for a moment. A course of electricity flowed through his fingers into mine, travelling through my hand and along my arm until it reached my heart.

"I know you," Oscar spoke tentatively. "I know you better than you think."

I cast my mind back to our conversation in the attic. "Through my dreams?"

"Yes," he reflected. "But it runs deeper than that. When I first saw you in your dream, I was…" he took a moment to contemplate his wording, "elated," he concluded. "It was as though I'd been waiting my whole life for you, and you'd finally been returned to me. There's something in your eyes that's so familiar to me..."

"I know that feeling," I told him quietly.

"The thing is, Rose," he continued, "eyes give away more about a person than anything else. People say that the eyes are the embodiment of the soul." He paused, a little unsure of himself, then cleared his throat. "I've never told anyone this, not even Caicus, but I have this weird feeling about you. I thought... I *think*... that you and I might be soulmates."

Bam. Everything suddenly became clear to me. It was as though a heavy fog had been lifted from my sight. I *had* met Oscar before—only not in this lifetime.

"I bet you think that's dumb," he said, smiling carefully at me.

"No," I replied in all honesty. "In fact, I think it's the one thing that actually makes sense."

He exhaled, then smiled to himself again.

There was a moment of quiet contemplation before he spoke. "That must be why I dream of you," he said at last. "Just as you were born into the prophecy, I was, too. I was born to find you."

"And to save me?" I added, naively optimistic.

He didn't respond.

I moved on. "So how did you know where to find me?"

"That's my power. Well, my *personal* power. You see, we all have heightened aspects: speed, strength, hearing, et cetera. My personal power is the ability to track anything, so long as it has a place in my heart."

"The chess pieces!" I exclaimed. "That's how you found them." I turned the torch on him so as to watch his expression.

"Yes," he grinned. "I told you, chess is important to me."

"And that's how you found me in Hutton Ridge?"

"I can always find you. It doesn't matter where you are."

"And Caicus?" I asked. "What's his power?"

That was an enigma that I'd been desperately trying to solve.

"His power is in his eyes. He's able to spellbind humans, to charm them into agreeing with everything he says."

"I knew it! That's why my aunt and uncle let you stay."

"Yes."

I frowned. "Why doesn't it work on me?"

Oscar fidgeted. "Well… you know… the *thing*."

I didn't need him to clarify, I had deciphered it for myself. "Because I'm not human."

"Something like that." He laughed nervously.

I laughed a little bit too, though I have no idea why.

Out of the blue, Oscar shuffled around to sit beside me.

"It'll be okay," he promised. But a distinct waver in his voice gave away a not-so-concealed uncertainty.

"I don't see how," I murmured.

I moved an inch or two nearer to him until our shoulders were touching. The heat of his body somehow percolated through the material of my clothes, like a furnace warming my blood as it swam through my veins.

"Can I?" he asked.

I wasn't sure what he was asking, but I said yes anyway. Then his arm wrapped around me, embracing me closer. And I was okay again.

THE GIRL WALKED ACROSS THE bleak terrain. She moved heavily, as though she were weighed down with lead. Beneath her feet, the desiccated amber ground was rough and unyielding, and the sky above was as thick as crude oil.

She was alone. But she sensed that he was there, somewhere.

In the silence of the barren land, her shallow breathing was deafening. The thud of her heart and the click of her footsteps fell into sync, composing the beat of a swan song.

Then something was different. There was someone else.

She couldn't turn her head to see him, nor could she hear him, but she knew he was there, reverently walking behind her. Instinctively she knew who it was.

"Oscar?" she whispered. The opaque air stole her voice away before it even passed her lips.

But he had heard her.

"Not this time," he replied, in a voice smooth and familiar. "My name is Oliver Sadler."

"Where are we going?" the girl tried to shout, but her question simply evaporated into the dense atmosphere.

"I'm following you," he told her. "You know the way."

"No, I don't. I don't know the way."

"You will."

"I don't want this!" She grew frantic now, and yet her stride remained steady, moving forward like the constant motion of a river.

And then she saw it. The crooked form hunched on the ground, shrouded beneath a black cloak.

She stopped walking.

"He's waking!" she cried.

"I know," Oliver responded calmly.

"Help me!"

"Go back."

She tried to turn her head to look at him, but her eyes refused to leave the demon.

Pulsating like an erupting volcano, the malignant form began to lurch towards her. A swarm of hornets circled him, their entirety appearing as a solid mass.

"Go back," Oliver urged again.

"I can't go back," she wept. "I can't move."

The creature was now so close that she could smell the decay on his putrefied bones. He reared up, growing to twice her size. The crevices of his skull teemed with maggots, and two sinister black eyes hungrily glistened with malice.

"Go back," Oliver pleaded.

The demon reached out, closer than he had ever been before. His contorted ivory fingers gripped her arms, holding her in place.

To her horror, the demon's claws penetrated her skin. And in front of her very eyes, the bony fingers grew a layer of tawny scales.

He was coming back to life.

"Goodbye," Oliver murmured remorsefully.

And he was gone.

Only two remained.

The demon's mouth parted and he inhaled.

Under his control, the girl felt her own lips part and her breath was drawn from her lungs.

With each breath stolen she grew weaker, until she could no longer hold herself upright. Only his toxic grip kept her on her feet.

And then, she was falling...

MY EYES FLASHED OPEN TO complete darkness.

"No," I cried, still lost in the limbo between reality and the dream world—not that there was much difference any more.

I felt a pair of hands grasp my shoulders.

"No!" I screamed.

"Shh, shh." The sound of Oscar's voice instantly soothed me. "It's okay. It's me."

"Oscar." I choked for air, frantically detaching myself from the nightmare.

"Yes, it's me. It's me," he repeated.

I couldn't see him in the darkness, but he was at my side. I leaned into his body and buried my face in his shoulder.

"It's so dark," I shivered, squeezing my eyes shut because at least that made my blindness seem intentional.

"The torch died a while ago," Oscar explained. His arms moved around me and the breath carrying his voice warmed my temple.

As my mind slowly caught up with itself, I registered that we were still in the tree house. I must have fallen asleep.

"Did you have a vision?" Oscar asked, twining his fingers through my hair.

"Nightmare," I replied, still clinging to him as though my life depended on it—which I suppose it did.

"You're trembling."

"He took my life," I stammered.

My statement couldn't have been more accurate. The fact was he'd stolen my breath right from out of my body. He literally took my life.

"Were you there?" I asked, remembering Oliver, who had been everything Oscar was, right down to the smell of his skin.

"No. I've been awake."

"There was someone else there. He called himself Oliver, but it was *you.*" I rested my cheek against Oscar's chest, listening to his steady heartbeat and slowly relaxing in the refuge of his company. "Oliver kept telling me to go back."

Oscar's shoulders tensed like a steel wall. "Go back to where?" he asked, his voice suddenly rigid.

"I don't know. Go back the way I'd come, I guess. I couldn't move, though."

It was a dozen or so seconds before Oscar let out a breath. And a dozen or so more before his shoulders relaxed.

"It's okay. You're safe now," he said, his tone restored to its soothing lull. He lightly trailed his hand along my back. "You're safe."

Having come through the initial shock, I cautiously opened my eyes. Everything was pitch black, but I was close enough to Oscar to make out the curve of his shoulder and the outline of his face.

"I don't remember falling asleep," I murmured, in what seemed to be quite a distant voice.

"How convenient," Oscar teased lightly. "I recall it was about mid-way through my life story."

I smiled to myself. "Oops. Sorry."

"Nah. You picked a good time to take a nap. Things got a bit uneventful during the pre-teen years. It's sixteen, seventeen and eighteen that you've got to stay awake for."

"I'll try," I laughed quietly. "Anyway, I don't plan on sleeping ever again. I can't take another nightmare."

"Don't worry," Oscar reassured me. "There won't be many more."

Wait. Not many more?

That didn't sound good.

PART FOUR
OSCAR

CHAPTER TEN

Pledge Your Allegiance

A STRIP OF DUSTY PINK SLUNK into the tree house. Dawn had caught up with us.

I could see Rose now, lit by the blush of sunrise. Perhaps it was the ethereal lighting, or perhaps I was impaired by the newly formed bond between us, but somehow at that moment, she was more beautiful than anything else on this earth. Akin to an angel in its purest form.

I toyed with a loose thread on the patchwork beanbag.

"Why did you stop?" Rose asked me.

Oh. Right. I hadn't even realised that I'd stopped talking.

"Sorry," I said. "So, where was I?"

"The other Valero witches."

"Right. They're family. Not in the biological sense, but in the animalistic sense—"

"Like a pack of wolves?"

I laughed. "Actually, yes."

"How many of you are there?"

"Valero witches? I'd say fifty. Maybe more. Most of them are elders. Caicus and I are the only ones of our age. That's why we're so close; we've only ever really had each other."

I felt a pang in my heart speaking about Caicus, with the knowledge that I would be responsible for his death.

"He's not only my brother, he's also my best friend."

"There are no other teenagers?"

"No. There's a few near, you know, their mid-twenties, that kind of thing. But they're pompous, jumped-up tools. I don't have time for that."

She laughed softly.

"What about you?" I turned the question around. "You've spoken about Mary, and Roger, and even the kid, but what about your family? Your parents?"

"I've got parents," she said evasively. "They're… somewhere." She swept a stray strand of hair from her face. Her fingertips were just visible from within the oversized sleeves of my jacket.

"They're somewhere?" I pried.

"Away," she clarified. "They work a lot."

I heard a remote sadness in her voice and my stomach knotted.

"Secret agents?" I said, trying to break the tension.

Apparently it worked, because she laughed again.

"Photographers," she replied.

"And they're away at the moment?"

"Yep. Africa."

I wondered how long it would take for me to run to

Africa. Probably a hell of a lot longer than it took me to get to Hutton Ridge.

"So you often come to Millwood?" I guessed.

"Yeah. Every summer. And some Christmases. The rest of the time I'm at boarding school."

"Boarding school?" I repeated, intrigued. "That sounds fun. Well, that's coming from a person who's only ever been around one peer." I smiled sardonically. "Not that I'm overly keen on befriending a bunch of angst-ridden humans. Present company excluded."

"Hey!" she gasped in mock horror. "I'm not angst ridden!"

"Eh," I shrugged indifferently. "You're up and down."

She swatted at me and I laughed.

"But for the record," she added, "it's not fun. It's school."

"I wouldn't know anything about that."

Her eyebrows shot up. "You didn't go to school?"

"I've never needed to. I'm a witch. I take my knowledge from books and the wisdom of elders."

"Lucky you."

"Not really," I disagreed. "I'm only taught what a witch needs to know. My education is in prophecies and incantations. Sometimes I wish I could just learn..." Hmm, what was it that they taught in schools? "Calculus."

"If you can say that, then you've obviously never had to sit through a maths lesson," Rose jibed. "But I think I can understand. When I found out about Lathiaus and the prophecy thing, I wished I could just go back to my normal, boring, maths-lessons life."

My heart ached for her. "You deserve a boring life."

Huh. That had sounded better in my head.

"Thanks," she grinned. "But it's kind of okay, because if I hadn't been doomed to the prophecy, then I never would have found you. So it all worked out in the end."

I felt a smile form on my lips, but I said nothing.

"Can I ask you a question?" she ventured.

"Don't let the cold light of day stop you," I smirked.

"If you could change, would you? If you could give up your life as a witch and just be normal" —she made speech quotes around the word normal—"would you?"

Interesting. Nobody had ever asked me that before. I wasn't sure if I even knew the answer.

"Hell, no," I replied, the certainty of my conviction surprising both of us.

"Good," she murmured. "I like you just the way you are."

Then I hope I don't let you down, I thought.

I cleared my throat. "Right. We should get back to the manor before the others start to wake up."

Rose groaned. "My aunt would have a fit if she knew I'd stayed out all night."

"Who, Mary?" I raised my eyebrow dubiously. "I'd hardly call her an authoritarian."

"No. She just worries about me."

"Can't be a bad thing," I reasoned.

"Not usually. But with this prophecy..." she trailed off.

Naturally, I had hoped that Rose wouldn't tell her aunt and uncle about Lathiaus. For starters, humans who knew nothing about demons were categorically useless when it came to dealing with—you've guessed it—demons. And in my experience, the fewer humans who knew about our business, the better. Too many cooks.

What concerned me most, though, was that she might 'out' us as witches. In other words, Caicus's power would be null and void, and I imagined all hell would break loose.

But I was officially done with influencing Rose. I'd lost control of this situation the moment I'd admitted to being a witch. Jeeze, lucky I wasn't responsible for guarding an imperative secret or anything like that.

Rose's voice broke through my reverie. "I'm not going to tell her," she said. "Mary, I mean."

Uncanny. If I hadn't known better, I'd have thought she'd dipped right into my mind.

I nodded my head. "Thanks."

"Will they be in any danger?" There was a selflessness in her eyes, like an obscured whirlpool brewing in a deep green ocean. I found it admirable.

"They won't be in danger," I assured her. "On the day of the awakening, we'll make sure your family is away from Millwood."

Rose's complexion grew ashen. "How?"

I shrugged. "Caicus will think of something. It shouldn't be a problem."

She stared at her hands.

"Come on," I said abruptly, "let's go." Believe me, I didn't want to go. What I wanted to do was stay in that tree house forever. Just me and Rose. But the real world kept plodding on, and sooner or later, we'd have to join it.

Rose moved first. I watched her climb through the

hatch and lower herself down the frayed rope ladder. Once she was back on solid ground, I dropped through the hatch myself.

The forest was shimmering with the first light of day. It painted the most mystical picture. Rows of evergreens cast silken shadows across the dull orange and purple of dawn. A gentle mist, conjured by the brimming sun's heat amalgamating with last night's lingering dew, graced the ground.

As we trod through the mist, it licked at our feet and parted with our strides. It was like nature's red carpet, laid out for two united beings. We walked side by side, content in a reflective silence.

When we emerged onto the dirt road and the manor came into view, the real world suddenly seemed a lot more *real.*

"I need to speak to Caicus," I muttered, mostly to myself.

I must have inadvertently picked up my speed, because I noticed Rose trotting to keep at my side. I had a tendency to move a little too quickly when I wasn't concentrating. I slowed down and smiled at her.

She smiled back.

We were almost at the house when I heard a noise from inside the walls. There was no way Rose could have heard it—not without witch's hearing—so I grasped her wrist and signalled for her to halt.

I pressed my index finger to my lips and listened attentively.

Kitchen.

Roger.

"What is it?" Rose mouthed.

"Roger," I said quietly. "He's awake. He's in the kitchen."

Rose stared at the closed door, probably wondering how I knew that.

"I don't want him to see us sneaking in," she said at last.

New plan.

"Close your eyes," I said.

Instead of closing her eyes, she rolled them at me.

"I thought we were past this—" she began.

"Just do it," I groused, rolling my eyes back at her.

She did it—pouting, though.

I hoisted her off the ground and swept her around to the side of the house, then carefully placed her onto the grass. All of which took place in under a second. I shouldn't have needed to explain why I'd asked her to close her eyes; the motion sickness from a manoeuvre like that would have been ghastly.

She blinked up at me, disorientated. "How did we...?" She touched the conservatory side door, evidently baffled by how we were no longer at the front door.

I rattled the conservatory door. It was locked. But this lock was old, and I figured I could probably bust through it without damaging *another* entryway. *Shame about the bathroom door,* I mused. Anyway, I gave it what I would describe as a forceful nudge, and it swung open.

We stepped into the conservatory and listened as Roger's shoes clacked along the hallway and out through the front door.

"Successfully averted," I commented once the door had clicked shut behind him.

"It must be around six o'clock if my uncle's setting off for work."

"Probably," I agreed, scrutinising the position of the rising sun. I liked this room; the walls were mostly glass, so it gave an impressive panoramic view of the grounds.

"We stayed up all night," Rose said with a yawn.

"Why don't you get some sleep?" I suggested. I obviously knew the answer to that, but I didn't want to validate her reasoning.

She lowered her eyelids. "No," she said quietly.

"Come on, now. Dreams can't hurt you. Besides, you've already seen tonight's episode."

I detected a weary smile.

"Go to bed," I implored her. "I'll sit with you if you like."

She looked up at me, her gaze soft. "Okay."

"Okay," I replied.

We slunk upstairs to Rose's room, glad that the rest of the house had not yet woken. I wasn't tired. Tiredness was not something that generally affected me. In fact, I could go days without sleep and still be as sharp as a razor.

Rose, however, crawled into bed with the rigidity of someone suffering from severe bruising. She half-heartedly pulled the covers over her and closed her eyes. My jacket still cosseted her like a coat of armour. It had never served a more worthwhile purpose.

I sat on the floor, in the same spot that I had been only

nine hours earlier. From my post, I watched Rose. Her hair curled like ivy over the pillow and her breathing fell into a steady rhythm.

The minutes ticked by, and, sitting in my own meditative state, watching Rose sleep, I was pleasantly contented. I could have quite happily stayed there for hours, but unfortunately I had other obligations.

Where the hell are you? Caicus's voice shouted in my mind.

In the attic, I responded to him silently. *Where are you?*

Where do you think I am? he fumed. *I'm in bed. Where else would I be at six in the morning? Imbecile.*

All right, all right. Don't get your apron all in a bunch. I'll be there in a minute.

Where the hell have you been all night? he demanded.

I groaned at his irritability. *I'm on my way down,* I told him.

Reluctantly, I stood up and stretched out my arms. This was most definitely a conversation that I'd rather avoid. I suddenly had enormous empathy for the Grim Reaper.

Poor guy. That must be a tough job.

Before I left the attic, I crept over to Rose. She was definitely sleeping, so I didn't wake her. But I brushed the hair from her face and kissed the top of her head.

I exhaled heavily.

Here we go.

It didn't take me long to get back to my own bedroom, and that was even with the dawdling I did along the way. I let myself into the room and shut the door behind me.

Caicus was sitting atop his daisy bedspread. He looked

surly, to say the least.

"Honey, I'm home," I joked.

He glared at me.

Point taken. Not a great time for humour.

He looked at me with his I-hate-you face.

"Tell me you got the talisman back."

Wow. He was still on that? He was way behind.

I'd almost forgotten that all of this had started with the stolen talisman. Boy, was he in for a shock.

"I did," I said.

"And? Where have you been all night?"

"With Rose. Did Mary ask about the hole in the bathroom door?"

He narrowed his eyes. "I said I fell into it. Why were you with Rose?"

This was what experts call the pull-the-plaster-off-quickly technique.

"I told her."

Caicus froze.

"Are you…okay?" I hovered at a safe distance from him, weighing his expression. Which was wide eyed and blank, by the way. Like a taxidermy rabbit.

"Hello?" I snapped my fingers in his line of vision.

"What did you tell her?" he asked in a stony voice.

"Um…" Lies or truth? Lies or truth? Truth. "Everything."

He squeezed his eyes shut and pursed his lips so tightly that they turned white.

"In my defence," I added, "she figured it out for herself. Well, most of it."

"You told her that we're witches?" Caicus seethed through clenched teeth.

"That's the part she worked out for herself."

"You told her about the prophecy?"

"Yes. I had to."

"Why?" he hissed.

"I don't know, Caicus. She just asked me."

"Then you lie!" he shouted.

"I couldn't. Anyway, what difference does it make? She'd already figured out that we're witches."

"So, then what? You told her we were sacrificing her to Lathiaus and she was just *okay* with that?"

"Well, not exactly," I stammered.

"Don't *not exactly* me!"

"I left out some parts."

"But you told her about the prophecy?"

"Yes."

He frowned at me. "What, you conveniently left out the tiny detail of her death? Which, you might say, features highly in the narrative?"

"No. I explained that her death is foretold..."

Caicus massaged his temples. Thick strands of blonde hair coiled around his fingers.

"I'm confused," he said.

"Me too," I chuckled.

"Oscar," he barked, "explain to me how it's possible that she's simply accepted the fact that we're going to kill her?"

"I didn't tell her that we planned to kill her."

Caicus hesitated. "Okay. That could work." He rubbed his chin thoughtfully. "Things will go somewhat smoother if she doesn't know what we're doing." He relaxed slightly. "Okay. Good work. Sorry I went all Sergeant Major on you."

"Yeah, no problem. But I should tell you one other thing."

He stiffened again. "Yes?"

"I'm not going to do it."

Caicus stared at me for a long, tense moment. I waited for his response with bated breath. It was taking a while. I considered offering to put the kettle on.

But then, he reacted. "What exactly are you *not* going to do?"

"Kill her. I can't do it."

Caicus fell silent again. He sat there so still that I was pleasantly surprised by how calm he was about the whole thing.

He was taking this better than expected.

And then he let out an almighty roar. He leapt off his bed and dived on top of me like a rabid dog.

We tumbled to the floor and scuffled around, colliding into furniture, and walls, and whatever else happened to have the misfortune of being in our path.

"Caicus!" I yelled. "Get off me, you lunatic!"

He took a swipe at my face, which I dodged, causing his fist to pound into the carpet. Ha.

"I knew you'd do this to me, Oscar!" he howled. "This is typical of you!"

"Typical of me?" I shot back. "Oh yeah, this is classic me. I'm always *not killing* people."

He heaved his weight on top of me and pressed my face into the carpet—which I'd only just noticed was the most putrid shade of brown I'd ever seen.

"You may be *not* killing her, but you're happy enough to be killing me!"

That hit me harder than any punch could have.

I stopped trying to wriggle free of him and instead just lay on the floor, defeated. I waited for him to dole out his beating. But it never came.

Caicus flopped down on the carpet beside me. Neither of us spoke for what may have been five or so minutes.

I made the first move. "So..." I said, sprawled out on the floor, twiddling my thumbs. "Is your hand okay?"

"Yes," he mumbled.

I waited a minute or two before I tried again.

"This carpet is ass-ugly, isn't it?"

Caicus let out a weary sigh.

"Yeah," he agreed. "It's vile."

Good. We were friends again.

"Sorry I... you know, took you down," he offered his olive branch.

I glanced at him. He was staring up at the ceiling.

"I deserved it," I replied.

"Oscar?"

"Yeah?"

"Please, don't do this."

I sat upright and shuffled back until I was leaning against the wall.

"What am I meant to do, Caicus?" The despair in my

voice was strange to hear. I didn't like it.

Caicus sat up, too. "Just stick to the plan," he beseeched me. "Don't do this. Not for some girl."

"She's not *some girl*." All of a sudden I was overtly protective, as though he'd slandered her somehow. "What can I do? I can't let her die." I pondered over it for a moment. "But I can't let you die, either."

"Well, you can't have it both ways," he pointed out.

"I know that."

"Stick to the plan," he said again. "Look, if you save her, then only she survives. Not even you. What would be the point in that? You won't even get the glory for doing it."

"I don't care about the glory. I just..."

"What?" he pressed.

"I don't know. I just don't want her to die."

Caicus raked his hands through his hair. "Oscar, please, I'm begging you, don't do this."

I swallowed. This was impossible. Sitting with Caicus, my brother, my best friend, I knew that there was no way—*no way*—I could let him die.

Funny, though. The most astonishing thing about tackling this dilemma was that there was one person whose wellbeing I had no interest in accounting for. Mine. It was an odd feeling. You naturally assume your own life will always be most precious to you, but when you're forced to choose between yourself and the two most important people in your world, *yourself* immediately becomes expendable.

It was either her, or him.

Time to pledge your allegiance.

CHAPTER ELEVEN

The Fractured Heart

ANOTHER HOUR PASSED BY AS Caicus and I remained on the floor.

We talked—mostly in short, emotionally charged bursts, followed by long spells of silence.

I despised the fact that I was beginning to yield. When I was with Rose, it was all so clear: I was saving her. End of story. But my mulish friend did a first-rate job of presenting the opposing argument. Caicus made damn sure to drill his standpoint into my head. I'm talking pneumatic power tools, here.

"You must think of the bigger picture," he said.

I stared at him, fearful that he was slowly breaking down what I'd thought had been an impenetrable wall.

"I know you want to save her," he went on, "and that's just...well, that's just swell. But think about what you're doing, Oscar. It's selfish."

I looked down at the carpet.

"This isn't about *the one*, it's about *the many*. You've known that from the start."

"I can't."

"You have to," he stated frankly. "It's not your place to interfere with her destiny."

I punched the floor in frustration. "Then why are we here? Why did I have the dreams? I was sent here to save her—"

"No, you weren't," Caicus cut me off. "You were sent here to save an entire race of witches. You were sent here for the greater good. Maybe this is your test."

I frowned.

"It's your time to step up," he insisted, "and do what you know is right. Save the world. Save *our* world."

I bit down on my lip until I drew blood. I wanted to feel the pain. I wanted to feel something other than the agonising ache of my impasse.

Caicus studied me watchfully.

I licked the trail of blood from my lower lip and then spoke again. "I can't do it."

"You won't need to. I'll do it." He gave me a look of loyal solidarity. The sunlight gleaming through the window caught in his powder blue eyes. "I'll do it," he repeated in earnest. "All I ask of you is to accept it."

My mind swam. Deep down, I knew Caicus was making sense. One life in exchange for many. And this was Rose's destiny.

But what was mine?

In the solitude of my head, I recounted the words of the

prophecy.

It is foretold, on the day of his end,
so doth life begin
At the stroke of the eleventh hour,
he shall awaken
All will bow before him
All will perish at his mercy
Only one can end the blood spill
She, the girl with the heart of a witch
Before the hour turns to twelfth,
she must grant him her death
Two will take her to him, and all will be spared
Two will turn away, and all will be slaughtered
Our fate awaits

I sighed. Damn it.

"Oscar," Caicus reached out and gripped my shoulder, "I'm sorry. You know that, don't you? If there was any other way…"

I nodded.

"I'll do it all," he assured me—as if the consolation was worth anything more than the breath it was spoken with. "The only thing I ask of you is to turn away."

Turn away, I thought, noting how ironic his choice of wording was.

"Can you do that?" he persisted.

What other choice did I have?

I nodded my head.

There was a knock on our bedroom door.

On reflex, I identified the scent in the air. It wasn't Rose.

"Come in," Caicus sang out.

Neither of us was surprised when Mary poked her head around the door.

"Hello, boys," she beamed, not venturing beyond the doorway.

"Hello, Mary," we replied in unison.

She peered down at us, to where we sat on the carpet, clearly thinking it strange.

Caicus and I shared a look.

"Now, boys," Mary carried on, lowering her voice to a hushed whisper, "I've come to talk to you about *the big day.*"

The hairs on the back of my neck bristled.

How the hell does she *know about the big day?*

Caicus began to babble. "No. Truly, Mary, it's not what you think—"

I cleared my throat to interrupt him. "Big day?"

Mary's eyes widened and she held her finger up to her lips. "Shh." She glanced over her shoulder into the hallway.

"Sorry," I mouthed. "Big day?"

"You know… the big *one-seven.*"

What's a big one-seven? Caicus asked me silently.

How should I know? I responded. *Must be some kind of woman thing.*

Mary looked at us expectantly.

"Yes," I said slowly. "The big one-seven. Very exciting."

She gave me an enthusiastic thumbs-up.

What was going on here?

I returned her thumbs-up, which seemed to please her.

Is the big one-seven something to do with Lathiaus? Even in silence, Caicus's tone was frantic. *She knows, doesn't she?*

No, of course she doesn't know. My brow creased in irritation. *She doesn't know a thing. She doesn't even know what day of the week it is.*

Out of the corner of my eye, I saw Caicus smile.

Hey, Oscar, he signalled to me mischievously, *what day of the week is it?*

I don't bloody know, I huffed. *And stop smiling; she'll think you're a crackpot.*

"So," Mary continued, deaf to our private conversation, "how about we go to Hutton Ridge and pick up a few things? We've only got a few days left."

"A few days?" I echoed.

"Yes. It's on Friday."

Oh, that's right. It was Wednesday.

It's Wednesday, I hissed to Caicus. Ha.

"Friday," Caicus chimed in. "The big one-seven."

"Yes," Mary's cheeks puffed out to allow for her enormous smile.

"What the hell is the big one-seven?" I blurted out.

Oh damn, I winced. I hadn't intended on saying that aloud.

Caicus laughed nervously.

But Mary didn't appear fazed by my brash tone. She merely smiled and said, "Seventeen. Rose's seventeenth birthday."

My jaw dropped. "She didn't tell me."

"No?" Mary wasn't particularly shocked by this. "Rose doesn't like to make a fuss over birthdays. Especially with her parents being away and all. That's why I'd like to do something special for her. Make it a really nice day."

I nodded my head, speechless.

"Great," Mary chirped. "Shall we head off now, before Rose wakes up? I've just checked on her and she's sleeping like a baby."

I felt a familiar twist in my gut. I was reluctant to leave Rose while she was sleeping, but Caicus answered for both of us, and the next thing I knew, I was on my feet and heading downstairs.

As we made our way out of the house, I heard Caicus call noiselessly to me.

Oscar...

I decided to ignore him. I wasn't in the mood for banter.

Oscar! he tried again.

What? I relented.

We stepped outside onto the gravel and Mary unlocked the minivan. Caicus rested his hand on my shoulder.

What? I looked at him. He was beginning to scare me now.

Her birthday, Caicus recapped what we already knew. *Friday is her birthday.*

Yes. I was there too, remember? I replied dryly.

Mary fastened baby Zack into the back seat and I climbed in beside him. Caicus hovered at the open car door.

"Get in then," I said to him.

He didn't move.

What? I demanded.

Her birthday. Caicus stared at me. *'On the day of his end, so doth life begin.'*

Suddenly it became clear to me.

Rose's birthday would be Lathiaus's resurrection day.

THE CAR JOURNEY TO HUTTON Ridge was glaringly tense. I didn't utter a word, not silently or aloud. My eyes were glued to the window, watching the trees whizz by. At one stage, I looked down to find that I was gripping the edge of Zack's car seat. My knuckles were white with the vigour of my grasp.

Mary and Caicus chattered casually in the front of the car and the radio crackled in and out of slushy love songs.

I envied how blasé Caicus was. He rambled on about God knows what and even sang along to the maudlin ballads. But of course, he could do that; he didn't care about Rose. He could belt out all the love songs in the world without it blitzing his heart to smithereens.

I glanced at the kid beside me.

Come on, child, say something, I willed. *Tell me something profound. Help me out here, friend.*

Kid made a few uncouth spit bubbles.

"Well said," I muttered, using my T-shirt to wipe the drool from his chin. "I'll send you the dry-cleaning bill."

Zack hiccupped.

"Another excellent point," I congratulated him.

Why did it have to be so soon? Today was Wednesday,

and that left only two days. Two days was not enough. It wasn't enough time to tell her everything. It wasn't enough time to sit with her, listening to her speak and breathe.

I closed my eyes. Sometimes if I concentrated especially hard, I could hear the sound of Rose's heartbeat. I tried to bring it to me now, but my consciousness wouldn't allow it. All I could hear was the purr of the car engine and the drone of Caicus singing Frank Sinatra's My Way.

Shut up. I covered my ears. The lyrics rang a little too close to home for my liking. One man's struggle to step up and see things through to the final curtain…

Caicus grew louder with each verse, his voice crooning above the stereo now.

Shut up, shut up, shut up. What angered me most of all, was that I didn't get a *my way*. It was their way or no way.

Caicus filled his lungs for the big note.

Don't do it, I warned him silently.

Too late. He was going for it.

"*My* Way."

"Shut up!" I kicked the back of his seat.

He stopped singing abruptly. Mary snuck a glimpse at me in the rear view mirror.

"Sorry," I mumbled.

"Sorry, Oscar," Caicus said as he peered over his shoulder at me.

"I don't like that song," I fabricated. But of course, Caicus knew the real reason.

He switched off the radio and we fell into stony silence.

The hush of the car didn't do much in the way of

alleviating the tension. And we resided in that prickly atmosphere until we reached Hutton Ridge.

Mary backed into a parking space on the high street and unfastened her seatbelt.

"Here we are," she sang merrily.

Obviously. I rolled my eyes.

With my tolerance already wearing thin, I stepped out onto the kerb.

"Okay," Mary began as she fussed with Zack's pushchair, "there's a nice little jewellery shop just up on Culver Street. What do you say we go there first?" She slung her handbag over her shoulder.

"Sounds splendid," Caicus set a flawless smile on his lips.

I kicked at the cobbled road. This was torture. I was away from Rose *and* I had to go to a jewellery shop. This was the worst day ever.

I stuffed my hands into my pockets and looked up to the sky. It was a greyish blue and a layer of fog loomed overhead. I was already feeling suffocated by it.

As we walked along the street, I trailed slightly behind, idly tuning in and out of Caicus and Mary's prattle.

If I didn't know any better, I'd think that Caicus was becoming fond of old Mary. Genuinely fond. Like the dutiful son he never was.

Mary stopped outside a shop and gestured to its huge black and gold sign.

"This is the one," she stated.

I joined her line of vision.

Cobalt's Jewellers.

The arched windows were barred and exhibited an array of gold and silver trinkets. Mary and Caicus gushed over the display before heading inside.

I followed, distinctly underwhelmed.

The shop itself was fairly small, with moss green carpeting and a domino arrangement of glass cabinets. A long counter ran along the left side. A podgy, snowy-haired man with round spectacles greeted us. Well, he greeted wholesome Mary and angel-faced Caicus. Me, he eyed distrustfully, as though he suspected I was seconds away from whipping out a pistol and ransacking the joint.

Mary toddled straight over to him and plonked her oversized handbag on the counter.

"Hello there," she said. "I'm looking for a birthday present. It's for my niece."

"Jolly good," the man replied. He linked his stubby fingers together. "Are you after anything specific?"

"Oh, I'm afraid I'm not that organised." Mary chuckled. Caicus did, too.

"Not a problem," the man said, peering out from behind his magnifying-glass lenses. "How old is the birthday girl?"

"She'll be seventeen," Mary answered.

I felt a gripping agony in my heart.

"How about a tennis bracelet?" the man suggested. He reached below the counter and heaved out a thick, laminated catalogue. Somewhat cumbersomely, he angled it towards Caicus and Mary and began flipping through the pages. The pair of them *ooh*ed and *aah*ed like good little shoppers.

I, however, wrinkled my nose in revulsion. This façade seemed to come far too easily to Caicus. The more I thought about it, the more I realised that perhaps he wasn't being so disingenuous after all. Not to Mary, at least.

The jewellery man paused on the current page and tapped it fervently. "How about a brooch?"

Did he just say *brooch*? I clocked the guy's name badge. It was pinned to the pocket of his thin white shirt, which clung like skin to his rounded frame.

Jim.

"That's not a bad idea," Mary mused. "A brooch. Something that she can keep forever."

Forever. There was that heartache again. Forever wasn't as long as it sounded.

"Yes," Jim agreed, "a brooch is a timeless artefact."

Get a grip, Jim, I thought cantankerously. *It's not a relic.*

"Which design do you favour?" he asked Mary. "We've got flowers, pearl cluster, bufferflies..."

Bufferflies?

"Hmm..." Mary pondered it. "Which do you like, Caicus?"

Caicus peered down at the glossy page. "What about the rosebud? You know, because her name is Rosebud."

"Rose," I corrected.

He scowled at me. "It's the same thing."

I didn't bother arguing. Anyway, Mary was visibly impressed by Golden Boy's idea.

"What a wonderful gift that would be," she cooed.

"No," I said bluntly. "Not the rosebud. Get the poppy. She's always preferred poppies."

Now both of them gawped at me.

"What?" I blinked.

"How do you know what she's *always preferred*?" Caicus mimicked.

Good question. It wasn't something I'd learnt in this lifetime, that was for sure. Funny what snippets of knowledge carry over.

"I just know her," I grumbled. "She likes poppies."

"Oh." Mary tried not to look too mistrustful. "Well, the poppy it is, then."

As Jim waddled off to find the elusive poppy brooch, I wandered around the shop, browsing the cabinets.

My attention fell on one in particular. On a shelf, locked behind glass casing, was a silver necklace. The pendant was half of a silver heart, cut through the middle in a jagged fracture.

"This one is broken," I said, my gaze still on the pendant.

Jim stopped shuffling for a moment. "What's that, my boy?"

I glanced at him. His round face peeked up over the counter top like a curious meerkat.

"The heart." I rapped on the glass. "It's in pieces."

"Oh." He pushed his spectacles up with his thumb. "No, that's the half-heart. The other half is behind the counter. One person takes one, and the other person takes the other. When they're put together, they are complete."

"How much for it?" I enquired instantly. "For both

pieces of the heart."

Jim leaned over the counter. "The price ticket should be below the necklace."

I examined the cabinet again. I had noticed a series of numbers marked beneath the necklace.

"That's the *price*?" I spluttered. "I thought that was some kind of barcode!"

"It's fine silver," Jim warranted.

I sighed very purposefully as I rummaged for my wallet. Producing it from my pocket, I opened up the brown leather slip and inspected the contents: a few small notes and a handful of loose change.

Being a witch didn't pay well.

Caicus, I caught his eye. *How much money have you got?*

None.

Didn't the elders give you any when we set off? I pushed.

Yes. But it's back at the house. Give me a minute and I'll charm the clerk; I'll make him hand it over free of charge. He smirked and winked at me.

I mulled it over. *No,* I declined. *I want to do this the right way.*

Are you sure? Seems a bit of a waste, don't you think?

I grimaced. *Why? Because she'll be dead on the same day she receives it?*

Caicus shook his head, sympathetically. *Oscar, I didn't mean that. I just meant, why spend your money when I can get it for free? Trust me, this guy will be easy to charm. And I'll make sure Mary goes under the spell, too. No suspicion.*

The offer was tempting, but my manner was set on honourable conduct. There would be more sentiment that way.

"Listen, Jim," I said, sizing him up for negotiations. "I haven't got enough cash. Will you do a deal?"

Jim fidgeted, clearly unsettled by the question. "I'm sorry, but I'm afraid I can't let it go for anything below the marked price."

Wow, Jim, thanks for nothing.

Mary put herself forward. "I'll cover what you don't have."

I raised my hand proudly. "Thanks, Mary, but I won't accept it."

I could tell she thought my stubbornness was a vice. Personally, I thought it to be a virtue.

"Right, Jim," I bartered, "how much for the pendant on its own?"

"Without the chain?" He cocked his head to one side.

"I believe that's what 'on its own' means," I said in a thin voice.

Jim reached for his calculator and began punching in numbers.

"I could sell it for…" he looked at the calculator and then at me, "half the marked price."

Half. Yeah, he really needed a calculator to work that one out.

"I'll take it," I confirmed. "But I want both pieces of the heart. Don't try to fob me off with some broken piece of silver junk."

"Uh, yes. Quite." Jim trundled to the cabinet, keys in hand. He collected half of my heart and took it to the counter to assemble it with the other half. Then he boxed up my full heart in a neat cream case that was lined with red silk.

That's a dumb present, Caicus teased. *It's a necklace with no neck-lace!*

It's a pendant.

With no chain to hang on? Naturally he was delighted by this.

As I marched to the cash register, I deliberately rammed my shoulder into Caicus, knocking him forward into the counter.

"Ooft," he grunted, winded by the impact.

"Oh, sorry," I said, for Mary's benefit only. "Clumsy me."

When Mary's back was turned, Caicus mouthed a string of delightful profanities at me.

I grinned.

Perched behind his cash register, Jim waited impatiently for the exchange of money. I handed over pretty much everything I had and took the box—which I tucked into my pocket with legitimate pride.

Ah, honest living, I mused, *there's nothing like it.*

"That's a lovely thought, Oscar," Mary said, kindly. She rose to her tiptoes and gave me a motherly kiss on the cheek.

What the...?

I stood back, stunned by her actions. Nobody had ever kissed me on the cheek before. Let me tell you something about our coven: it was widely recognised that you didn't kiss each other.

I stared at Caicus and we shared a moment of deep

understanding. This had been an experience that neither one of us had been prepared for, and one that had infinitely changed our lives in a way that we could not ignore. And I'd never noticed this before, but I saw it then—Caicus was sad. We both were. Without a doubt, we would miss the wholesome life we had created for ourselves.

He tried to force a smile, but damn, he couldn't do it. I hadn't seen his sadness before. I didn't like it.

Choked by my own helplessness, I called to him silently, *Don't worry, you've still got me.*

He brightened a little. *You, too. I'll always watch your back. Just how it's always been.*

I focused on the catalogue, feigning a sudden interest in brooches. I didn't want Caicus to see that 'just how it's always been' would never be enough for me again.

CHAPTER TWELVE

This Is Where We Stand

AN HOUR OR SO AFTER arriving in Hutton Ridge, our little quartet returned to the minivan, armed with provisions for Rose's impending birthday. On my counsel, Mary had purchased the poppy brooch and an assortment of other small gifts. Caicus oh-so-generously used the last of my change to buy Rose a birthday bar of chocolate. However, he now sat in the front passenger seat, quite happily devouring his gift.

On the route back to Millwood, the minivan chugged along at a snail's pace. That's Mary's driving for you. If I had been in the driver's seat, things would have been massively different. I drove as I moved—in other words, fast.

But I held my tongue and tried not to sulk over it. Neither of which was easy to do, because of my sulky and opinionated nature, not to mention that I was insanely desperate to get back to Millwood. Not a good combination.

Anyway, after light years of watching the trees monotonously pass, Mary steered the car onto the estate access road. It was only a mile to the manor, yet this part of the journey felt like the longest of all. Perhaps because Mary insisted on slowing down to tackle the narrower road. Each to his own, I supposed. But put it this way: if I were a kettle, a torrent of steam would have been pouring out of my every orifice.

By the time we finally lurched to a stop, my patience had worn down to the bone. I flung the car door open and paced across the gravel. The others dallied behind while I let myself into the house and bolted upstairs.

At the top of the attic staircase, I tapped on the closed door.

There was no response, but there was an intense scent lingering in the surrounding air. I knew Rose was near.

I suddenly became aware of my hammering pulse.

I twisted the door handle and crept into the room. Rose was sleeping soundly in her bed, still in the same huddled position where I'd left her much earlier, with my jacket tucked up to her chin. It seemed like she'd had a restful slumber, at least.

I stepped over to the bed and perched on the edge.

"Hello," I whispered.

She didn't stir.

I lay my hand on her arm.

"Wake up now," I said smoothly.

Her eyelashes fluttered and she gazed up at me blearily.

Huh. It worked.

"Hello," I smiled.

"Hello," she mumbled back. "You're still here."

"I had to go away for a little while," I admitted, "but I came back as soon as I could."

"Oh." She rubbed her eyes and sat herself upright. "Where did you go?"

"Caicus," I replied, not exactly keen to divulge the entirety of my morning. "And other stuff."

"Oh. Are you okay?"

I attempted a smile and a weak nod.

"Any dreams?" I asked.

She turned to the window, her focus resting on the feathery clouds as they floated by.

"Yes," she told me, in a hazy, distant voice. "I had dreams. But good dreams. He wasn't there."

It was blissful to see the look of gratitude on her face.

"A dream without Lathiaus," I noted, joining her relief. "Must have been nice." I moved closer to her, sitting at her side now, with my legs slouched on the bed.

She leaned into me. "It *was* nice," she murmured.

"Yeah? Tell me about it."

"Trees," she explained vaguely.

I grinned. "Trees?"

"Lots of trees. And you. You were there, too."

"What was I doing?"

"Watching the trees."

"Sounds thrilling."

She went on, "I was here, and you were there, but we were both watching the trees. And I knew that even though we were apart, you were with me. You didn't leave me. Not for a moment."

I laughed quietly.

"What?" she asked.

I reached my arm around her and held her as though she were fused to me. "I think your dream was more of an instinct."

I could hear her heart beating now, and I instantly felt at ease.

She glanced up at me. "Was I on your mind?"

"Yes," I told her. "Always."

My chest tightened. I had been so keyed up to see her that I'd barely considered the darkness that would follow.

"Rose," I began, staring down at the bedding that cocooned her, "you didn't tell me about your birthday."

She groaned. "I was hoping I could avoid it altogether. Did my aunt tell you?"

"Yes."

She giggled. "I was so close! I almost had a birthday-free year."

"Why would you want that?"

"I don't have the best luck with birthdays. They never seem to work out all that well for me. It's laughable, really."

"Rose," I said.

She let out a forlorn sigh. "Go on. Hit me with it."

"I… uh… I'm sorry."

"It's going to happen on my birthday, isn't it?" she guessed.

"We… Caicus and myself… we think Lathiaus will

awaken on Friday." I held my breath, waiting for her to burst into tears or faint or something.

She mulled it over. I couldn't see her face—to be perfectly honest, I didn't dare look—but she folded her arms across her chest.

"Typical!" she exclaimed. "On my birthday? The brazen nerve of it..." she ranted. And I listened. It was quite amusing actually, as far as grim, end-of-the-world conversations go.

"The brazen nerve," I agreed, ever one to encourage a tirade.

She wagged her finger as though she was rebuking Lathiaus right there and then. "Well, I'm not going to take this lying down. It's not over yet," she huffed. "This is Judy Timmons all over again."

I frowned. "What's a Judytimmons?"

"The worst creature imaginable."

"Demon?"

"Worse. School bully."

I cocked my head with intrigue while Rose recounted her tale.

"Judy, a girl at my school who convinced everybody not to come to my birthday party," she seethed, clearly still harbouring resentment towards this Judytimmons thing.

"Do you want me to hunt it down?" I offered.

She chuckled sweetly. "No, that's okay. As tempting as it is, I don't think hunting her down is quite necessary. I'm taking the high road. Lathiaus, on the other hand..."

"Yeah," I exhaled heavily. "He's a lot bigger and badder than the Judytimmons."

"Doesn't mean I'm going to run scared, though."

I hesitated. That wasn't a bad idea. If Rose wasn't around, then there wouldn't be much anyone could do about it.

"Run," I told her, a note of urgency in my voice.

"What?"

"Run," I repeated. Yes, this made so much sense. Why hadn't I thought of it before?

"I can't run away," she vetoed the idea.

"Why not?" I pressed.

"My family—"

"I'll make sure no harm comes to your family."

"I can't leave them."

"Then take them with you."

She appeared to be contemplating it. "What about you? Will you come with me?"

My mouth went dry. I couldn't. I simply couldn't leave Caicus to face Lathiaus alone. And I could hardly bring him along with us; that would defeat the point of running in the first place. Oh, I could just picture it: hey, let's run away, but be sure to invite everyone we know to come with us—including those we're running from.

Not to mention the fact that Rose still had no idea that her survival depended on my death, and vice versa. I wouldn't want her to bear witness to my superb demise, in whatever gruesome means it might be bestowed.

"Oscar," she gripped my hand ardently, "what do you think? Will you run away with me?"

Her wording could not have been more attractive if it

were doused in chocolate. I felt like I'd been plonked down in the Garden of Eden without so much as a paddle. Apple? Yes, please.

Her fingers curled around mine. She was waiting for my decision.

"No," I said, regretfully.

She sighed again. "Well, I'm not going anywhere without you."

"Just promise you'll think about it?"

"No."

Oh. Stubborn as all hell.

"Please," I demanded.

"No."

I tut-tutted.

"So, we face Lathiaus," she declared, with courage in her tone.

"On Friday," I uttered. "During the final hour."

"Eleven at night?"

"Yes. Everything that happens will happen in that hour. When the clock strikes twelve, it'll all be over."

"Just like birthdays."

I closed my eyes.

Just like us.

PART FIVE
ROSE

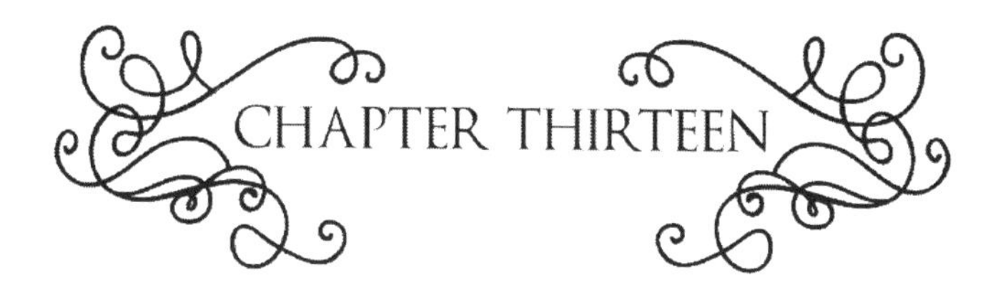

CHAPTER THIRTEEN

Out of the Game

ON THURSDAY I AWOKE AT sunrise. The morning had scarcely begun, but I could tell from the oppressive sky that it would be another grey day.

I had no interest in going back to sleep, so I crawled out of bed and threw on a pair of jeans and a butterscotch top. I sat down at my dressing table and inspected my reflection in the mirror. At this early hour the lighting was poor, so the left side of my face was shadowed with what looked like deep bruising. Even my eyes looked murky and dark—a sort of seaweed green. I pulled a brush through my hair and watched the strands settle on the cotton of my top.

One more day.

Staunchly, I stood up and made my way out of my room.

As I stepped onto the attic staircase, my heart leapt into my throat.

Oscar was sprawled across the bottom step, half sitting, half lying.

"You scared me," I gasped. "What are you doing down there?"

He shrugged, and his auburn eyes met mine. "I don't feel like sleeping. I'm more at ease when I can keep watch. You know, just in case."

I tiptoed down the steps.

Oscar courteously rose to his feet. "Did you have another vision?" he asked, taking my hand.

"Yes," I replied. "It was the same as the night before. You..." I paused. "Well, *Oliver* was there again."

"Did he say anything?"

"He kept telling me to go back," I relayed.

We stood in the hallway now, standing face to face and breathing quietly. Oscar was several inches taller than me, so I looked up to meet his eyes.

His expression was unreadable. "Go back?" he repeated.

"Yes, but I couldn't move. It's horrible. My body feels like rock. And then Lathiaus comes towards me... It's the same every time."

Oscar placed his hand on my shoulder and then idly trailed it along my arm. He opened his mouth, as if he were about to say something imperative, but he stopped himself.

"What is it?" I pressed.

A dashing smile shaped on his lips. "Chess?"

I laughed quietly. "Okay."

As we crept downstairs, I studied Oscar's footing. It was incredible. He moved with such effortless agility. Compared to his steps, my own seemed awkward and lumbering.

Oscar led the way into the conservatory, holding the

door open for me to duck through.

I took a seat, watching the concentration on his face as he arranged the table-top chessboard. He was so careful and accurate, lining up the pieces without any room for error.

Once the board was efficiently in order, Oscar rubbed his hands together.

"Get ready to lose—again," he teased.

I mimicked his self-righteous expression. "I don't think so. This time, I'm playing to win."

"Oh, right," he scoffed. "Because the other times you've intended to lose."

"They were practice rounds," I replied haughtily. "This time, I'm serious."

He snorted. "We'll see about that."

"Yes, we will." Ha. Last word.

"Ladies first," he said as he gestured complacently to the board.

I went for what was swiftly becoming my trademark first move. I pushed forward the centre pawn. Yep, well played.

Oscar clapped his hands once, then bent over the board. His fingers hovered, poised eagerly to make their move. I noticed that his foot had begun to tap in anticipation.

"Come on," I muttered.

After a lengthy deliberation, he moved his first pawn. Although it appeared to be a tactical manoeuvre, I was ninety-nine per cent sure it was random.

We played a cut-throat game for a further twenty minutes before Oscar called a time out.

"No, no, no," he sighed irritably. "Don't you see what's happening here?"

I inspected the board. "Nope. Am I winning?"

He groaned impatiently. "No. You're losing. And you're not paying attention."

I yawned. The truth was, I'd stopped caring about nineteen minutes ago. The bold competitiveness had quickly fizzled out—as it usually did.

Oscar looked at me sternly. "You're in check."

"Oh. So, you've won?"

"No, not yet. Winning would be check*mate*. Check means your king is in danger, remember?"

I yawned again. "Shall we just call it a draw?"

"No!" he exclaimed.

"Fine. You win."

"No! I'm not winning by default. We have to finish the game."

I rolled my eyes and made a half-hearted attempt to slide my king one space over.

My renewed participation pleased my opponent. He rubbed his chin thoughtfully, carefully assessing every remaining piece on the board.

The conservatory door rattled open.

Oscar scarcely noticed. I, however, waved a greeting to my uncle, who ambled into the room dressed in his shirt-and-tie work clothes.

Roger propped his briefcase against my chair and peered down at the coffee table.

"Dear, oh dear!" he let out a good-natured chortle.

"He's got you, Rose. Oscar's got you in checkmate. There's no escape!"

I tucked a strand of hair behind my ear. "Can't I move one space to the left?"

"No," Roger shook his head solemnly. "I'm afraid it's game over. You're dead." He used the word so blithely. Little did he know.

"Okay," I relented without protest. "It was only a practice round."

I glanced at Oscar. He sat rigid in his chair. The muscles in his jaw contracted and his eyes had darkened.

Roger gave me a commiserative pat on the shoulder. "Someone has to lose. That's the game."

With that, Oscar sprang up and snatched my king from the board. He stormed out through the side door, pacing into the garden.

Roger and I swapped a bemused look as the conservatory door gently swung shut. Oscar was already out of sight.

"My, my," Roger uttered, "that was rather odd. He took your player off the board."

I shrugged and smiled innocently.

Roger craned his neck to peer outside. "I'd call it poor sportsmanship, but he was just about to win! How curious." My poor uncle was clearly baffled by the whole state of affairs. "What a peculiar young man."

I grinned. "Yes, he is peculiar. Maybe the pressure got to him."

"The pressure of winning?" Roger's brow creased.

"Winning can be very stressful."

"Quite," Roger murmured. "Any rate," he said, his voice brightening, "I'm off to the office. You have a nice day, dear." He patted me on the head awkwardly and trundled away.

THE MOMENT I HEARD THE front door close behind Roger, I hopped up from my seat and set off in search of Oscar. I trotted outside and scanned the meadow garden, speculating in which direction my playmate had gone. To my right was Mary's flower patch, and straight ahead was the forest.

Taking a gamble, I headed for the forest.

"Don't look for me," Oscar's voice called out, though I couldn't tell from where. "I want to be alone."

I whirled around. "Where are you?" I shouted.

No response came, so I continued walking towards the boundary of evergreens.

"Don't go into the forest," his voice came again.

I strained my eyes. Where was he?

"Is that where you are?" I asked. "The forest?"

Again he didn't reply, so I continued forward.

When I reached the first tree, I tried again. "Are you in there?" I called, peering into the shadowed carnival of tree trunks.

"No." His voice was much nearer now.

I laughed to myself. "Okay. I'm going into the forest. It's up to you if you want to join me."

"Emotional blackmail," Oscar yelled.

I put my hands on my hips. "It's not blackmail. I'm just

updating you on my whereabouts. That's what considerate people do," I added.

"I don't need updates, thank you. I can see you perfectly well."

I looked up sharply. I could have sworn his voice had come from above me. But all I saw was a tangled web of leaves and branches blocking out the glimmer of daylight.

All of a sudden, an incredible thought occurred to me.

I sucked in my breath. "Are you… flying?"

"Of course I'm not flying!" Oscar snorted. He sighed loudly. "Take a step to the right."

I took a generous sidestep.

There was a rustling in the tree tops and a few green leaves floated down to the ground. Then, high above me, I saw Oscar sitting on a sturdy branch. It bowed with his weight as he adjusted position.

I gawped at him. "How did you get up there?"

"I flew," he remarked wryly.

Effortlessly, he slid from the branch and landed on the ground—on the exact spot where I had been standing only a few seconds earlier. The breeze stirred by his landing fluttered through my hair.

I stared at him, then up at the soaring branch, then back to him again.

"You can really…" What was the word I was searching for here? "Jump."

"Technically it was more of a drop."

I blinked at him.

He spun on his heel and marched off towards the

garden.

I stared after him, astounded.

Oscar glanced briefly over his shoulder. "I'm storming off, now," he told me. "Are you coming or not?"

"Oh. Right." I shook off my starry-eyed wonder and skipped alongside him. "So, what was all that about?" I asked, struggling to keep in stride with him as we marched across the lawn.

"I took you off the table."

"Um, yeah," I said quietly. "I noticed."

"It was a stupid thing to do."

"I thought it was okay."

He stopped in his tracks. "It was not okay. It was not okay at all."

We stood on the spongy grass alongside Mary's patch of garden. The dainty flowers grew in graceful sequence—with exception of the snapdragons, which seemed to have taken a battering.

"I know why you did it," I told him softly.

Oscar bowed his head. "Caicus is right about me. I'm acting irrationally. I can't just take people off the table." He kicked the ground with the toe of his shoe.

"You can do whatever you want to do," I disputed.

He stepped over to Mary's roses and idly touched the silky red petals.

I stood behind him, inhaling the delicate scent of the flowers as it mingled with the familiar scent of him.

"Roses," he noted, turning to face me.

I nodded my head, watching him curiously.

"Do you still like poppies?" he asked.

That took me by surprise. I racked my brain, but I was certain that we'd never discussed it.

"How do you know I like poppies?"

He offered me an ambiguous smirk. "So, you do?"

"Yes."

"Do you know what flower I like?" he coaxed.

"Roses," I whispered, more impulsively than logically. It was as though I'd answered from my soul, rather than my consciousness.

He grinned and nodded his head. "Do you know why?"

"Because they have thorns," I answered immediately. The inexplicable certainty and accuracy of my words staggered me beyond belief.

Oscar's eyes sparkled in delight. He traced his fingers along the stem, stopping when he reached a sharp thorn. He allowed the thorn to prick his thumb, without even a flinch as it pierced the skin.

"You're bleeding," I murmured, watching a drip of ruby blood spill over his thumb.

He laughed ironically. "Does it bother you?"

"Blood?" I generalised. "Or your blood?"

"Blood."

"No."

"My blood," he revised.

"Yes."

He wiped his thumb on the rose petal. The ruddy colours blended together almost flawlessly.

"Gone," he said in a tender voice.

I didn't know exactly why I felt compelled to do this, but I simply couldn't stop myself. I reached out to him and enfolded my arms around him, resting my chin on his shoulder.

His breath faltered.

"Is this okay?" I tested.

Oscar cautiously returned the embrace.

"Yes," he said. "This is okay."

So, there we stood, at six in the morning, in Mary's flower garden, holding on to each other as though we may not get another chance.

And I wished for it never to end.

CHAPTER FOURTEEN

Reinforcements

AROUND MID-AFTERNOON, SOMETHING HAPPENED that subsequently changed the course of events in a way that could never have been foreseen.

We had a visitor.

Oscar and I had been in the garden at the time. It wasn't a warm day, nor was it particularly pleasing to the eye, what with the murky fog curtaining the landscape. But neither of us made any attempt to move back indoors, so we silently agreed to stay put. Anyway, from where we'd planted ourselves, there was a direct view to the front driveway. Parked on the gravel was Mary's sky-blue minivan and the Valeros' sleek black Lamborghini. There was an empty space between them, where Roger's gold Volvo would usually slot. Of course, he was at work, ergo the space was empty.

Not for long.

We heard the rumbling engine before we saw the car. It snarled like a tiger, rising louder and louder until the impressive vehicle swerved into view.

Oscar and I frowned at one another. And for a second, I thought my eyes and ears were playing tricks on me. Now, it might have seemed odd to feel so disbelieving that a car would come to Millwood. But, it was *Millwood.* Cars didn't come here. The rest of the world was miles away, and we went to *it.* Not the other way around.

At first we were both a little perplexed. However, when the royal blue BMW shot across the gravel, perplexed changed to worried. I didn't know why I felt worried—as far as I knew, I had no reason to be—but Oscar froze like a deer in the headlights. My own anxiety naturally emulated his.

The car screeched to a halt, sliding with impeccable precision between the minivan and Lamborghini.

"That traitorous back-stabber," I heard Oscar mutter under his breath.

"What?" I looked to him for answers, but his focus was glued to the BMW. A stream of grey smog poured from the exhaust pipe, merging with the fogged air.

"Who is that?" I asked, trying to peer into the blackened car windows.

Oscar didn't seem to hear me; his mind was elsewhere.

The engine cut out and the driver's door opened smoothly. Out stepped a man. He was tall and smartly dressed, with hair the colour of vanilla ice cream. He looked to be in his late twenties, though from this distance I couldn't be sure.

"Don't let him see you," Oscar hissed.

I shrank back into the flowers.

"Who is he?" I asked for the second time.

"Marco," Oscar spat out the name with vicious detest.

"Who's Marco?"

"My brother," he responded grimly.

From our hiding place we watched Marco stride to the front door and ring the bell. He moved with long, agile steps, his head held high.

Oscar edged forward to get a better view. He gave me a warning *stay back* look. I'd never seen that expression before; it was almost animal.

Personally, I wasn't close enough to see the front door, but I heard it all go down.

"Marco," Caicus greeted the newcomer, not surprised or troubled as Oscar had been. "Do come in."

"Hello, Caicus," Marco replied, in a voice that oozed superiority. "I trust I find you well?"

"Very well, thank you. And yourself? How was your journey?"

I didn't hear Marco's response, because he crossed into the manor and closed the door behind them.

Oscar swivelled around to face me. His expression was thunderous.

"Family reunion?" I quipped.

"An unwelcome one," he grumbled. "And one I haven't been invited to." He let out an enraged breath and kicked at the grass.

"Why is he here?" I shuffled forward to sit beside Oscar.

"Because Caicus doesn't trust me," Oscar fumed. He sprung to his feet and marched across the lawn towards the house.

"Wait!" I called after him, scrambling off the ground and rushing to catch up.

"No, stay there," he yelled over his shoulder.

"No!" I snapped. "I'm in this, too, remember?"

Oscar paused his stride.

He pinched the bridge of his nose. "Fine," he muttered. "Stay behind me and *don't* look into his eyes." Without further explanation, he stormed off towards the manor, flinging the door open and bursting into the hallway.

I followed closely behind, not sure if I should be scared or angry. I decided on angry—mostly because I didn't like the sound of scared.

Oscar made a beeline for the kitchen.

The first person I saw was Mary. She was standing at the breakfast bar, apron on, rolling pin in hand. Zack was in his highchair, bashing his rattle on his tray.

"Hello," Mary waved at us. She placed her rolling pin down and wiped her floury hands onto her apron. "Oscar, your brother has come for a visit. How nice." By the sound of her voice, she was as confused as I was.

On the other side of the breakfast counter, Caicus and Marco stood, both smiling cryptically.

I could see Marco up close, now. His skin was bronzed and his hair and eyes were as pale as clotted cream. Without a doubt, he was outstandingly handsome. Striking, even. It was difficult to peel my eyes away.

"Hello," Marco purred. He offered me his hand. "My name is Marco Valero. And you are?"

I warily shook his hand, all the while conscious of Oscar's barbed body language.

"I'm Rose," I said, a little more meekly than I would have liked.

When I stepped back from him, I noticed Oscar's shoulders relax a fraction.

Then Marco pivoted towards Mary. He extended his long fingers out to her.

"Pleasure to meet you both," he charmed her, sinuously.

Mary took his hand, staring deep into his talcum powder eyes. "Hello," she managed, utterly tongue-tied.

Caicus stood aside, smiling amiably. Thick strands of caramel hair curved into a neat frame around his own frosted eyes, which he now cast upon Mary, breaking her connection with Marco.

I didn't like this. I didn't like it at all.

"Mary," Caicus said, "as I was saying," he glanced briefly at Oscar, "Marco is our brother. It's okay if he stays with us for a few days, isn't it?"

Completely spellbound, Mary nodded her head. "Of course."

"Thank you," Caicus cooed in delight.

Now Marco joined the game, directing Mary's eyes back to him. "How very generous of you. You have a lovely home."

Mary's jaw dropped open. Dumbfounded, she plonked down onto a kitchen stool and gawped at the new guest.

Marco cocked his head towards me. "Rose," he spoke my name as though it tasted sweet on his lips, "my brothers informed me of your beauty, but their praise does not do you justice."

Oscar groaned. "Give it a rest, Romeo. Nobody likes a kiss-ass."

"Little brother," Marco glanced at Oscar, and then at me, "have you no etiquette?"

Caicus cleared his throat. "Uh, Mary," he said, severing through the tension, "would you be so kind as to take Zack outside for a moment?" He thanked her before hearing her response.

Entranced by him, Mary obliged. Two humans down, one to go. I stood in the kitchen with three Valero witches. Three fiercely handsome witches—though I had a feeling that things were about to get ugly.

"What a great surprise," Oscar jeered through clenched teeth. "Marco's here." He looked accusingly at Caicus.

Caicus shrugged his shoulders. "Three heads are better than two."

Oscar's eyes narrowed. "I'll bet they are."

The boys fell into a hush. I had been in their company for long enough to spot when they were communicating telepathically. Like now, for instance.

After a lengthy silence, Marco spoke. "So, this is her." He motioned to me. "The infamous prophecy girl."

I shrank away from his intrusive gaze. Despite his placid beauty and refined demeanour, there was something about Marco that frightened me to the core. My beware-of-the-dark-alley radar was spiralling off the scale.

As if sensing my discomfort, Oscar stood in front of me, which I was infinitely pleased about.

Marco sneered. "Well, isn't that something?" he remarked contemptuously. "Oscar's found himself a pet."

Oscar stared steadily at him.

"I thought you were exaggerating, Caicus," Marco went on, "but now I see your words ring true. Seems I arrived just in the nick of time."

I stood, motionless and vulnerable; it was all I could do. To my surprise, I noticed Caicus was doing the same. Oscar and Marco, on the other hand, were like two lions, ready to pounce at the drop of a hat.

"Come now, Oscar," Marco said in a low, fluid murmur, "aren't you going to let me talk to the girl?"

Oscar laughed bitterly. "Nothing you can say will be of any interest."

Marco flashed his perfect white teeth, but it was more of a snarl than a smile. "Are you afraid I'll work my magic on her?"

"Your magic is useless on her," Oscar retorted. "She's immune."

Marco signalled to Caicus for confirmation.

"It's true," Caicus verified. "My power doesn't work on her. Yours probably won't either."

"May I see this for myself?" Marco requested, in an unnervingly polite manner. "Not that I don't trust you two boys, but let's face it, you hardly have the greatest track record."

Caicus and Oscar glanced at one another, and I could have sworn they grinned.

"Well?" Marco pushed. "Step aside, Oscar."

Oscar remained faithfully in front of me.

"No, thanks," he replied coolly.

I peeked around my protector. Marco was glaring at him, and Caicus was bursting with nervous energy.

"You want to talk to me?" I said, boldly. Well, as boldly as I could when I'd been scared out of my wits.

Marco's lips crooked upwards and he met my eyes. "I'd like that very much."

All of a sudden, I felt sick. Dizzy, too. Looking into Marco's vanilla eyes was like looking at the world through distorted mirrors. Kind of appealing, but mostly it just made me want to vomit.

"Pleasure to meet you," Marco uttered seductively.

I tore my gaze away from him and waited for my head to stop spinning.

"Well?" Caicus urged, virtually salivating in anticipation.

"Well, what?" I asked.

"What do you think of Marco?" Caicus spoke with such jumbled excitement that his words came out disjointed.

"Umm… He made me feel sick," I clarified.

Oscar and Caicus exploded into a fit of laughter. Evidently unimpressed, Marco shot them a vicious glower.

"Sick?" Caicus repeated, still battling to catch his breath. "So, no uncontrollable feelings of love or adoration?"

"For him?" I pointed sceptically at Marco. "No. Just sick."

Marco struggled to remain impervious, but I could tell he wasn't accustomed to being anything other than irresistible.

Caicus sniggered quietly, but Oscar continued to laugh openly.

"That's that, then," Oscar concurred, distinctly satisfied.

"I think we've all learnt something today. A valuable life lesson."

Marco raised his chin.

Oscar's grin broadened. "Caicus, care to tell big brother what we've learnt?"

"That you're never as hot as you think you are," Caicus offered.

He and Oscar guffawed again.

Marco straightened the collar of his shirt. "Tomorrow is the resurrection," he barked. "There's no time for childish games. We have work to do."

Oscar rolled his eyes. "*We* are on top of it. *We* have been working on this for weeks. Or have you forgotten who was assigned this mission?"

Marco arched an eyebrow. "You were not assigned to the mission as a reflection of your capabilities, Oscar. Do not for a second think that any of the coven elders were pleased about your involvement. My only solace is that Caicus had the sense to call for reinforcement."

"No, I didn't," Caicus objected. "I merely called to update you on our progress."

"And sell me out," Oscar griped.

"No!" Caicus cried. "But… I'm worried about you, Oscar. You're acting…"

All three of them looked at me, as though they'd just remembered I was in the room.

"You did the right thing," Marco told Caicus. "There is no shame in requiring assistance. We recognised a cry for help; we had anticipated as much."

Oscar gave him the finger.

"Now, now," Marco scolded him, "I am your brother. And I'm here to help you. You certainly need my help."

"The coven may not have chosen me for this task," Oscar acknowledged, "but the prophecy did. This is my mission, not yours."

Marco's air was indifferent. "Yes, you have visions. But that does not deem you able. The coven has lost faith in you. Even your cohort has lost faith in you."

"Hey!" Caicus protested. "I haven't lost faith in him."

Oscar tusked loudly. "You've got a funny way of showing it, back-stabber."

Caicus clutched his heart. "I would never stab your back. All of my stabbing is done upfront."

Huh? These boys were eccentric, to say the least.

I raised my hand. "Excuse me."

They all stared at me.

"What's going on here? Why have you lost faith in Oscar?" Something told me I was way out of my depth.

Oscar knotted his fingers through his hair. "Forget them, Rose," he replied tautly. "Their faith means nothing to me. I'll do what I have to do."

Now it was Marco and Caicus who exchanged a private look.

I gripped Oscar's sleeve as he abruptly steered me out of the kitchen.

"We can still stop Lathiaus, can't we?" I whispered.

He answered with a reassuring smile, but I could tell that on the inside he was falling to pieces.

CHAPTER FIFTEEN

Something Old, Something New, Something Broken in Two

"HAPPY BIRTHDAY!"

I groaned and pulled the bedcovers up over my head.

"Happy Birthday!" Oscar sang out again. He peeled back the covers and grinned broadly at me.

I squinted, adjusting to the sudden influx of daylight. A few seconds ago I had been deep in slumberland.

"Are you having a nice day?" he asked.

"I'm not sure yet," I garbled.

"Oh. Never mind, then. What would you like to do today?"

"Sleep." I wriggled further under the covers.

He shook me. "No more sleeping. Eight hours is enough."

"Eight hours?" I peered up at him quizzically. "That's the most I've slept in weeks."

Oscar's eyes glowed like hot embers and his dark hair fell tousled around his brow. "Happy Birthday," he said again, winking.

I yawned and kicked off the bedding.

"That's more like it!" Oscar applauded. "Shall we go downstairs? They're all waiting for you."

Okay, my tatty, purple-checked pyjamas were hardly the most glamorous birthday ensemble, but they'd have to do for now. I rolled out of bed, moving at a comfortably sluggish pace. Well, until Oscar intervened, jostling me out of my room and practically frog-marching me downstairs.

We swept into the kitchen and Oscar presented me to Mary, Roger and Zack, who were seated around the breakfast table.

Roger and Mary cheered.

"Happy Birthday!" Mary hooted.

"Happy Birthday!" Roger clapped his hands as though I'd achieved something momentous.

I grinned. "Thanks. You're not at work, Uncle Roger?"

"I told them I'd be late this morning. It is a special day, after all."

"Open your presents," Mary insisted, sliding three gold-wrapped boxed across the breakfast bar.

I took a seat on one of the stools. "You didn't have to get me presents."

"Of course we did," Mary gushed. "It's your birthday!"

I stacked my gifts in a neat pile and tackled them one by one. Four pairs of eager eyes watched me on tenterhooks.

The first box I opened contained a pack of bath salts, all

shaped like mini cupcakes—very cute. Next I unwrapped a book.

"*Double Jeopardy*," I read the title aloud.

Mary nodded her head enthusiastically. "It's a thriller," she informed me. "I've never read it, but I think the idea is that if a man's been convicted of a crime he didn't commit, then in theory, if he ever *did* commit the crime in future, he's already served his time for it. Is that right, Roger?"

Roger leaned over to see the book cover. "Hmm. Could be. I believe that 'double jeopardy' is the term used for the second prosecution of the same crime. I don't know about all that 'getting away with it' business, though."

"It's only fiction, Roger." Mary waved her hand to hush him.

"Looks good," I said, placing the book down on the table. "Thanks. I'm in need of a new book. I've already read all of yours."

Mary chortled warmly. "Now this one," she urged, nudging the final gold present.

I tore the wrapper off and opened up the dainty jewellery box.

It was a brooch.

"It's a poppy," I murmured, lifting it to the light. Under normal circumstances, I probably wouldn't have been overly keen on a brooch. But today I absolutely adored it. I knew instantly that it had been bought for me out of love. I saw the influences that had each played a part: my aunt and Oscar. I knew they'd chosen it together.

They looked at me, nervously, trying to measure my

reaction.

Mary cleared her throat. "If you don't like it, we can take it back to the shop—"

"No," I stopped her. "No. I love it." I hopped off my stool and hugged her. Then I hugged Roger and baby Zack. And lastly, Oscar.

His arms linked around me.

"Good choice," I whispered into his ear.

"I never make a bad one," he whispered back.

I returned to my stool, temporarily pinning the brooch onto my pyjama top.

After the customary present giving, Roger left for work and Mary produced a tray of freshly baked breakfast muffins.

Halfway through my second one, the phone rang.

Mary picked up the cordless receiver and held it to her ear. "Hello? Mary Clements speaking."

There was a pause and then her face lit up. "Hello, David! How's Africa?"

I dropped the muffin onto the tabletop.

Dad.

"Oh, how wonderful," Mary gushed into the phone. "I'll pass you over to Rose. Take care, dear."

She handed me the phone.

"Hi!" I exclaimed. I was rather excitable—after all, this was the first time I'd heard from my parents since they'd left for their trip a month ago.

"Hello, Rose," my father's voice came through faintly on the poor telephone line. "Happy Birthday!"

"You remembered."

"Of course we remembered." He seemed a little disgruntled by my comment. "How are things in Millwood?"

"Great!" I replied.

"Really?" He sounded shocked.

Actually, even I was a little shocked by my over-zealous response. It was odd, but despite the drama and catastrophic bombshells, this had still been the best summer of my life.

"Really," I assured him.

The telephone line crackled, and his words began to break.

"That's… other… Africa… but we… again?"

I wrinkled my nose. "What was that? I can't hear you."

"Oh, that's… Must… bad connection. Here's your mother to speak to you." He moved away from the mouth piece, but I heard him call to my mother, "Adele, Rose is on the phone."

Then her eloquent voice drifted into my ear.

"Hello, Rose. Happy Birthday!"

"Thanks. How are you? How's Africa?"

"Terrific," she stated. "We've got some excellent shots… work with such wonderful… once in a… experience."

"The connection is really bad." I jammed the phone closer to my ear.

"Oh dear. We'll have to call again… better line."

"When will you be home?" I asked. The plan had been for them to stay in Africa until the end of August, which was only two weeks away. That meant I'd be seeing them in fourteen days—assuming I survived the night, of course.

"We've been commissioned… stay out here… longer than planned."

"How much longer?" It was hard to disguise the sudden frostiness in my tone.

Out of the corner of my eye, I noticed Mary and Oscar busy themselves clearing the table, pretending not to listen to my conversation.

"Six months," my mother replied.

My heart sank. "Six months?"

"Hopefully we'll… after Christmas."

"You won't be back for Christmas?" I spluttered.

"I'm afraid… for Christmas... but… in the new year."

I sighed. I supposed I should have seen that coming. I'd heard this story one too many times. Even if they had been back for Christmas, they'd swan off somewhere else again within a few months.

"Okay," I muttered, resigned. "If you have to…"

"Remember, Rose, this is how we're able… afford… send you to such wonderful schools."

I pulled a face. I couldn't care less about the wonderful schools.

"So, what about you… have any news?"

News. Now there was a question.

Tonight a demon will rise, and there's a pretty good chance that I'll die at his hand. Oh, and I got a new brooch.

"No news," I said.

"Oh. Have you made… friends?"

"Yes."

"Oh!" My mother seemed astounded by this revelation.

She'd probably have had an easier time believing me if I'd told her the demon thing. "What's her name?"

"Oscar."

"Oh." There was friction in her voice now. "And where did you meet Oscar?"

Well, he put a spell on my aunt and uncle to trick them into letting him stay at the manor so that he could stop a prophecy that foretells the end of all witches. And me.

"Millwood," I answered.

"Is he a nice boy?"

Hard to say. He's a deadly witch.

"Yes."

She clucked disapprovingly. "I shouldn't… remind you that your focus… on school… at this stage… life."

"Okay."

"Not to mention… boys should not… with school… throw it all down the drain… we've worked so hard to… plenty of time for boys… older… Do you understand?"

"Okay."

"I'll call again."

"Okay."

"Send my love to Roger and Mary."

"I will. And Zack," I added.

"What? Who?"

"Your only nephew."

"Oh, yes, of course. The little one."

"Bye," I said into the cold, plastic phone.

"Bye…"

And the line went dead.

I SLOUCHED IN A SALMON pink armchair in the conservatory, pensively watching the rain pour down outside. The drops fell like bullets, pattering on the evergreens and slowly turning the garden into boggy, waterlogged slush.

Oscar perched on the edge of the coffee table, twitching restlessly.

"You're upset, aren't you?" he said. I could tell he'd wanted to ask that for a while.

"Nope."

"About your parents?" he deduced.

I shrugged.

He pressed his knuckles together. "Because they're not coming back?"

"It's not the end of the world."

We exchanged a momentarily troubled look, unsettled by my wording.

I sighed and returned my gaze to the garden. The sky churned with a brewing storm. Bulging grey rain clouds hovered over the estate like enemy aircraft.

"Why am I what I am?" I asked distantly.

Oscar scratched his head. "Can you elaborate?"

"Why do I have a witch's heart? And what have I got to do with Lathiaus?"

"I don't know."

I was sick of hearing that. "Does anyone know?"

"I don't know," he answered again.

"But there must be a way of finding out. Someone must

know."

Oscar stared down at his hands. "Well..."

"Well?" I prompted.

"There are ways..." he trailed off.

I sat up straighter in my seat. "Ways for you to find out?"

"Ways for *you* to find out," he amended.

My breath caught. "How?"

Oscar glanced to the closed conservatory door. We were alone.

"There is a spell," he confessed.

I regarded him carefully, watching his gaze as it darted between me and the door. "What kind of spell?"

"I... I think there's a Retracing spell."

"Retracing spell?" I echoed.

Weird. I was chatting about spells now. Very weird.

"It's like regression," he explained. "It shows you your roots. How it all began, that type of thing."

"Sounds good," I mused.

Oscar rubbed his hand over his face. "No. Not necessarily. I've never done it before, and it's heavy magic. Besides, I'm not sure how safe it would be for a human."

I pretended not to hear that last part.

"Could we try?"

"I don't do magic unless I'm sure of its consequences," he flatly rejected the idea.

"But, people—*witches*—have done it before?" I argued. "Isn't it worth a try if it means the chance of piecing together the puzzle?"

"Witches have done it before, yes. But I haven't. I don't know what it entails..." He winced. "I don't know why I mentioned it in the first place."

"Can't we just try—"

"Forget I said anything," he cut me off. "It's not safe. It's..." He shook his head. "Forget I said anything."

Yeah, right, I thought, folding my arms across my chest.

"Do you really need to know?" he asked wearily. "Can't you just accept that you are who you are?"

No, I thought.

Oscar stood up and walked over to the window. "It's really raining," he stated.

Not-so-subtle subject change.

"Yes," I grumbled. "I've noticed."

"How about a walk?" he suggested.

I looked up at him and frowned. "Now? Out there?"

He flashed me a charming smile. "Sure. Why not?"

I laughed. "You're crazy."

"Maybe," Oscar smirked. "Are you?"

He crossed the room and ducked out through the side door.

For a moment, I contemplated leaving him to it, letting him be crazy all on his own. But my hesitation was short lived. I hopped to my feet and set off after him. I ran out into the rain, cringing as the cold drops splashed onto my skin. I covered my head with my hands, but the downpour drenched my hair and streamed over my face.

"Oscar!" I cried. "We're getting soaked!"

"I know," he exclaimed. "Isn't it exhilarating?" He

stretched out his arms and turned his face up to the sky, like a fallen angel spreading its wings.

I shrieked as the water washed over me. In a way, it was exhilarating. Or liberating, at least. I had no inhibitions or reservations—I was simply *there*. Out in the epitome of wild nature with Oscar, freeing our untamed souls and allowing them to play together. It was the truest form of happiness.

I extended my arms, just as Oscar had done, and twirled around until I felt dizzy. When I stopped, I collapsed onto the soggy ground and sank into the mud without a care in the world.

Oscar jogged over to me. He crouched before me, his shirt soaked through and clinging to his skin.

"I got you a present," he said, biting his lip to suppress a grin.

I sat up. "You did?"

Oscar held up his index finger, signalling for me to wait. He reached into his pocket and pulled out a small, cream-coloured box.

"It's just something," he said, sliding the box into my hand. "I liked it. I don't know… You might not."

I opened the lid. Inside were two halves of a silver heart, nestled amidst a bed of red silk.

"It's beautiful," I breathed. I lifted one of the pieces and held it as though it were the most precious object I'd ever touched.

"There was supposed to be a chain with it… It was supposed to be a necklace…"

I shook my head, water spilling from my hair. "It's

perfect just the way it is."

Oscar's mouth curved into a smile. "You like it?"

"I love it." I examined the piece in my hand. "This is my half," I decided, holding it up to the murky sky.

He nodded.

I passed it to him. "You keep my half."

He gestured to the remaining piece in the box. "And you keep mine."

I reached up and pulled him down to the muddy ground, and we lay, giggling like children… until the shadows of two tall figures darkened our light.

The Valeros were here.

"Oscar," Marco snapped. He towered above us, intimidating and dominant.

We sat upright, startled by the intrusion on our private moment.

Marco gripped the handle of a striped umbrella, while Caicus loitered on the outskirts of its shelter, kicking light-heartedly at the pooling rainwater.

Where my focus rested on Marco, Oscar's immediately went to Caicus. He grinned and splashed water at his friend, and the game rapidly escalated until they were on the verge of an all-out water fight.

Marco swiftly put his foot down.

"Oscar," he barked. "Caicus and I have reached a decision on how best to remove the humans."

"Remove the humans?" I echoed, squinting through the misted rain.

Marco peered down his nose at me. "Get them out of

the house," he elaborated.

Oh.

Marco went on, "Caicus will persuade them to stay at a hotel for the evening, on the pretence of permitting us to throw a birthday party for Rose."

"They'll never agree to that," I objected.

But, of course, I'd forgotten who I was dealing with.

"They'll agree to anything Caicus asks of them," Marco retorted condescendingly.

Oscar licked his lips. "That seems satisfactory."

"Then we are agreed," Marco solicited.

Oscar nodded his head.

"Caicus," Marco said, disrupting his game of raindrop catching, "go now. Do your duty. Make sure they're out of the house by nine o'clock this evening. The ritual will begin at precisely eleven."

Caicus nodded once, then jogged away like an obedient puppy, and Marco stalked back to the house.

I looked anxiously at Oscar. "Ritual?"

He snaked his arm around me, but said nothing.

BY SEVEN O'CLOCK THAT EVENING, I was showered and getting ready for my customary birthday meal. I rummaged through my limited clothing options in the hope of finding something to wear.

It was no surprise to hear that Mary and Roger had approved the fake birthday party, and had compliantly agreed to stay at a hotel for the night. Not before my birthday meal, though.

I glanced at the clock on my nightstand. Time was slipping away right before my eyes.

A bolt of fear surged through me, and I reminded myself for what felt like the thousandth time that everything would be okay. Oscar wouldn't allow anything to go wrong. I was safe with him.

Taking a deep breath, I resumed rummaging through the pile of clothes strewn over my bed. Yuck. I hated them all.

Back to the wardrobe. I riffled through the hangers.

No... No... No... Absolutely no.

Defeated, I dropped cross-legged onto the floor. And it was a good thing I did, because I caught sight of a pink shopping bag stuffed into the bottom corner of the wardrobe.

The dress! How could I have forgotten about *that* dress? Especially after making Oscar jump off a cliff to retrieve it.

I hauled the bag out from its hiding place and emptied the contents onto the carpet. The dress had gained some creases from its confinement, but it was still just as stunning as I remembered: a rich mulberry colour, delicate fabric, and a long flowing skirt.

I wasn't entirely convinced that I had the confidence to wear it, but I was definitely in the mood for a dress rehearsal.

I wriggled into it and pulled up the zipper.

Okay. Mirror time.

It was probably fortunate that my mirror was the size of a melon, because as a self-confessed non-dress wearer I didn't think I was ready for the full-length view. That said, my cantaloupe-sized view was kind of pleasing.

I crouched, and knelt, and stood on tiptoes until I saw more-or-less the whole outfit.

I flipped my hair and let it tumble over my shoulders. Then, I paraded around my tiny bedroom, strutting my stuff down the world's best imaginary catwalk.

I had all the confidence and coolness known to mankind.

And then someone knocked on my bedroom door.

No longer cool, I virtually pole vaulted over my bed and dived for my discarded bath towel. Scrambling around like a frantic maniac, I shrouded myself in the towel.

"Are you all right in there?" Oscar called from the other side of the door.

I guess my belly-flop landing had caused quite a thud.

"I'm fine," I shouted back, hastily clambering to my feet and patting down my dishevelled tresses. "Everything's fine!"

"Can I come in?" his muffled voice returned to me.

I sat on the end of my bed and tugged the towel down until it covered as much of the dress as possible.

"Okay," I beckoned.

The door opened and Oscar poked his head in. He greeted me with a familiar boyish grin. "Nice towel."

"What?" I said, feeling my cheeks flush. "I can wear a towel if I want." I tugged at it again and flattened it over my knees.

Oscar's eyebrow cocked. "Yes, I would never suggest otherwise. I think it's a very nice towel."

"It is," I said, sounding more petulant than I would

have liked.

"Uh... right," he stammered. "I'm sorry. I didn't mean to..." He paused and his brow furrowed. "Are you mad at me?"

I sighed submissively. "No. I'm wearing a dress," I confessed.

"Yes. I can see that. It's very stylish. Unique."

"No, not the towel. The dress is underneath."

"Oh. Okay. Can I see?" He edged further into the room, letting the door fall shut behind him.

I fiddled with a thread on the towel. "I'm not sure yet. I'm feeling a little self-conscious."

"But... it's me."

Exactly! I thought.

"Why would you feel self-conscious around me?" he asked, clearly mystified by the notion.

"Because you're so confident and gorgeous." I laughed in good nature. "And I'm just the girl in the bath towel."

Oscar suppressed a grin. "You're not the girl in the bath towel; you're Rose. And I'm Oscar." He sat down beside me on the bed. "Don't sell yourself short. You're confident and gorgeous, and so much more."

I leant my head on his shoulder. In response he draped his arm around me.

"Do you not like the dress?" he asked.

"No. The opposite. It's the dress my aunt bought me in Hutton Ridge. You know, *the* dress."

"Oh, *that* dress! Well, then, you *have* to wear it," he declared animatedly.

I gazed up at him.

"Show me, show me," he teased, tugging at the edge of the towel.

"If I show you, will you promise not to laugh?"

He rolled his eyes.

"Just promise," I repeated.

He crossed his heart with his forefinger.

I stood up and tossed the towel onto the bed.

No laughter. That was a good sign.

"What do you think?" I ventured timidly.

He let out a long breath. "It's…"

"What?" I could feel the colour rushing to my cheeks again.

"Beautiful," he finished. "Really, really beautiful." He smiled unassumingly.

"Thank you."

"You're beautiful," he said.

Now my face was a blazing inferno. But I kept smiling.

"The meal," I blurted out, promptly redirecting the attention. "We should go. The others will be wondering where we are."

"Right," said Oscar, blinking. "Right. The meal." He stood up. "Let me escort you." He held out his hand in what I considered to be a chivalrous gesture.

I quickly threw on a pair of black ballerina flats and took his hand.

As I closed the door to my bedroom, I had a sinking feeling that I wouldn't be opening it again.

Here we go.

CHAPTER SIXTEEN

Dark Secrets

MARY SWITCHED OFF THE DINING room lights and struck a match, igniting the candles on top of the birthday cake. When seventeen tiny flames flickered to life, she brought the cake to the dining table and set it down in front of me.

"Happy Birthday to you..." she sang.

"Happy Birthday to you..." Roger joined in and they had themselves a little barbershop duet.

Only the three Valeros abstained from the singalong. They looked between one another as though it were the most absurd tradition they had ever witnessed. Singing! Whatever next?

My aunt and uncle finished the final note and then erupted into a round of applause.

"Make a wish!" Mary cheered, nudging the cake closer to me.

I instinctively recoiled from the festive, amber flames.

Even dancing above a bed of white icing, they still seemed threatening. I glanced at Oscar. In his eyes the pyramids of fire returned to me—reflecting off the irises, yes, but also imprisoned inside. Tiny blazing bonfires trapped beneath the surface.

I turned back to the cake and let out a huge puff of air. I wished for everything that I might never have again—in other words, everything that I had right then.

The flames were extinguished in one breath, and the room plunged into utter darkness. In cliché horror-movie fashion, a loud eruption of thunder rumbled outside. I guessed it was voicing its disapproval of the nature of my wish.

"Ooh, spooky," Mary chortled, simulating a series of ghostly moans.

The faint aroma of candle smoke wafted to my nose. Opposite me, Roger's chair scraped the floor as he stood up to switch the lights back on.

I heard the click of the switch, followed by Roger's disgruntled voice. "The power's out."

"Oh, you're not serious?" Mary wailed.

The switch clicked again.

"I'm afraid so," Roger confirmed.

In one beat, the darkness had gone from spooky fun to chilling defencelessness.

"What about the party?" Mary gasped. "What time are the guests arriving?"

The boys were silent.

"Don't worry," Marco pacified them in a creamy voice. "This will not be a problem."

"Does anyone have a torch?" Caicus asked.

Roger fumbled clumsily around the dining room. "Somewhere around here..." he muttered, rummaging through drawers and cabinets.

"Darling," Mary called to her husband, "I don't think we should leave the kids tonight. Not during a power cut."

"Yes, you're right," Roger agreed. "We won't leave tonight."

I figured that wouldn't go down well with the Valeros. And I was right. I didn't know if it was possible to literally feel tension, but right then, it was so glaring that it made the hairs on my arms stand on end.

"No, you must go," Caicus intervened. "It'll be fine."

"No, I don't think so, dear," Mary let him down gently. "Not tonight."

Huh? I'd never known Mary to decline Caicus before. And then it occurred to me.

Of course! Caicus's power source lies in his eyes. In the dark, he's pretty much redundant.

I heard him swear under his breath. "Have you found that torch yet, Roger?" he persisted.

"I can't think where I would have put it..." Roger mumbled to himself.

"Not to worry, Rose," Mary continued, as though she suspected I'd need to be placated. "Roger and I will keep out of the way tonight. We'll stay upstairs."

Caicus huffed in irritation. I heard him stand up and march across the room. A moment later he struck a match and held it at nose level.

"Mary," he said, obdurately, "you must stay at the hotel

this evening." His eyes were so bright that they eclipsed the match's flame.

I squinted to see her reaction, but she was lost in an abyss of darkness.

"Yes, dear," she murmured back.

"Thank you," Caicus beamed. His smile was wicked, hauntingly enhanced by the eerie match light. "Roger, are you in accord?"

"Uh. Yes."

The match burnt down to Caicus's fingers. He carelessly dropped it to the floor and stomped out the dwindling flame.

Throwing fire on the floor! Is he trying *to give me a heart-attack?*

"Got the torch!" Roger suddenly announced.

A yellow spotlight hit the table and travelled along the surface until it landed on the cake.

We weren't the sort of family that let a power cut stop us from eating cake, so it was more-or-less a given that the meal would go on, albeit messily.

Mary groped for the china plates and I lifted the kitchen knife. It was heavy and cold to the touch. Guided by the light of the torch, I plunged the knife into the cake. But when I happened to glimpse down, I saw two crow-like eyes reflecting off the silver blade.

I gasped and let go of the knife. It clattered onto the table and slid off the edge, heading tip-first for my leg.

With miraculously sharp reflexes, Oscar stretched out his arm and caught the knife before it hit me.

A bated hush fell over the dining room.

And then came Mary's fretful voice, "Are you hurt, Rose?"

I stared at the glinting blade in Oscar's hand. "No. I'm okay."

Brazenly, Oscar flipped the knife and caught it by the handle. "I'll do the honours."

"Oscar, you seem so very at ease with a knife in your hand," Marco joked inappropriately.

Oscar laughed it off. "You'd be wise to remember that, Marco." He sliced the cake into several pieces, at a speed that would be gawped at by even the most experienced of dicers. And I could guarantee, if I'd taken out a ruler, every piece would have been meticulously equal.

Oscar shared out the slices and we ate in silence. It felt very much like the final meal of condemned men. And I supposed that was exactly what it was.

After we'd finished, Mary stood up and patted her mouth with a napkin. "There we are, then," she said. "A lovely birthday meal. Roger, did you bring the overnight bag downstairs?"

"Yes, it's in the hallway."

"Wonderful. I'll get Zack ready and we'll set off." She took the torch from Roger and shuffled out into the hallway.

We were reduced to blindness until she returned.

"Shall we?" she gestured to my uncle, shining the torch on us.

He heaved himself up and followed Mary into the hallway. I went with him. I didn't want them to leave without saying a proper goodbye to them. To my surprise, Caicus came, too. Probably to give them that final push out the door.

Standing in the porch, I hugged Mary and Roger. Baby Zack was snuggled in his carry cot, almost swallowed beneath a heap of blankets. I kissed him on the cheek. When I stepped away, I noticed Caicus was huddled to my aunt and uncle, bidding his farewell with sincere affection. And I realised that maybe Caicus and I had something in common after all. We both loved Mary and Roger.

"Mary," Caicus said quietly, "I want to thank you for your kindness. You've been superb company these past few weeks, and…" he hesitated, "I hope you don't mind me saying so, but you're an excellent mother." When his eyes weren't so icy white, they were a tranquil shade of ocean blue.

Mary was visibly choked by the sentiment. "Caicus, it has been an absolute pleasure having you here, and you are welcome to stay for as long as you choose."

He smiled sadly.

"Rose, dear," she said to me, "enjoy yourself tonight. Make sure it's the night of your life."

Roger handed me the torch and I lit the path to his Volvo. Rain poured down like a waterfall in the spot of light. The little family rushed to the car and bundled in.

Caicus and I remained in the open doorway until the car disappeared out of sight. We hovered a little while longer, not really knowing what to say to each other, but sort of feeling as though we should say something.

"You were fond of Mary," I said.

"Yes," he agreed, wistfully. "And I liked who I was when I was with her."

"Who were you?" I asked.

He smiled sadly. "Whoever I wanted to be."

Perhaps that comment threw me, because I was totally caught off guard when Marco appeared behind us.

Noiseless footsteps and unlit corridors are a bad combination, I thought. *Well, unless you're the one with the noiseless footsteps.*

"The ritual will take place in the dining room," he asserted sharply. "I will prepare the brew."

"What's the brew?" I asked.

They ignored me and stalked away.

I closed the front door. My hand lingered on the handle for a little longer than necessary.

Right, this was my chance, I realised. If I was going to run, now was the time to do it.

I pondered it. My family was safe, out of the house. I was alone. I could do it. I *wanted* to do it. So why wasn't I doing it?

I guessed it was the same reason that had stopped me from running any of the other times. With all the frightening things I'd discovered over the past few days, I should have run, but didn't. And it all boiled down to this: I was in over my head with Oscar Valero. And I would never run. Never.

Then I felt a breath on the back of my neck.

"Oscar," I whispered.

"Go," he whispered back.

I spun around. "No. I'm not going anywhere."

He was close to me. Closer than I had anticipated. I relished the sensation of it, listening to the rasps in his breathing and feeling the rise and fall of his chest against mine.

"Go," he urged again. "Remember your visions. Remember what Oliver told you."

"He told me to go back," I recounted slowly.

"Yes. To run."

"No," I shook my head, "he didn't tell me to run. He told me to go back." It was as though I was suddenly able to see things from a different perspective. "To go back… to the start."

Oscar kicked at the floor. "He was telling you to *run*. Just like I am."

"No," I was resolute on this, "he was trying to help me. He wanted me to go back." I paused. "The spell."

"The Retracing spell?" said Oscar huskily. "I've already told you, I can't do that."

"But what if it holds a clue to defeating Lathiaus? If I could go back to my origins, I might be able to understand why I'm connected to him."

Oscar groaned. "What does it matter? It won't change anything."

"Can I at least see the spell?" I pleaded.

Oscar glanced to the staircase, twitching with nerves. "It's in the book."

I envisioned a giant phone book, an A to Z of spells. How very handy for the modern-day witch.

"Do you have the book here with you?" I pressed.

"Upstairs."

"So...? Can I see it?"

Oscar's eyes darted anxiously around the dim corridor. "No one is allowed to see the book. It's sacred to Valero witches."

I rolled my eyes. "That's an unreasonable rule."

He smiled roguishly. "All rules are unreasonable."

"Please?"

He grumbled unintelligibly. Nevertheless, he caught my hand and towed me swiftly up the staircase.

We snuck into his bedroom and closed the door with a click. It was pitch black, apart from the circular torch light. Oscar ushered me to the space on the floor between the two beds. He reached under one of the beds and hauled out a hefty trunk. I slanted the light while he fiddled with the combination lock, and then rummaged inside for his oh-so-precious book.

When he eventually raised it from the trunk, even I had to admit that I was reverently surprised. It was, without doubt, the most extraordinary book I'd ever seen. The leather-bound cover was engraved in gold with intricate patterns. And, judging by the texture of the aged pages, it had been around for centuries. I gazed at it, awestruck.

Midway through the tome, a piece of string bookmarked a page. But Oscar disregarded it and opened towards the front. He began hurriedly flipping through the pages.

I shone the torch onto the paper, peeking over his shoulder.

It was incredible; all of the passages were handwritten,

mostly in old-fashioned script. I scanned the words as Oscar turned the coarse pages—though I could tell he was uncomfortable with my scrutiny.

Banishing Thy Enemy…

The page turned.

Potions, Poisons and Antidotes…

The page turned.

Drawing the Blood of a…

The page turned, thank God. I wasn't too keen on finding out the end to that one.

Retracing.

"This is it," he spoke sombrely.

"What does it say?" I huddled on the floor beside him.

Outside, a flash of lightning illuminated the night sky.

Oscar read from the page. "Retracing. For he who wishes to visit the start, another must bestow his blood…"

Blood?

He carried on, skimming the text. "The root of a yellow flower, placed on the heart, and the blood of a witch on the lips…"

I cringed. "Blood of a witch?"

"And a yellow flower," Oscar pointed out.

"Yellow flower? Like a buttercup?"

"Yeah, anything. Buttercup, daffodil, sunflower…" He returned to the page. "There's an incantation, too."

"Is that the spell part?"

"Yes. It's a verse. I'd have to say it."

My heart rate quickened. "So, we can do it?"

Oscar thrust the book into my lap. "No."

"Why not?" I demanded.

"Because we don't have a yellow flower, for one thing. And do you really want to drink my blood?"

I pulled a face.

"Didn't think so," he smiled wryly. "Besides, there's no time. The others are downstairs waiting for us."

I stared longingly at the yellowed page. Oscar was probably right, but I couldn't shake the feeling that this spell held answers. Answers we needed.

As Oscar rose to his feet, focused on listening intently to the sounds beyond the closed door, I flipped to the string-marked page in the book.

THE PROPHECY OF LATHIAUS

Oh my God. My breath caught in my throat. *This is it. This is my prophecy.* I read on…

It is foretold, on the day of his end,
so doth life begin
At the stroke of the eleventh hour,
he shall awaken
All will bow before him
All will perish at his mercy
Only one can end the blood spill
She, the girl with the heart of a witch—

I gasped as Oscar reached over my shoulder and slammed the book shut.

"That's my prophecy," I stuttered.

"Don't read it," he snapped.

I shone the torch at him. "Why not?"

He pursed his lips. "Come on," he said. "Marco will be getting suspicious. He'll probably come looking for us."

Before Oscar could take the book from me, I opened it towards the front and flipped through until I found the Retracing spell. In one quick motion, I tore it from the spine. A fine layer of dust sprinkled down from the split paper.

Oscar sucked in his breath and yelped.

I glanced up at him. "We might need it," I justified.

He pressed his knuckle to his mouth. "Rose, you just desecrated a worshipped, sacred book."

"Sorry," I said. "It was an accident."

There was a beat of silence, and then Oscar laughed.

Well, he kind of laughed. He made a noise, anyway.

I folded the page and slipped it into my shoe—my chic dress didn't provide many inconspicuous hiding places. How *did* those Bond girls do it?

Oscar returned the book to the trunk and rammed the chest under the bed. With our hands linked, we snuck out of the guest room and back downstairs.

Caicus and Marco were in the kitchen. I could hear them chanting in velvety, hushed voices.

"What are they doing?" I whispered, lingering in the shadows of the hallway.

"Summoning Lathiaus," Oscar replied.

I cowered back. "Why? Surely that's what we *don't* want to do, right?"

Oscar's eyes were trained on his brothers' backs. "This is war," he said darkly. "It's happening whether we want it to or not. They're just letting Lathiaus know we're ready for him."

I watched Marco sprinkle some sort of herb into a black clay pot. The contents steamed and fizzed like a wayward chemistry experiment.

"What's that?" I shrank back further.

"The brew."

"What is 'the brew'?"

"It's a potion."

"For what?"

"You'll drink it."

Yes, he was answering my questions, but not in the form I'd intended. I was beginning to think his responses were tactical. After all, he was too clever to miss my point so entirely.

"What will it do to me?" I articulated myself as concisely as possible.

"It's for the ritual."

I placed my hands on my hips. "Oscar..."

He half-heartedly relented. "There's a ritual to stop Lathiaus. Part of the ritual will involve the brew."

Okay. That was the most I was getting out of him. It would have to suffice.

An abrupt reverberating noise made me jump out of my skin. The hollow chime of the grandfather clock. Ten thirty.

Half an hour to go...

PART SIX
OSCAR

Who I Am

THE GRANDFATHER CLOCK CHIMED. TEN forty-five.

We sat around the dining table. The torch was our centrepiece, creating a path of light over the table and directly to the patio doors.

Any form of conversation had declined from polite, to occasional, to non-existent. My brothers and I sat like waxworks. Caicus stared at Marco. Marco stared at me. I stared at my hands. Rose, however, fidgeted like a hyperactive kitten. She crossed and uncrossed her legs, and chewed on a strand of hair. She looked at all of us. But none of us looked at her.

The rain lashed down outside and the wind shook the glass doors. This was menacing weather if ever I saw it. The demon was waking up from nap time, and he was letting everyone know he was cranky.

I listened to the tick of the pendulum as it swung

mechanically back and forth. My breath fell into sync with it. Breathing away the seconds.

Breathing away her life… or mine.

Without shifting my gaze, I reached under the table and entwined my hand with Rose's. Her warm fingers tightened around mine.

I saw Marco fold his hands on the table.

Oscar, he said, only perceptible to mine and Caicus's ears. *Are you ready?*

I flinched. *No*, I replied.

Marco's eyebrows knotted together. *Then get ready*, he hissed silently. *You must be the one to do this. She only trusts you.*

And that's exactly why I can't do it. Please, Marco, I beseeched him, *understand that, at least.*

Pathetic, Marco scoffed.

My teeth clenched.

I understand, Caicus jumped to my defence. *I'll do it.*

No. She will be suspicious of you, Marco shot him down. *This must go smoothly. It has to be Oscar.*

I will not give her poison, I denied him point blank. *I would sooner die.*

I'll do it, Caicus repeated. *There's no need for it to be Oscar. She won't be suspicious. She won't expect him to sit back while she drinks poison.*

That stung.

The clock struck the eleventh hour. I held my breath as the eleven chimes began their fatal melody.

Marco slid a half-full crystal brandy glass to Caicus.

Now, he ordered.

Caicus lifted the glass. The murky brown liquid sloshed around in its crystal confines. When the torch light hit it, its hue looked almost coppery. If I didn't know any better, I would have thought it truly was brandy in the glass.

I felt sick.

One in exchange for many. One in exchange for many. One in exchange for many... How many times did I need to drill that into my mind before I actually gave a damn?

I must have squeezed Rose's hand a touch too hard, because her fingers squirmed in discomfort.

"Drink this," Caicus said aloud, passing the glass to Rose.

She looked at me for confirmation. "What is it?" she asked.

I couldn't speak.

"An elixir," Caicus replied vaguely.

"What will it do?" She examined the liquid warily. Rightly so.

Caicus swallowed. He didn't dare look at me. "It will protect you."

I didn't know what the hell was happening, but I started to wheeze and pant for breath. It was as though someone was wringing the air out of my lungs. I began to tremble, too. Uncontrollably and violently. I gripped the table, but that only made it shake along with me.

"Oscar!" Marco barked. "Get a hold of yourself!"

"Oscar," Rose gasped. She set the glass down and coiled her fingers over my hands. "What's wrong?"

"Nothing's wrong," Marco snapped. "He's *fine*. Aren't

you, Oscar?"

I nodded my head—although I imagined that was part of my general convulsions.

"Drink," Marco turned his authority onto Rose. "Drink *now.* Lathiaus will be rising. We don't have time to waste."

Rose slipped her hands away from mine.

"What will it taste like?" she whispered, blissfully unaware.

I met her eyes. "I don't know," I choked.

"Will it be bad?"

I shook my head, gripping the edge of the table until my grasp almost dented the wood.

Rose gave me one final look before raising the glass to her lips.

The three of us watched through three very different outlooks. Marco hunched forward like a baying beast, vibrant with expectation. Caicus shrank back, his hands balled into fists. Me? Well, I quaked off the Richter scale.

I prepared to enact the most important moment of my life.

To be perfectly clear, what I was about to do was neither wrong nor right. It was just, plain and simple, what I *chose* to do. Deep down I never doubted that this would be my decision, because, quite frankly, I couldn't live my life—however short or long—knowing that I had not done it. For it was, and forever will be, the greatest and proudest moment of my life. This moment would define not only who I was, but more importantly, who I would become from that second on.

I knew that some people would deem my choice the

wrong one, but I would tell anyone, hand on heart, that I was damn glad I did it.

In one motion, I swooped in and switched off the torch, then struck my arm out like a snake, knocking the glass from Rose's hand. It hurtled across the room and smashed against the patio doors in an explosion of crystal.

"No!" Marco bellowed. He lunged across the table and dived on top of me.

My chair skidded backwards and thumped against the wall. I toppled to the floor and my head smacked against the mahogany cabinets.

Dazed, I heard the scuffle of Rose leaping up.

"What's going on?" she cried. "What was in the glass?" There was a frantic quaver in her voice.

I staggered to my feet. "Run!" I shouted to Rose. "It was poison."

Marco roared. I couldn't see all that well in the dark, but I wouldn't have been surprised if his chest ruptured out of his shirt, Hulk style. Anyway, what I did see was him lifting the dining room table and hurling it at us.

I jumped in front of Rose and used my arm to shield us from the airborne table.

But my arm only took the brunt of it, because the impact still knocked us both down to the floor.

We were trapped now. The overturned table had us captive against the wall. And to make matters worse, Marco's boot smashed through the thick, varnished wood. I dodged it by a fraction of an inch.

"You were going to kill me," Rose wept.

I had no defence.

"You lied to me, all this time." She was really sobbing now. "How could you?"

"I can explain," I said. But it sounded weak. It was the sort of thing people said when they had no justification. Unfortunately, now was hardly the time to have a deep and meaningful.

Marco's fist came through the table.

In the darkness, I could just about make out the shadow of the adjoining kitchen door. Before I'd even had a chance to think it through, I shoved Rose through the table legs and sent her in the direction of our only escape route.

She clambered out.

And that was the last I saw of her.

CHAPTER EIGHTEEN

Sealed

MARCO'S FIST POUNDED WILDLY AGAINST the upturned table. Sometimes the force split the wood, other times it just dented it. I pressed myself flat to the dining room cabinets, dodging the blows.

So, Marco was going to kill me. Tear me limb from limb, probably. Okay. That wouldn't be as bad as it sounded. I mean, if not Marco, then Lathiaus. Either way I'd be dead by midnight, so who really cared how it happened? I'd probably put up a good fight, too—with Marco, at least.

But there was one slight problem. The sooner Marco finished with me, the sooner he'd move on to Rose. And she wouldn't stand a chance. I had to get her out of Millwood.

I glanced to the adjoining doorway. I could make it. Marco was so enraged that I still had a few more minutes of random destruction before he really went in for the kill. The thing was, though, that the moment I left that room, I'd be gone. No turning back. I had an hour to live, and I would spend that time getting Rose as far away as possible. That meant away from Marco and Caicus. Hence, I'd never see Caicus again.

In my life, I'd tended to go by three primary emotions: happy, sad and angry. I wasn't sure what they called the one that was sadder than sad, but I was it. It made my eyes sting and my chest burn. I'd betrayed my brother. I'd *killed* my brother.

I fumbled my way through the table legs and staggered to the door.

"I'm sorry, Caicus," I choked, suspended somewhere between them and her.

I couldn't see him, but his boot smashed through the table.

"Go to hell, Oscar," he seethed.

With my head bowed, I squeezed through the doorway and burst out into the hall. I didn't have long, but I didn't need long. I ran from the manor, grabbing everyone's car keys from the porch hook as I went. If I was driving us out of there, I could do without tailgaters.

In seconds, I was in the Lamborghini, the engine hissing to life. It felt good to be back in the low-set, leather driver's seat. The past few weeks, Caicus and I had kept up the façade that something was wrong with our baby. What a joke! As if I would have let anything happen to her. I lovingly fondled the steering wheel.

With my trigger-happy foot poised on the accelerator, raring to go, I closed my eyes and thought of Rose, bringing her whereabouts to my consciousness. I heard her voice in my mind, I saw her smile, and the olive colour of her eyes…

And then I saw her, stumbling down the access road, drenched, shivering and scared.

I slammed my foot down and the car ripped down the path. The torrential rain obscured the windscreen, but it didn't hinder me. I found her.

I skidded to a stop, the back wheels sliding across the mud until I was facing Rose, blocking her path.

I stepped out of the car, into the icy wind and rain.

"Oscar," she said my name.

"Come with me," I called. My eyes narrowed at her expression. She looked at me with such coldness. Of course she was angry, but there was no time for resentment. I had to get her into the car and out of Millwood.

"Get in the car," I appealed through gritted teeth. She didn't move. "You are so… stubborn."

"How could you do this to me?" she cried, exposing her fragile heart to me.

I moved forward, closing the gap between us.

"I didn't."

Damn, that was a weak response.

"Yes, you did!"

I ran my hands over my face. "Get in the car, Rose," I raised my voice, kicking the ground in frustration.

She didn't budge.

"Get in the car," I tried again, "or you will be killed."

I glanced in the direction of the manor, not that we could see it from there. All we saw were the winding walls of evergreens. If Marco was coming for us, we wouldn't know it until it was too late.

Then Rose looked at me. Even in the darkness I could see her eyes, as green as emeralds and warm with spirit. Rain spilt over her skin, and I wanted to offer my jacket to cover her bare arms.

"Trust me," I begged.

But she had no trust left for me. I supposed I didn't blame her.

"*Trust* me," I kept on at her, reaching out now. I willed her to take my hand.

"No!"

This was impossible. She was so mad at me. Everyone was. Well, maybe I was on my own then. Maybe she was, too. If she was stubborn enough to refuse my help, what more could I have done?

"Then you will die," I said to her. Harsh, I knew, but true.

I paced back to the car, climbing into my seat and slamming the door shut.

I flipped on the headlights. Now I could see her, but she couldn't see me. I was glad of that. It meant that I could hide the pain on my face. She could hate me if she wanted. *And, hell, let her think I hate her, too.*

I revved the engine and tore off down the road.

Goodbye, Millwood. Good riddance. I hope you choke on my dust.

I swear, I got about one hundred yards before I slammed on the brakes and got back out of the car.

So much for my tough talking. And it had been going so well.

I ran down the path, back to Rose. My clothes were already soaked and clammy against my body.

"Rose!" I called. "Be mad at me if you want, but please let me help you."

She stood trembling, tears and rain flowing freely over her face.

"You were going to kill me," she whispered.

I grabbed her hands. "I never would have killed you," I avowed wholeheartedly to her. "Things just got so complicated. There's something I didn't tell you about the prophecy. It's us or you. The line of witches or you. It was never possible for both of us to survive."

A small breath escaped from her lips. "So, either I die or you die?"

I nodded. "Yes. And I want you to live. I always want you to live."

"But… you?" She threw her arms around me. "I don't want you to die!" Her wet hair clung to my cheek.

"I don't mind. I've lived my life the way I wanted to." The wind howled so loudly that it almost drowned out my words. "And if I die saving you, then that's a pretty damn good ending."

Now, the next instant brought about the greatest thing anyone could ever wish for, in their final hour or otherwise.

Rose kissed me.

She kissed me! Right there, in the middle of a demonic storm. Who said romance was dead, eh?

It was strange how familiar her kiss was; it was as though I'd felt it a thousand times before. Obviously I kissed her back. And I didn't plan on stopping, either. Incidentally, all of that running didn't seem so imperative anymore. Marco who?

But luckily for us, Rose had the sense to stop. And while I stood around all gooey- eyed, she went all proactive on me. She took my hand and hauled me into the forest.

Interesting. I was so deliriously happy that I didn't particularly care where I was going. Though, the downfall to this was, I didn't have the brains to concoct a more level-headed plan, either.

We kept pacing, deeper and deeper into the evergreens. Somewhere in my awareness, I knew where she was leading me.

"Rose," I said, "we need to get out of Millwood."

She paid me no attention. "Look!" she cried.

The tree house.

I considered talking her out of it, but she was already scrambling up the rope ladder. I didn't have the resolve to fight her on this. In fact, I didn't really have the resolve to fight anyone on anything at the moment. So, with no fortitude but plenty of contentment, I hoisted myself up after her.

Oh, yeah. I remembered this. Dingy, damp and rotting. And yet I associated it with the greatest night of my life. Simple pleasures.

We huddled against the wall, shivering. It was dark and we were soaked through, but at least we were sheltered and together, which was enough for me.

Rose drew in several shallow breaths.

"Are you okay?" I asked.

"You're not going to die," she stated.

I pulled her closer to me. "Not before Marco, anyhow," I quipped.

"Not before *anyone*," she amended.

It would have been in my character to correct her on the technical inaccuracy of her comment, but I couldn't be bothered.

So instead, I said, "Let's not talk about macabre things."

She surrendered surprising quickly. Apparently because she had other ideas. She slipped off her shoe and emptied the contents into her lap.

It took me a few seconds to register what was going on.

Not that damn Retracing spell again. The girl's relentless.

"No," I groaned.

"Why not?" she implored me.

"Because I don't know how to do it," I reminded her. How many times would I have to drum that into her head? "It's not safe."

"I don't care," she protested. "I'm doing it, with or without you."

I laughed derisively. "Good luck with that."

"Thank you," she said, pretending not to notice my sarcasm.

"Just one small catch, girlie." I playfully rapped on her skull. "How do you plan on undergoing a witch's spell when you're not a… oh, what's that word again… witch?"

"Well, I'm a something," she argued.

"Yes. But *something* just won't cut it. Unless you have powers, you can forget incantations and rituals. You've got no chance."

"Then you'll have to help me," she persisted.

"I wouldn't be helping you. I'd be putting you in danger." I rubbed my hand over my brow, sweeping away the droplets of water as they leaked from my hair.

"Please, Oscar." She was inexorable. "I need your help. I *know* this is right. You came to my dreams as Oliver, and you tried to warn me. Let me do this. I have to do this."

I sighed loudly. "Even if I wanted to, I couldn't. It calls for the root of a yellow flower, and there's no way either of us is going back outside. Not with Marco on the rampage."

"Well, it just so happens…" she fumbled around for her shoe treasures.

Oh no.

She waved something around in my line of vision.

"Yellow flower!" she declared.

I sat brooding for a while. Rose continued to twirl the flower before my eyes—which annoyed me greatly.

"Stop being so stubborn," she jibed.

I spluttered in outrage. "*You* stop being so stubborn!"

We went back and forth for a few rounds. Ashamedly, I was the one who broke first.

"What if I did it, and the magic is too strong for you?" My willpower was flagging slightly. "You could fall ill, or worse…"

"I'll risk it."

"Then you're a fool."

She took my hand. "Everything I've done since I've met you has been a risk. But I don't regret a single thing."

I smiled inwardly.

"And I'm not about to stop taking risks now, especially at a time when I need to most of all. I'm going to do this," she told me, adamantly. "And I'm asking you to stand by me."

Ugh. Not the stand-by-me card. How could I say no to that?

"Let me see the page," I yielded an inch. After all, if it was too dark for even *my* eyes to read the words, then the decision would be made for us.

Time to let fate roll the dice.

Rose made no attempt to conceal her glee as she unfolded the crumpled page and handed it over.

I held the paper, still astounded that she'd actually torn it from the book. *The* book! And Rose had shredded it like yesterday's newspaper. Shameless!

Casting my bewilderment aside, I relished the feel of the antique paper, which was now wrinkled and damp in places. I was afraid to look at it. For once in my life, I could do without the benefits of having heightened sight. But I put my game face on and peered down.

Hell. There were the words.

"You can see it, can't you?" Rose murmured.

I made a sort of 'yes' noise.

She exhaled in relief.

I exhaled in regret.

"Let's do this," said Rose.

"Now?"

"Now," she echoed.

How odd it seemed that I'd spent weeks wary for her to trust her life in my hands, fearing that I would disregard it. And now, as I fought for her salvation, she was the one who was disregarding herself. But one thing remained the same—I held her life in my hands.

"Lie down," I said.

She did her best to lie flat in the cramped tree house. I took the flower from her. It was a buttercup—a squashed one, but a buttercup nonetheless. I placed it over her heart. And then I took off my jacket and blanketed it over her for warmth.

Step one, complete.

"I'll need to say the spell now," I talked her through it. Though I was just as much talking myself through it.

Rose nodded. I sensed she was scared.

"Please," I begged her one last time. "Reconsider? It's not too late to stop this. You don't need to do this—"

"No," she cut me off without hesitation. "I'm doing it."

I imagined that behind all of her bravado, she was feeling like a feather in a tornado. She must have been terrified. Even I was getting palpitations.

I attempted to emotionally detach myself. "Okay, when I say the spell, you might feel light headed, but I'll be right here with you. When the incantation is finished, I'll seal it with a drop of my blood."

"What happens then?"

"I don't know."

This was where never having done the spell before set us at a disadvantage.

"I guess we'll soon find out," she said.

We both laughed nervously, which, as it happened, proved to be a dose of much-needed relief.

I bent down and kissed her lips and then I began…

"*Grant memory to the soul,*
Return it to a life so old,
Let the truth be seen,
Cast back by the power of a witch's dream…"

Rose let out a whimper and her head rolled to the side.

I wanted to stop, at least to check that she was okay. But the first rule of witchcraft was, once you'd started a spell, you could not stop. So I kept going…

"*What was born into life,*
Was thus born before,
Uncover what it seeks to find,
Through the channels of the unconscious mind…"

Her head thrashed towards me, and then back in the other direction. I swallowed and kept going…

"*A witch's blood will grace it same,*
And send the soul back to whence it came."

I bit down on my lower lip until I tasted the coppery hint of blood. Then, I kissed her. Her eyelashes fluttered.

I saw the blood trickle into her mouth. Her eyelids drooped and I watched in dismay as she drifted away from me.

"Rose?" I pushed the hair from her serene face.

When she didn't react, I gently shook her shoulders, but her body was limp and her eyes remained shut.

"Rose!" I shouted.

She didn't move.

"Rose!"

What had I done?

PART SEVEN

ROSE

CHAPTER NINETEEN

I Face Myself
1692 Salem, Massachusetts

EMILY SADLER UNTIED HER PINAFORE and folded it neatly on the stone work surface. She stood back and proudly admired the kitchen. She'd stake her life that they had the cleanest pots in the whole town. And why wouldn't they? She'd spent near three hours scrubbing them at the brook today. The finished products now hung glistening from the stone wall.

Emily patted her hair, double checking that no strands had fallen loose. She then took a seat on a stool beside the front door, awaiting her husband's return. Oliver Sadler had been out since the break of dawn, working with his Uncle John, the blacksmith. At last, an honest day's labour—something that Oliver had kicked and screamed about, fighting tooth and nail to resist.

"Why?" he had argued. "I know not why I should. Not when I already possess all the power conceivable, and could be a wealthy nobleman if I so chose. Instead, I'm out at just past

five of the clock, on a bitter cold morn'. Pah!"

"Oliver," Emily had pleaded with him, "thou would not wish the townspeople to talk—"

"I care nothing of the townspeople!"

"Reckless." She shook her head despondently. "There will be a witch hunt."

"So be it!" he exclaimed. "My goodwife, Emily, thou hast nothing to hide. Thou art human. It is I *who am the witch. And I say, let them run afraid."*

"They shall not run; they shall hunt and bring trial."

"They shall try…"

"And they shall take thee from me," Emily finished. Her mossy green eyes brimmed with tears.

Oliver softened and enfolded his arm around her. "Dear maiden, if ye truly wishes, then I shall work with my uncle," he yielded. "I shall be Oliver the Blacksmith, and none other!"

Emily dabbed at her watery eyes. "I do wish. I do."

He snapped his fingers like a genie granting a wish. "Then so it will be done."

And that was that. Oliver Sadler had become a working man.

Now, as the sun began to set, Emily awaited his return, praying, as she always did, that no harm had come to him during the day.

She crossed her ankles, the material of her dress skimming the grey floor. The smell of broth filled the air as it cooked on the stove. Everything was prepared for Oliver's return, and Emily longed to see him.

Her gaze remained glued to the gap in the wooden door. She watched as the day's light dimmed.

"Oliver, where art thou?" she muttered. He usually returned

home before sundown, and yet here she sat, in darkness, still waiting.

Her mind raced with terrible thoughts. What if today had been the day that they'd come for him? What if he had been caught and exposed as a witch? What if he was, at that very moment, locked in the stocks, awaiting trial?

Emily couldn't bear it. She began to weep into her hands. The idea of life without Oliver was too horrible to imagine.

I'll go in search of him, *she decided.* I'll plead with the townspeople to let him go.

If only she could turn to someone for support. But the Sadlers had few friends in Salem. Oliver was known to be a displeasing character at the best of times. But never where Emily was concerned. To her, he was wonderful.

Emily rose to her feet and dried her eyes. There was no room for weakness.

Just as she was about to set off in search of her missing spouse, the front door swung open.

"Oliver!" Emily gasped.

His step was light and he smiled roguishly. His dark hair was swept to the side and his cheeks were ruddy from the cold.

"Where hast thou been?" Emily asked. She opened her arms and enveloped him into a loving hold. She adored the scent of his skin and the warmth of his embrace.

Oliver kissed her on the temple. "My sorrow it is if I worried thee."

"Where hast thou been?" she asked again.

"Detained," he answered, puckishly.

Emily's stomach knotted. "How so?"

"Ah, broth," Oliver breathed, his russet brown eyes travelling

towards the kitchen area. "I am famished!"

Emily took his face in her hands, directing his focus back to her. "My love, what hast thou done?" Panic began to rise in her throat, for she knew Oliver too well.

He grinned and then passionately kissed his wife.

It was a kiss so familiar to Emily. The kiss of the one she loved. But today it made her sad, as it came with a sentiment of foreboding. That of a kiss goodbye.

"Please," she whispered to his lips, "tell me what hath detained thee?"

Mischief exuded from Oliver's air. "I showed that old hag Dolores Rapp the importance of affable manners." He winked.

Emily felt a rush of blood surge to her head. "I am faint," she murmured.

Oliver assisted her back to the passageway stool.

"What did thou do?" she begged him for answers.

"I set free her livestock!" Oliver announced, beaming with pride.

Emily relaxed slightly. Yes, that's another friend lost, but at least no witchcraft was done.

"You unbolted her fence?" Emily guessed.

Oliver's eyes glinted wickedly. "I did not."

"Then, what?" she pressed, weary from his games.

"I granted her animals the gift of flight." Oliver doubled over laughing. "Thou should hath seen her face!"

"Oliver, no!" Emily cried. "Please tell me thou speak untruths!"

"She deserved it," Oliver huffed. "She did not pay my uncle, and after he shod all three of her fat horses."

"But she will know it was thee, Oliver! She will accuse thee of witchcraft and thou will burn for it." A fresh batch of tears

brewed.

"Let her accuse," Oliver replied complacently. He looked to the kitchen, ready to feast and put the day's events behind him.

"Oliver," Emily clung to his arm, desperate never to let go. "Her husband is Lathiaus Rapp, and he fears witchcraft most of all. He will come for thee and they will take thee from me."

Oliver crouched to the floor, levelling himself to where Emily sat. "My dearest love," he said earnestly, "no one in the world could take me from thee. Mine heart is Emily's and we shall never be parted."

Emily tried to dispute, "But—"

Oliver cut her off. "We shall live together until we are old and senile! And then we shall die together, also. And when we return in the next life, we shall return together."

Emily smiled sadly and played along. "What if we do not return together?"

Oliver gripped his chest theatrically. "Then I shall not rest until I find thee. That is mine eternal oath."

"What if I am forgotten?" she challenged in good humour.

"Impossible. I will always come for thee. And when thou ask how I found thee, I shall tell thee, my love lives in my heart."

Emily wound her fingers through his hair. "My Oliver," she said, "thou art dear to me."

"Always. Now, I go in search of broth. For I knoweth what I love, and it is my Emily and her broth!"

She watched him trot away with a spring in his step. And she knew the routine that would follow. Oliver would sit beside the fire with his meal, and then take a short nap in his best chair.

That gave her time. Time to make sure that Oliver's actions had not caused chaos in the town; to put her mind at ease once and for all.

She quietly left the house and paced along the cobbled streets of Salem.

The town clock chimed eleven, and a flock of crows cawed raucously overhead.

Emily spotted a gathering of men assembled by the town hall. They were in uproar, some of them carrying flaming torches and batons.

"What is it?" Emily called, rushing to them.

The town grocer turned to her. "Witch hunt."

He raised his torch, causing the flame to waver in the breeze.

"Who hath been accused?" Emily demanded urgently.

"Oliver Sadler, thy very husband!"

Emily's heart stopped. She could no longer feel the ground beneath her feet.

"Oliver is not a witch," she protested. "He is a good man."

"Burn the witch!" The grocer cheered.

"No!" Emily wailed. "I beg of thee, not my husband." She fell to her knees, pleading with them.

But her pleas were drowned out by the commotion of the mob.

"Burn the witch! Burn the witch! Burn the witch!" the men chanted, their torches pulsating up and down, moving as one fierce monster.

"No!" Emily screamed. She lunged into the crowd and grabbed the arm of the ringleader. "Please, Oliver Sadler is not a witch."

The man looked into her eyes. His gaze was cold and as black as the eyes of the crows above. He sneered and pushed her to the floor.

Emily crawled on her hands and knees, tangled in her own dress.

"Look at the pitiful maiden," the leader bellowed. "Her husband is a witch, and she is crawling the floor like the peasant that she is!" He cackled wildly.

Emily clambered to her feet, regaining dignity. "Lathiaus Rapp, I beg of thee, do not harm my husband Oliver."

Lathiaus spat at her, "Thou art not permitted to speak."

Emily squared her shoulders.

"Stop!" she commanded the others.

She took a deep breath, suddenly overcome by an inexplicable sense of peace.

"It is I who am the witch," she declared boldly.

The horde hesitated, all eyes upon her now.

"Yes," she continued. "It was I who bore flight to Dolores Rapp's livestock. And I am proud, for she deserved it."

Lathiaus stood before her. Their eyes met in a harrowing stare. He seized her wrists, and then in a low, menacing voice, began to chant.

"Burn the witch, burn the witch…"

The crowd joined in, growing louder and louder. "Burn the witch! Burn the witch!"

Lathiaus had caught his first witch.

OLIVER AWOKE FROM HIS SLUMBER with a jolt. The embers glowed in the fireplace, warming his feet.

"Emily?" he called, glancing over his shoulder. Her chair was empty.

When there was no reply, Oliver's heart skipped a beat. It didn't take long for him to realise that something was wrong. In a house as small as theirs, it would have been absurd to think that she had not heard him—or he her, for that matter.

Oliver leapt up from his chair. "Emily!" he yelled, frantic now.

He strode quickly out of the house and ran down the cobbled street.

A huge gathering of people congregated around a bonfire, chanting and cheering like feral hyenas.

Oliver ruptured through the crowd. "Hast anyone seen my goodwife Emily?" he shouted, but his voice was lost in the din.

"Emily!" he shouted until he was hoarse, shoving through the people, his heart hammering.

And then, it was as if he'd been struck down. His life ended at that moment—the moment he saw Emily drowning in flames.

"No!" he howled like a wounded animal. "No!"

The town clock chimed the stroke of midnight.

"No!" Oliver shoved people aside, trampling them in his race to get to the bonfire.

"Emily!" he sobbed.

Oliver charged to the front, cursing himself for not being able to run faster. The fire hissed and crackled and smoke filled his lungs. He had to get to Emily.

With his last ounce of speed, Oliver dived into the flames.

And that was where they took their last breaths.

Together.

I AWOKE SOBBING, RAPT WITH grief and screaming for Oscar.

I heard his voice immediately. "I'm here, I'm here!"

He lifted me into his arms. Only then did I realise that I had been lying down. It was dark, but I recognised that I was in the tree house. The smell of damp wood and the restricted walls were unmistakable.

I buried my face into the groove of Oscar's neck.

"I saw it all," I whispered.

He stroked my hair, soothing me. "What did you see?" he murmured tentatively.

"I saw us. I saw how it all began. Lathiaus…"

His arms tightened around me as I trembled.

"He was human," I whispered. "He was a human who killed in cold blood, like a demon. He led a witch hunt. They were coming after you…"

Oscar nodded his head. "If his human soul was so corrupt, then it seems only fit for him to have evolved into a creature that reflects that." I felt his breath brush against my face as he let out a sigh. "I thought…" he struggled to speak, his words quiet and sombre.

"What?" I urged.

"I thought you were gone," he managed. "I thought the spell's power was too strong for you to survive."

"I went back to the beginning," I explained quietly. "I watched it as an outsider, but I knew that the girl I was watching was *me*. Emily. And I knew that Oliver was you. It wasn't our bodies, but it was our souls. The first life we shared together."

Oscar laughed gently. "What were we like?"

"The same."

He laughed again.

"There's something else," I went on. "When I read the prophecy back at the manor, it called me the girl with the heart of a witch."

"Yes."

"Well, you always said that was because my heart was a witch's heart."

"Yes." He seemed curious as to where I was heading with this.

"But, I have another theory." I tested his reaction before I continued. "What if I'm the girl with the heart of a witch because I have *your* heart? Now, then and forever…"

A minute or two passed before Oscar replied.

"Oh," he said, stunned. "It pains me to acknowledge my mistakes, but there could be some truth in that. Hmm... *Your* heart is not a witch's heart, but you *have* the heart of a witch. *My* heart." He paused, allowing the premise to sink in. "Now, then and forever."

We fell silent for a moment, almost as though we were paying respect to the depth of the eternity that we shared.

"I think I know what I have to do," I said at last.

"Oh yeah? What's that?"

"I have to face Lathiaus."

"What!" Oscar spluttered. "Are you out of your mind? You must be suffering some sort of delirious after effects." He touched my brow with the back of his hand.

I sat upright. "The spell did what I hoped it would. It helped me to understand all of this. You, me, Lathiaus… I'm part of this. I *am* this."

Oscar groaned under his breath. "I *knew* I shouldn't have carried out that spell. I should have trusted my instincts," he ranted fervently. "I knew no good would come of it—"

"But good *did* come of it," I insisted. "I found out why it has to be me. I was Lathiaus's first kill, and I have to be his last."

"You will *not* be his last kill!" Oscar shouted, his temper mounting. "You will not be his last *anything*! I will not allow him to even *look* at you."

I placed my hand on his forearm. I could feel the muscles tense beneath his skin as his fists clenched in anger.

"This is my destiny," I said, for the first time feeling quite accepting of it. Proud, even. "It's my prophecy."

"And what about *my* prophecy?" he retorted. "It's my responsibility to protect you."

"You'll die!" I exclaimed. "Along with the line of witches. And then Lathiaus will have won—*again*."

"He won't have won, because he won't have got you." Oscar's tone was pleading now.

I flinched. I hated putting him through this, but I couldn't give in. I couldn't let a demon prevail. Not after what I'd seen—and what I'd *lived* hundreds of years ago.

The insight into my previous life had changed me. It was the missing piece of the jigsaw. For one thing, it explained my *not*-so-irrational fear of fire. But more importantly, I'd died for Oscar, and he was offering me the same sacrifice in this lifetime. I adored him for it, but I didn't accept it. I wanted to fight.

I felt around in the darkness for Oscar's face and then held it in my hands, just as Emily had held Oliver.

"I have to do this," I told him.

His eyelids dropped. "Then don't expect me to watch. If you insist on this *suicide* mission," he spat, "then you'll go alone."

"Okay," I accepted valiantly. I savoured the touch of his skin for one last time, and then I crawled across the tree house and lowered myself through the hatch.

"Yeah, that's right!" Oscar yelled after me. "Just go!" I heard him kick his feet.

"Bye, Oscar," I whispered back as I descended the rope ladder. It was still raining heavily, but I was already soaked through so I didn't care anymore.

When I reached the bottom, Oscar peered out of the hatch. "If you think I'm going to follow you, you can think again!"

I looked up at him. "Okay."

He scowled.

"Bye," I said, giving him a heroic little salute.

He pursed his lips tetchily. "What is this? Some kind of reverse psychology? Because it's not going to work!"

"Nope." I waved at him. "Bye."

"Oh, so this is how it's going to be, is it?" Oscar drawled. When I didn't answer, he tried again. "Rose?" He paused. "You're not really going, are you?"

I smiled obscurely. "Yes, Oscar, I'm going."

He muttered a few profanities. "Wait for me, then."

The next thing I knew, he'd jumped to the ground and

landed beside me. The wind swept through our hair and the branches of the trees swayed overhead.

Oscar took hold of my hand. "So, you want to fight a demon?" he said as he gave me a look of reluctant cooperation.

"Yes, please."

"You'll die," he told me matter-of-factly.

"Or you will."

He returned my salute. "Our destiny awaits."

"Well, we'd better hurry up then. We wouldn't want to keep destiny waiting."

And on we walked, hand in hand, heading back towards the manor. We took our time, because I, for one, was sick of running.

Invictus

OUT OF THE NIGHT THAT covers me,
Black as the Pit from pole to pole,
I thank whatever gods may be
For my unconquerable soul.
In the fell clutch of circumstance
I have not winced nor cried aloud.
Under bludgeoning of chance
My head is bloody, but unbowed.
Beyond the place of wrath and tears
Looms but the horror of the shade,
And yet the menace of the years
Finds, and shall find, me unafraid.
It matters not how strait the gate,
How charged with punishments the scroll,
I am the master of my fate:
I am the captain of my soul.

—William Ernest Henley

I led the way through the forest, walking with a confident stride. Each foot seemed to hit the ground with strong, controlled determination.

I guess there's a certain strength that comes with clarity. For the first time in a long while, I knew exactly what I was doing—and more importantly, why I was doing it.

Oscar didn't speak, but he marched loyally at my side. We were like soldiers, front line until the end.

We stepped through the trees, emerging out onto the road. Probably around the same spot where Oscar had found me. We weren't far from the house now.

Oscar stopped in his tracks.

"No!" he wailed.

The sound made me jump.

"What is it?" I asked frantically.

"No!" he howled again. "That sadistic *animal*!" He broke into a run—heading in the opposite direction from the manor.

"Who's a sadistic animal?" I called, hurrying after him.

"Marco!" Oscar shouted back.

I saw him drop to his knees and hunch over something that lay on the road.

It was too dark for me to make out what it was. My legs felt like jelly at the thought that it might be Caicus.

I sprinted the last few metres and, with bated breath, peered over Oscar's shoulder. The object of his despair lay on the ground.

It wasn't Caicus.

In fact, I didn't know what it was.

"How could he do this?" Oscar murmured. "Have you ever seen anything so horrible?"

"No," I agreed sympathetically. "What is it?"

Oscar collapsed onto the ground and slung his arm over a deformed lump of metal. "The engine," he grieved, wretchedly.

It dawned on me that the dented object was Oscar's car. Or part of it, anyhow. I glanced along the road and noticed the rest of the vehicle scattered in chunks every few metres for as far as the eye could see.

I sat beside Oscar. He was taking this badly.

"It was just a car," I tried to console him.

He sat upright and glared at me. "*It* was not just a car. *She* was a Lamborghini Gallardo, and she was beautiful."

I tried a more sensitive approach. "I'm sorry for your loss."

"Thank you," he sighed, mournfully.

I looked back to the other parts: slashed metal, crushed hubcaps, bits of seats…

I grimaced. "You think Marco did this?"

"Yes." Oscar's eyes narrowed. "It's got Marco written all over it."

"But how could he have…" I trailed off. I didn't need Oscar to answer that question. Marco had torn the car apart with his bare hands.

I shuddered.

All of a sudden Oscar sprang to his feet, hauling me up along with him.

"They're near," he hissed.

"Marco and Caicus?"

"Yes. I can sense them."

I looked around. We were alone.

"Are they at the manor?" I asked.

"No," he murmured, gazing into the dark maze of evergreens. "The forest. They're in the forest. Moving quickly, though."

He frowned as though he were listening to something. I tried to listen too, but all I could hear was the moan of wind and the lashing rain.

Oscar's hands balled into fists. "They're coming for us," he stated.

My breath caught in my throat. "What should we do? Run?"

"You won't outrun them," he told me.

Of course, he was right.

"Go to the tree house," Oscar said abruptly. He gave me a little nudge in the direction of the forest.

"Without you?" My eyes widened. "And with Marco in there?" I gestured loosely to the trees.

"You'll be fine. They can't track you—it's not their power—but they'll pick up my scent and I'll draw them out to the road."

"What about Lathiaus? I have to find him—"

"Forget Lathiaus!" Oscar shouted at me. The severity of his tone made me shrink back. "Forget Lathiaus. Go to the tree house and just… be safe." His eyes blazed with urgency.

"But—"

"No," he yelled again. "Please, do as I say. I don't have time to argue about it. Go to the tree house and stay there until midnight. Please." His hands clasped together.

Hot tears stung my eyes.

Oscar's expression softened. "Don't cry, Rose."

I swallowed the lump in my throat. "I don't want to leave you."

"I don't want to leave you, either," he whispered.

I took his hands. "Then don't. We'll stay together."

Oscar stiffened. "They're onto my scent," he said. "I have to move. Please, go to the tree house and stay there." He kissed me with a heartbreaking passion. "Take care."

And he was gone, leaving only a tingle on my fingers from where his touch had once been.

I SPRINTED DOWN THE ROAD as fast as my legs would carry me. I probably should have gone back to the tree house, but I didn't. I couldn't hide away while there was still a chance. Granted, I wasn't exactly sure what I planned to do. I kind of assumed something would just come to me. I was banking on that, anyway.

My feet crunched down on gravel. I was almost at the house now.

Oh my God.

My aunt's minivan had been overturned. Oil seeped from the exhaust pipe like a river of black blood.

More of Marco's handy work.

I decided not to linger, and instead made a final dash

for the manor.

Once inside, I took a moment to catch my breath. I leaned against the door, looking straight ahead into the chasm of the unlit hallway. As far as I could tell, there was no one else there. No Marco, no Caicus. No Lathiaus.

Now what?

I flipped the light switch, just in case. Zilch.

Blindly, I edged forward, feeling my way through the house, still waiting for that fantastic plan to miraculously pop into my head. Several steps into my totter, my hand brushed against something. It was bigger than me and dressed in coarse, woollen material. I flailed my arms around in distress and the thing wobbled and crashed to the floor, landing in my path.

"Demon!" I screamed, then covered my mouth reflexively.

Breathe. It was just the coat rack.

What? It was an easy mistake to make.

Okay, phase one of The Plan, I strategised with myself: *toughen up.*

I kept going, heading for the dining room.

Phase two of The Plan: find the torch.

When I reached the dining room, I crashed straight into the upturned table, right on the shin.

Ouch. Good start.

I crawled through the table legs, feeling less cat woman and more elephant woman. Somehow I managed to clobber every limb during my sightless table-assault obstacle course. When I finally made it to the other side, things didn't get much easier. Marco had turned the room into complete disarray:

toppled cabinets, snapped chairs, smashed windows… He'd pulverised the place.

I stayed low—less chance of tripping if I was already on the floor. Unfortunately, that meant substituting tripping for another of my favourite pastimes—cutting my hands on broken glass. Which I did. A lot.

I felt around for the torch, but it was like searching for a needle in a haystack. A very sharp-toothed haystack.

Come on, torch, where are you?

"Ouch!" I yelped. Chair leg to the eye.

I'd been told that everybody has a breaking point, and apparently that was mine. I drew the line at chair leg to the eye. Abort phase two of The Plan.

Phase three of The Plan: get a new plan. Which was not impossible. There was one other way of obtaining light. And I decided I was up to the challenge.

I backtracked to the hallway, sustaining a few more see-you-in-court-Marco injuries on my way. I now had a clear run to the staircase and, hopefully, to my bedroom. As it turned out, this was easy. That saying 'I could do it with my eyes closed' was actually true in this case. I burst through the attic door and was instantly in sanctuary. My room.

I rushed to the dressing table and picked up my toffee candle. The silken wax cylinder soothed my sore, nicked hands. I rummaged through the top drawer until I found the box of matches. I was going to light a candle. Me!

I wondered if my bravery came from a needs-must mentality, or if my vision of the past had actually turned out to be therapeutic. I mean, it was safe to say that my fear of fire originated from my death by fire, so perhaps revisiting that moment had given me some sort of closure.

Whatever the reason for my courage, I was eternally grateful for it.

I struck a matchstick on the box and a tiny flame darted out. Of course I flinched, but the mettle of my action also made me feel kind of fearless. Like if I could overcome a lifelong phobia, then I could overcome anything.

I lit the candle wick and listened as the dust sizzled.

"You're living out your destiny, too," I said to the candle. I suddenly felt a deep affinity for that inanimate tube of wax. And as it burnt, I could smell the sweet aroma of toffee. The smell of victory.

I took a moment to recap.

Bravery? Check. Light? Check. Plan?

Hmm.

The prophecy seemed like a good place to start. My candle companion and I set off for Oscar and Caicus's bedroom. I snuck in and seated myself cross-legged in the gap between the two beds. I took a pillow from Oscar's bed and cuddled it to my chest, breathing in the scent on the material. It was the closest thing I had to Oscar.

I placed the candle on the floor and heaved the trunk out from under the bed.

Oh, what the…?

The stupid trunk was locked.

I fiddled around with the combination, not really applying any logic to my guesses. Who had time for logic?

Unfortunately, randomness wasn't getting me anywhere.

I felt like the loser contestant on some low-budget cryptic maze game show. I glanced around the room.

Hello, heavy object.

I grabbed a hefty, old-fashioned lamp from the bedside table and brought it down as hard as I could on the lock. My first attempt had no effect, but I learned that if you kept bashing a lock with a lamp, then it would eventually bust open. Good old brute force!

I lifted the trunk's lid and scooped the book out. The piece of string still marked the prophecy page, so I flipped straight to it.

Laying the open book on the floor, I hovered the candle above it.

THE PROPHECY OF LATHIAUS

It is foretold, on the day of his end,
so doth life begin
At the stroke of the eleventh hour,
he shall awaken
All will bow before him
All will perish at his mercy
Only one can end the blood spill
She, the girl with the heart of a witch

Okay, that was the part I'd read up to before, when Oscar had closed the book on me.

So that was me, the girl with the heart of a witch. The girl who had Oscar's heart.

I read on...

Before the hour turns to twelfth,
she must grant him her death
Two will take her to him,
and all will be spared
Two will turn away,
and all will be slaughtered
Our fate awaits.

I glanced to the window. The weather was wild. I tried not to think about how somewhere out there, a demon lurked. And I tried not to think of what may or may not have happened to Oscar. I was in survival mode—*his* survival. As far as I was concerned, it wasn't midnight yet, so the war was still on.

I returned my focus to the candlelit prophecy.

"Before the hour turns to twelfth, she must grant him her death," I murmured into the empty room. "Two will take her to him, and all will be spared. Two will turn away, and all will be slaughtered…"

I leaned back against the bed.

Was that really it? Was it really that cut and dry—I died or they died?

"Before the hour turns to twelfth…" I said the words again. It was strange hearing myself use such old language. My voice became almost unfamiliar, different somehow.

All of a sudden, it was as though Emily was speaking through me. It was not my voice that I was hearing—it was hers. "She must grant him her death."

And then I understood.

PART EIGHT

OSCAR

CHAPTER TWENTY-ONE

Final Thoughts

COME ON. SHOW YOURSELVES.

I could sense them, and they could sense me. Why weren't they coming for me?

I lingered on the estate road, a mile from the manor. I was hoping to lead Caicus and Marco out of Millwood, but they weren't taking the bait.

Standing completely motionless, I listened to every noise. I was losing them. As much as I was trying to draw them out, they were trying to draw me in. And I had no choice but to go. Because if they didn't have me, they'd go after her.

So I went. I tracked them, heading knowingly into their hands.

I couldn't pinpoint their exact location, but there was no denying that they were close. Hesitantly, I strayed off the path and into the forest. It was even harder to see amidst the shadows of the trees, but at least the foliage provided shelter from the downpour. The constant barrage of raindrops was getting on my last nerve.

Somewhere between me and the road, I picked up a sound. I stopped and listened. They were in the evergreens, probably no more than a stone's throw away. In the craters of my mind, I could hear the slow thud of their heartbeats.

I whirled around. But I was alone.

Where the hell were they?

And then I heard Marco's filthy snarl.

This was it.

Out of nowhere, I felt a fist plough into the back of my head. I dropped to the ground, face first.

Behind me, Marco let out a rippling bellow. He grabbed me by the scruff of the neck and hoisted me upright, only to knock me back down again with another iron-knuckled punch. This time I skidded across the mud like a hockey puck.

I spat out a mouthful of blood and flipped over onto my back. Marco was already on top of me, frothing at the mouth.

"Well, this is cosy," I said with a grin.

Seemed Marco wasn't in the mood for banter. He raised his fist.

I swiftly rolled out of its path, just in time to see Marco's punch dent the ground.

I was on my feet. "Come on, brother," I goaded, "you can do better than that."

He swung for me again and I jumped back. But, the truth was, I was no match for Marco. I didn't know how long I could keep this up for. Of course, I wasn't about to let *him* catch onto that. To him I planned on being Mr Invincible. Or at least, Mr Put-Up-a-Good-Fight.

"Too slow," I taunted, dodging left, then right, then left, then back, then right…

Marco was ferocious now, growling and seething and occasionally gnashing his teeth—more animal than human. His eyes bulged and the falling raindrops sprayed off his lips in angry rasps. He swung at me, his stamina only increasing with time.

Huh. Probably shouldn't have riled him up so much. Damn hindsight.

Thinking fast, I reached up for a low-hanging tree branch and snapped it clean off the trunk. The branch was thick and heavy, and I used it like a bat, swiping it at my opponent.

It backfired.

Marco seized the other end and slammed it against me, forcing me backwards and pinning me against the tree.

I gripped my end of the branch, trying to match Marco's strength as he attempted to drive the weapon into my stomach. My muscles shook and burnt from the strain. The splintering wood pressed into my body, cutting into the skin. Marco was winning. And just as I was about to accept defeat, he made a fatal error.

"After I've finished with you, I'll move on to the girl," he sneered.

Well, what do you know? Taunting really could make people angry. I flipped out.

With a second wind, I thrust a gap between me and the branch, ducking aside and letting the bough stab through the tree trunk where I had previously been.

Marco baulked in disappointment.

In an instant I was behind him. I locked my arms around his throat, forcing him to lose his footing and splutter for air.

Ha. Now who's the boss?

Then a new voice came from behind me.

"Oscar, no!" It was Caicus.

Startled, I lost my concentration. It was only for a fraction of a second, but it was enough for Marco to slip free.

Damn. We were on an even footing again. Except this time, he had reinforcements.

Marco struck out and smacked me in the jaw. His punch threw me backwards, and I hit the ground hard.

Dazed, I tried to stagger to my feet, but Marco's boot met my face. I was down again and choking on my own blood.

"Caicus," I spluttered.

There was no response.

"Caicus," I called for my brother again, louder this time. But it seemed as though that ship had sailed.

From the ground I saw Marco's feet approach. He kicked me full-force in the gut and cackled.

"Ooh," he mocked. "Looks like that one hurt."

I squinted through the pain. "Itches a bit."

"How about this?"

He booted me again.

"Feels nice. Keep going," I said. Blood dripped from the corner of my mouth and merged with the dark, boggy mud.

So, this was how it would end. Flattened by brother dearest. Eh. Could have been worse. I figured I'd lose consciousness soon, which would be pleasant. I could have used a good sleep.

As Marco carried on, I blocked out the pain and thought only of Rose. It really took the edge off the beating. I pictured her safe in the tree house, away from all of this brutality. She'd come out after midnight, and we'd all be gone. She'd be safe, and she'd go on to have a wonderful life. A normal life. I could finally rest assured that, for once, I had done the right thing. I'd given life to my girl. A life away from demons, and witches, and anything else that threatened to taint her world. I'd done what I'd set out to do. I'd saved her.

That was my prophecy.

I smiled deliriously.

"I'll wipe that smile off your face," Marco spat.

I vaguely saw him raise his fist high into the air. His scowl was vengeful, murderous, and satisfied.

Oh well.

I love you, Rose, I thought. *See you in the next life.*

And I kept smiling.

CHAPTER TWENTY-TWO

My Way

MARCO STOOD OVER ME, HIS fist poised above my head.

"You've had this coming, Oscar. You're *done*," he spat, salivated at the thought.

I could feel a stream of thick blood spilling from my mouth and nose.

"Get on with it, then," I said hoarsely, "before I keel over from boredom."

"Still proud," Marco scoffed, pressing his foot down on my chest. "Even in your final breath you're conceited." He shook his head and laughed bitterly. "I've always hated you."

"I know," I wheezed. "I've always hated you, too."

He brought his fist down and I squeezed my eyes shut, waiting for the impact.

I heard a heavy thud, and the next thing I knew, Marco's weight had slipped from my chest and landed on my leg. I didn't dare open my eyes.

Was I dead? For a dead person I was in a lot of pain. What about all that no-more-pain junk? Wasn't that death's major selling point? Refund, please.

I opened one eye. I was still in the forest. I glanced down to see Marco slumped over my leg, dazed.

Now someone else stood tall. My saviour and his weapon of choice—the Lamborghini's exhaust pipe.

"Well, it's about bloody time!" I said to Caicus.

He grinned quickly at me, then turned to Marco with a scowl.

"You," he said in his favourite bad-ass voice, as Marco was attempting to sit upright, "I may have let you trash my car, but nobody, and I mean *nobody*, trashes my best friend." He clunked the exhaust pipe on Marco's skull, this time knocking him unconscious.

"Ooh," I winced for Marco. "He'll feel that in the morning." I wriggled my trapped leg free and Caicus helped me to my feet.

"Cutting it fine, weren't you?" I said, acutely aware of the torrent of blood running down my face.

"Eh," he shrugged casually, "I wanted my dramatic moment. Everybody else got one."

Now, I wasn't really sure where this came from, but I gave him a hug. Patted him on the back a few times too—you know, to man it up a bit. He did the same. It was our way of saying thanks, sorry, forgiven, clean-slate.

I wiped a trickle of blood from my mouth. "Hey, Caicus," I said, cocking my head to the side. "All these years and I never knew you were left-handed."

"Huh." He stared down at his hands in fascination, the left one still gripping the exhaust pipe. "Neither did I."

"Strange. You know, I'm left-handed, too."

"Are you? Well, isn't that something."

We chuckled pleasantly.

"Oh, wait!" I smacked my brow with the heel of my hand. Our blithe reunion had distracted me from fast-approaching midnight. "Lathiaus. We should do something."

"Like what?"

"I don't know."

Come on, brainwave, do your stuff...

"Let's fight him!"

Caicus laughed. "Good one."

"No, I'm serious. What's the worst than can happen?"

"Um, we die?"

"We're going to die anyway," I reasoned.

He swept the rain-soaked hair from his eyes. "It's such an effort," he sighed.

I took that as a yes. "That's the spirit!"

"What about him?" Caicus nudged Marco with his foot.

"He'll wake up eventually," I guessed. "Then it'll be a case of see who gets us first."

"Place your bets," Caicus cheered. "Where's Rose?"

"I've hidden her," I declared proudly. "In a tree house."

"Oh," he said. "That's nice."

We began walking. We were surprisingly chipper considering that we were heading to our doom. Again.

Caicus mimed the act of raising a glass. "I'd like to take this opportunity to tell you that it has been an honour working alongside you." He propped his arm on my shoulder as we walked. "I've had a heck of a time being your best friend."

I smirked. "Never a dull moment."

"I feel good about this, you know," he mused. "This was how it was meant to be. This was always our destiny."

I was sure he didn't truly believe that, but I nodded my head. "Thanks for sticking by me."

"Get real, Oscar. What else was I going to do?"

I smiled.

"You look like hell, by the way." He prodded at my bruised face.

I smiled again.

"So," he went on, "let's think up some last words."

I cleared my throat. "I regret not the things I've done, but those I did not do—"

"Snooze."

I tried again. "Et tu, Brute?"

He rolled his hand for me to continue.

"Last words are for fools who haven't said enough?"

Caicus sniggered. "How about, 'Either that wallpaper goes, or I do!' "

I laughed. "Yeah, that about sums up my life."

"Hey," his eyes lit up playfully, "I bet you go first."

I snorted. "Bet *you* do."

We trundled along, humming the tune to that Sinatra song, My Way.

Hmm. I think I just found my last words.

I did it my way.

BY THE TIME WE REACHED the manor, I felt like I'd done ten rounds in the ring. I'd taken a hammering from Marco, and now my body was more-or-less running on pure adrenaline.

Caicus and I stepped onto the gravel and I let out a slow whistle at the sight of Mary's overturned minivan.

"Brother spat his dummy out," Caicus commented.

"Yup."

I looked around. The house was dark and vacant. Across the waterlogged lawn, I could see Mary's flower garden. The quaint rose bushes suddenly seemed sinister, as though the gale had bent them into distorted, hideous figures.

"Now what?" Caicus asked, shoving his hands into his pockets.

I feigned confidence. "We wait for Lathiaus to show up."

Caicus groaned impatiently. "Any idea when that'll be?"

I rolled my eyes. "How should I know? I'm not his PA."

He huffed. "Well, it's almost midnight. Shouldn't he be here by now?"

I listened to the secret sounds of the night. "He'll be here," I muttered. "You summoned him. He'll be here."

Across the yard, the manor door flew open. Caicus and I jumped, caught unawares.

I was even more shocked when I saw who came pelting through the door.

Rose!

"What are you doing out here?" I yelled at her, gripping

my head in dismay.

She raced over to me and flung her arms around me.

I returned her embrace. "What are you doing out here?" I asked again, tenderly now. "I told you to go to the tree house."

"Oh, I didn't go," she replied simply.

Figures. Nobody listens to me.

"Go now," I implored her. "There's still time."

She drew away from me and gasped at the sight of my face.

"What happened to you?" she cried. "You're bleeding—everywhere!" She glanced at Caicus, who kind of waved at her.

"Marco," I answered. "Sibling rivalry."

"Where is he?" Rose pressed.

I shared a look with Caicus. "Taking a nap."

"Bashed him with the exhaust!" Caicus hooted.

Rose furrowed her brow, confused and probably shaken.

"It's okay," I assured her, twining my fingers through her hair.

I wouldn't have expected her to kiss me with a face like that, so I was pleasantly surprised when she did. It hurt a little—but in a good way.

"I'm so happy to see you," she breathed.

"I'm happy to see you, too. You have to go, though."

"Too late," I heard Caicus murmur.

A tearing sound came from the forest, and before our eyes, one of the trees uprooted and soared through the air like a javelin. It crashed into the house, shattering the windows.

Rose shrank back, and I angled myself in front of her.

"Lathiaus?" she choked.

"No," I muttered, shaking my head. I raised my voice. "Marco!" I shouted into the shadowy evergreens. "Fight *with* us on this. We're not the enemy. Lathiaus is."

"Oscar," Caicus whispered, edging closer to me, "I can't see him."

I kept my eyes fixed to the trees, watching for any sign of movement. I saw a flash of blond hair, and the next thing I knew, Marco stood before us.

"Help us," I appealed quickly. "Fight alongside us."

Marco glowered at me. His chalky eyes were rabid, bloodthirsty. He was past the point of reason.

However, if there was one thing I knew about Marco, it was that he was painfully predictable. And it didn't take a genius to suss out his next move. He'd go for Rose. And he'd be going for a quick kill.

As he lunged forward, I turned my shoulder on him, using my body like a shield. I managed to knock Marco backwards. But he was by no means beaten.

I held my ground as he charged again. This time he went for me. He gripped me by the throat and effortlessly tossed me aside.

I hit the gravel with an excruciating smack.

As I clambered to my feet, I was surprised—and grateful—to see that Caicus had thrown himself in front of Rose. Alas, his gallant gesture didn't last long. Marco batted him away with the flick of a wrist. Caicus was hurled through the air, landing on the grass and sliding along with the momentum until he crashed into a tree trunk.

"I'll get to you next," Marco threatened him.

While Caicus staggered to his feet, I pulled Rose out of the way.

Marco growled and thundered towards me.

Again he clamped his hand around my throat and lifted me off the ground. I scrambled to get my footing, but Marco held me high.

Rose pounded her fists on Marco's back, but to him she was nothing more than a pesky fly.

As I rasped for air, I scanned the yard for Caicus. He stood motionless, his face ashen. But he wasn't looking at us. Something else held his attention. And I was willing to bet it was something big.

All of a sudden, the ground began to shudder. At first it came in short, sharp bursts, but it swiftly progressed into a low, continuous ripple.

Earthquake? No such luck.

I didn't waste time asking questions. Instead I took the opening to clout Marco around the head. Startled, he released his grip and dropped me to the gravel.

Rose was immediately at my side. I drew her closer. I needed her closer. Something immense was about to go down.

Understatement.

Actually, it was surreal the way it happened; it was as though the world stood still for a moment. The war between our little group took intermission and all eyes gravitated towards Mary's flower garden. It was as if there was a magnetic pull beyond our control. As witches, when we sensed true evil, we found it very hard not to stare.

I set my focus on one of the rose bushes. The long-stemmed flowers swayed, crooked and arched, almost as though they were trying to take human form.

"That's him," Rose murmured.

I didn't reply. There was no need to. Instead, I watched as what had once been an innocent rose bush began to warp and grow into a giant skeleton swathed in a long, black robe. Its beady black eyes peered out at us, visible even in the dark of night.

Rose clung to my arm and I linked my fingers over hers.

Lathiaus was there. In the flesh. Or lack of flesh, as the case may be.

He lurched across the lawn with a stride that appeared rusted and stilted. The closer he got, the clearer I could see his rotten, ivory bones and his claw-like, hooked fingers. What repulsed me most of all, though, was that his jagged teeth remained perfectly intact, despite the rest of his body having long succumbed to decay.

Rose looked at me, and I looked back at her.

I saw her through the rain, incomparably beautiful and eternally etched on my mind.

"I'm not afraid," she said. "Tell me I'm not afraid." She kind of smiled, shivering at the same time.

I smiled back in a similar, jittery way. "You're not afraid," I reassured her. "And neither am I."

With my gaze so absorbed in Rose, I barely noticed Marco swooping in on us. And that was something I'd never forgive myself for.

He took Rose and flung her across the yard.

My heart stopped.

"No!" I cried as she collided against the minivan. In an instant I was beside her, stooped over her protectively. She was unconscious, but breathing.

Marco darted towards us again.

"Oscar, look out!" Caicus shouted.

I held my arm up and, using the last of my dwindling strength, I struck our attacker away.

He tumbled backwards onto the gravel. But it didn't keep him down for long. In seconds, he was on his feet and blind with rage. He was feral now—and clearly couldn't see sanity from lunacy, because, to my surprise, he went for Lathiaus.

The demon extended one withered ivory finger and curved it into a hook shape.

Marco stopped in his tracks. Then something strange happened. Marco clutched at his stomach, suddenly gripped by agony. As his pain worsened, his cries grew louder and more tortured. The sound was like nothing I'd ever heard before. It was unimaginable.

No matter what issues I'd had with Marco—and believe me, I'd had many—there wasn't a soul in the world who would not have felt empathy for his suffering. I glanced at Caicus and he looked back at me, helplessly.

Marco crumpled to the ground, screaming and thrashing.

I covered Rose's ears. I was sure it wouldn't make much

difference, what with her being unconscious and all, but it was something I did nonetheless.

Across the yard, Lathiaus's unnerving smile broadened. It made me feel empty to look at him. Violated, even. I was looking into the face of evil. I was looking into the face of death—literally.

I held Rose close to me, distractedly rocking her back and forth. This was bad. Very bad. I snuck a glance at Caicus. He didn't look too healthy—although, for the first time, I noticed the advantage of his location.

Silently, I spoke to him, *Go,* I told him. *Get out of Millwood.* He was close enough to the forest to escape without being detected.

But he didn't budge. He didn't even blink. He was frozen to the spot in terror.

I weighed up the odds of saving Marco. I knew it would be tricky at best, if it was even possible at all. I knew I'd have to try, though. What could I say? I was a glutton for punishment.

Sadly, the decision was made for me; I didn't get the chance to try. Marco's number was up.

He let out a gut-wrenching howl. Through his open mouth came an explosion of flames, which spilt over his body until he was engulfed by them.

I bowed my head away from the disturbing scene, and hoped, for Caicus's sake, that he was doing the same.

I had to admit, to my shame, that I was completely powerless. By the time I returned my focus to Marco, there was nothing left of him but a pile of ashes, extinguished by the rain.

Lathiaus basked in the glory of his kill. The slaughter seemed to have strengthened him. His corroded body moved differently now, prowling forward with a serpent-like slither. His clawed fingers massaged the air as he approached us.

It was hard not to gawp at his face, mostly because he was so damn revolting. I retched at the sight of maggots teeming in and out of his mouth and around his eyes, feeding off the parched bone.

Go! I ordered Caicus, willing him to move. *Run!*

With a slow creak of his neck, Lathiaus turned upon his next victim.

Caicus.

The demon pointed his finger, then bent and twisted it into a hook—just as he had done with Marco.

"No," I staggered to my feet.

He was going to kill Caicus.

I left Rose beside the minivan and sped out into the open. Now I stood staunchly in the path between Caicus and Lathiaus.

Run! I urged Caicus.

Oscar, I can't, his voice came back weakly. *He's going to kill us.*

Lathiaus's tormenting stare was on me now.

I tried to hold my nerve. *I'll buy you some time,* I assured Caicus. *Just get out of here. And take Rose with you.*

I'm not leaving you here! he whimpered.

I gave him a fleeting look. *Go. And don't let anything*

happen to Rose.

It was funny what I learned about myself when I was facing death. Like, I actually was stubborn. Wasn't that a kicker? I'd spent eighteen years denying it, only to admit it in my final hour.

I rubbed my hands together. "Okay, bones," I said to Lathiaus. "You don't look all that. Do your worst."

Taunting a demon? I really needed to sew my mouth up sometimes. Nah. Too restrictive. I'd take death, thanks.

Lathiaus bared his teeth at me.

"Lovely," I muttered, gagging at the view.

He extended his finger and curved it upwards.

The pain came quicker than I'd anticipated. It was instant. And it was not like anything I'd ever experienced before, either. It burnt from the inside, as though my blood was boiling and my organs were on fire.

I clenched my teeth, fighting the urge to cry out. My legs buckled and I dropped to the ground. I was on the gravel now, my head spinning and my mouth filling with blood. And, to my dismay, I realised I was screaming.

I vaguely heard Caicus's sobs, but I could barely hear anything above my own cries. I thought of two things: one being, *Run, Caicus, you moron*! And the other being, *Rose.*

And then I heard her voice, smoother and more fluent than it had ever been. So much so, it made me wonder if she was an angel, coming to take me to the other side.

"Stop," she said, quite simply.

The pain stopped.

I opened my eyes, but all I saw was gravel, and my body

didn't seem to obey my order to move. So I lay there, looking at the granules of stone.

"I'm the one you want," she stated calmly. "Come here."

"Rose, I can't," I tried to speak, but my throat was singed. "Where are you?" There was no way she could have heard me. Even *I* couldn't hear me.

She spoke again. "Come here, *now.*" It was only then that I realised she had not been talking to me.

From where I lay, wrecked and immobilised, I saw Lathiaus pass me, gliding towards the minivan.

My heart began to race.

Caicus! I called frantically. *What's going on? Am I dead?* Apparently my silent voice had a lot more potency than my vocal one.

Oscar? his words came back to me. *You look dead, but I don't think you are. How do you feel?*

I feel dead. What's going on? I used all of my willpower to tilt my head just enough to see across the yard.

Rose has summoned Lathiaus to her, Caicus explained.

Through my bleary eyes, I surveyed whatever was in my line of vision. In a nutshell, Rose backing away from the minivan as the demon closed in on her.

"Rose!" I tried to shout, but it translated as a feeble groan.

I heard her speak. "Two will take her to him," she began reciting the prophecy, "and all will be spared." She paused. "Well, one took me to you. Will that do?"

I held my breath. What was she thinking? This was suicide. I expected to hear her screams at any moment. And there would be nothing I could do about it. This was, hands down, the most petrifying moment of my life.

"One took me to you," she repeated, talking only to Lathiaus. "Oscar took me to you. I went all the way back to 1692. Do you remember that year, Lathiaus Rapp? It was the year you killed your first witch. The year that set you on course to become a cold-blooded demon."

'Two will take her to him, and all will be spared'? Oh hell.

Could that be true? I wondered desperately. *Our salvation doesn't depend on us sacrificing her to him—it depends on us performing the Retracing spell?*

Caicus's voice drifted into my mind. *Do you think she's right?* he asked urgently. *Do you think we were wrong all this time?*

I wasn't ready to respond yet. Was it possible that centuries of witches had read the prophecy wrong? Were we really that stupid?

'Two will turn away, and all will be slaughtered.' Oh hell. We were that stupid.

Two will turn away, I replied to Caicus. *Not turn away from our duty, but turn away from* her! *Two will turn away from her, and all will be slaughtered.*

So, what does this mean? he pressed.

It means we're idiots. We pretty much misunderstood every line of that entire cursed prophecy!

Hey, lucky you're such a pain-in-the-ass rule breaker, then, he teased. *Does this mean we've won?*

I felt the gravel move as my lips tried to smile. But my

rejoicing was premature. There was another line to the prophecy. A line which I would rather have forgotten.

'Before the hour turns to twelfth, she must grant him her death.'

We have to help her! I appealed to Caicus. I hated my limbs for refusing to comply.

Wait, Caicus responded, with an air of nonchalance. *I want to see where she's going with this.*

Caicus! I was outraged by his remark.

Shh, he hushed me. *Give her some credit. She is the prophecy girl, after all.*

"I'm told that I have to grant you my death," Rose carried on, oblivious to our muted conversation—and seemingly oblivious to us as well. "I don't want to do that, so I'll give you the chance to leave now. Go back and lay to rest."

Oh good God, she's crazy.

The poor girl had officially cracked. She thought Lathiaus was going to listen to a peace talk? That he was going to suddenly see the light and say, 'Okay, I'm off back to hell, catch you on the next demonic rising'?

Rose kept going, "I'm giving you a choice."

I squinted to see her. My vision was blurred and my eyes stung, but I couldn't let her down. I had to fight through this.

Through my distorted sight, I observed Lathiaus stretching out his arm and curling his finger into that lethal hook.

"No!" The word came out that time. Though I didn't

know how loud it was, because no one paid me the slightest iota of attention. No change there, then.

Caicus, help me, I begged. *Do something! Put me in Lathiaus's path. Don't let him hurt Rose.*

There was no response.

"Caicus!" I managed to get another word out. But the sheer effort of it sapped me. Why wasn't he answering?

What's going on? I demanded.

Finally his voice came back. *Nothing.*

That wasn't a sufficient answer. *What do you mean?*

Nothing's happening. He's trying, but it's… it's not working.

Then Rose spoke. "Double jeopardy," she simplified. "I haven't read the book yet, but I think I get the gist. It's all about being prosecuted for the same crime twice. If you didn't commit the crime but you were still tried for it, then you can't get tried for it again." She shrugged her shoulders. "I was burnt for being a witch, but I wasn't one. And now you want to do it again." She wagged her finger disapprovingly at him. "By law of double jeopardy, you can't touch me this time." There was a brief hesitation. "And I'm guessing that's why I was immune to Caicus and Marco's powers, too. I was executed for being a witch, so now I'm out of bounds. I'm off the table."

Lathiaus made a strange guttural rumbling sound. The sound of an angry demon.

It was perhaps a good thing that I couldn't get up, because I probably would have collapsed right back down again. Was this really happening? Was she off the table?

Rose continued, coolly, "One last chance, Lathiaus

Rapp. Go back to where you came from. I don't want to grant you my death."

I saw Lathiaus's silhouette reflecting off the minivan. Even his reflection was intimidating. And Rose seemed so tiny compared to him, like a mouse facing a lion. But she held her ground.

Lathiaus turned his body, evidently bored of Rose now. What followed was a sound that made me wish for death.

Caicus let out a howl of distress.

Lathiaus had found a new toy.

Just as I was about to give up hope, Rose shouted, "I warned you."

My focus went to her. She was holding something, but I couldn't make out what it was. Well, not until a tiny flame flickered in her hand. She had matches. With a slow breath, she allowed the lit match to drop onto the driveway. I watched in awe as the flame instantly spread into fire, igniting on the oil spill of the overturned minivan. The flames travelled along the river of oil until they reached Lathiaus.

"This was my death," Rose told him, "and now I grant it to you."

The blaze reared up to him as though it had a mind of its own. Spitting fire leapt skywards, enveloping Lathiaus and swallowing him whole. He screeched and hissed for what felt like an eternity, and then… silence.

I closed my eyes. I was out of the game. And so was the demon.

The fire fizzled out in the rain, and all that was left of

Lathiaus was a black cloak and a putrid heap of bones.

Grant him her death. Ha. That she did.

There was a long hush. I couldn't have found the words, even if I'd had the voice to speak them. I was woozy, and my eyelids felt like lead.

I took a final peek, just in time to see Caicus walk over to the remains. He stomped on the debris, turning the bones into nothing more than dust that would wash away with the rain.

It was over.

"Rose, you vanquished Lathiaus," Caicus said, looking at her in awe. "You'll go down in history as a hero... Hey, if anyone ever asks, will you tell them I did it?"

And then I lost consciousness.

EPILOGUE

Christmas Day

MY NAME IS OSCAR VALERO.

That's one of the three things I know for sure.

The other two are these:

One—It's snowing.

Two—My heart is incomplete.

I trudged inside from the winter snow, passing beneath the grand, arched doorway. My footsteps echoed off the high stone ceilings and marble floors.

Home bitter home.

In fact, it wasn't until I'd experienced life in a *real* home that I'd noticed how much like a museum this place was. I supposed it actually had been a museum at one stage. Before we staked our claim on it.

I kept walking, ascending a wide marble staircase. My shoes clicked on the floor. I missed carpet. Good old soundproof carpet. A few of the elders passed me, heading in the opposite direction, but we didn't acknowledge one another. That was nothing new. They thought me to be insolent. I thought them to be pompous. Eh, it was swings and roundabouts.

I strode along the first floor and followed the corridor around. If this really had been a museum, the exhibition rooms were now our bedchambers. Saying that, most of the bedrooms resembled exhibitions even now. Mine was okay. It was *me*. Lots of dark colours—browns mainly. It was fairly big. You know, standard for a dwelling like this. I had a balcony though, which I liked.

I reached my room and stepped inside, closing the door behind me. No more Christmas merriment. Just me.

I manoeuvred my way through the thin, brown drapes that marked the entrance to my balcony. Back outside again, the bite of frost stung my face. But it didn't bother me. I sat on my chair, high above the world, looking out onto the white blanketed mountains. I saw nothing else. No people. No animals. Just mountains. That was our world: no one got in, no one got out.

Okay, that wasn't entirely true. I could have left whenever I wanted. Although what would be the point? Hell, I had nowhere to go.

There was a scuffle at my bedroom door.

I groaned inwardly.

"Leave me alone," I muttered.

Caicus bounded in. His hair and clothes were dusted with snow. I expected mine were, too.

"Where did you go?" he asked, fumbling through the drapes to join me out on the balcony.

"To my room," I replied, deliberately stating the obvious.

He rolled his eyes. "It's Christmas. Come outside and play."

Now it was my turn to roll my eyes. "I don't want to *play.*"

"So, what do you plan on doing? Moping around up here all day?"

"Yes."

"Suit yourself." He shrugged, still in annoyingly high spirits. With a hop, he pounced onto the metallic railing of the balcony and jumped down onto the snow-coated ground below. It was a fifty-foot drop, so he really made a splash when he hit the bottom.

He whooped in delight and threw a snowball at me, then scampered off like an excitable puppy.

The missile shot past my head and exploded against the balcony wall. I scarcely glanced. It was obliterated now, just powder on the granite. How easy it was for something with such a seemingly solid mass to instantly reduce to nothing.

I closed my eyes indignantly.

I was a snowball.

I used to be a solid mass, ready to cause mayhem, but now I was spent, scattered and broken. Sure, my battle wounds had healed—the literal ones, anyway. They always did. It was only my heart that would not mend.

I wasn't looking for pity. I chose it to be this way. I chose to leave, and I chose never to recover. I sent myself to emotional purgatory. And that was where I was determined to reside.

After *that night,* what followed was merely a blur of irrevocable events. This was how I remembered them…

I regained consciousness around an hour after Lathiaus was vanquished. I was unable to move or speak, but Rose…

I winced. It hurt to think her name.

…Rose sat beside me through the night, easing the pain and listening patiently as I tried to speak. Gradually my body healed. By morning, my voice had returned, and my limbs were my own again. Mary and Roger came home and we spun them a yarn about storm damage.

"Uh, yeah, the storm knocked over your minivan. And, uh, it knocked a couple of holes in your dining room table, too." Et cetera.

They didn't question us. They were good people. They probably gave allowances to us, assuming the party had got a little out of hand. Which I supposed it had. Ha.

For a long time, I truly believed that I would stay with her. With Rose. I could picture it, in a blissfully ignorant sort of way. But even in my modest fantasies, it seemed too good to be true. In hindsight, it was too good to be true.

I think that realisation first came to me when Rose started griping about the bores of returning to school. I suddenly became aware that she was human. She had a human life, and she was fragile and precious. The severity of what I'd put her through began to dawn on me. I couldn't bear the thought of it. She was a human and I'd dragged her into a violent, ferocious world—one which she should *never* have been exposed to. It was reckless, selfish and irresponsible of me.

And what exactly did I plan on doing? Bringing her along on every mission I had? Taking her to every underworld battle that I'd be assigned to? Being a witch was a vocation. We were warriors. And she was just a girl.

It would have been cruel to take normality from her. How could I have done it? My altruistic side could see how much freedom was in her grasp, and what a great life she could have—and *should* have. I'd have envied her if I hadn't been so magnanimously in love with her.

So, I left. In the middle of the night. No warning. No goodbye. Hardly surprising, really. Goodbyes were too difficult for a coward like me. Instead, while she was sleeping, I snuck into her room and placed my half of the silver heart on her pillow, then I kissed her head and walked. And I didn't stop.

Once we were out of Millwood, Caicus charmed us a car. It wasn't a Lamborghini Gallardo, but it was okay. We didn't speak on the journey home. He drove, and I stared out the window.

When we returned to the coven, we told them everything: about Marco, Rose, Lathiaus… We didn't get the heroes' welcome we'd hoped for. They kind of nodded and reluctantly congratulated us. A few of them were peeved about Marco—not because they cared for him, but because he was a damn good combatant. I could vouch for that.

As the weeks passed by, I thought only of Rose. Sometimes I considered going to her, but I never did. And I knew that she wouldn't find me. That was another thing about being a witch—you didn't get found.

The seasons changed and the leaves turned orange and fell from the trees. I watched their lives deteriorate until the trunks were all but bare. Their gradual demise happened alongside mine, so I took solace in them. We faded together.

And then the snow came, thick and heavy and not going anywhere anytime soon. People said that nothing would grow beneath the winter snow. That was me. Beneath snow. Standstill. I didn't grow. I didn't live. I was frozen.

Purgatory.

Caicus bashed on my door again.

"Go away!" I shouted.

From the balcony, I heard my bedroom door open and he stomped in.

I kept my gaze transfixed on the white mountains and the opaque silver sky.

"Go away," I sighed.

He halted at the gap in the drapes and lobbed something at the back of my head. It was small and sharp and sent a bolt of electricity down my spine.

I looked to the floor where the bullet lay.

What the…?

I spun around.

"You can have your stupid heart back," she said.

My jaw dropped. I didn't know if I smiled, or laughed, or wept…

"Rose," I whispered.

She paused. Her expression gave away the fact that she'd probably had a whole angry speech rehearsed, but was too thrown to remember any of it.

"I don't want it anymore," she blurted out. I guessed that was around line seven of her speech.

Actually, I wasn't having much luck, either. I'd had four months to think of all the things I would say to her if ever I saw her again, and yet there I was, my moment to shine, and all I could come up with was, "Hi."

Line, please?

"Hi," she said back. "I'm very angry at you."

I nodded my head. But it was hard to look understanding while beaming with joy.

"I'm very angry at me too," I offered.

"How could you leave like that?" she demanded.

I stood up now, face to face with her where she hovered, veiled behind the thin drapes.

"I wanted you to have a better life," I told her honestly.

She didn't seem to like that.

"You *ruined* my life," she screamed at me. "You took away the thing I love most."

"Caicus?" I tried to joke.

Uh, oh. That didn't go down well. Eh, maybe she'll laugh later.

"Look," I said, sincerely, "I know what I put you through last summer, and I care about you too much to involve you in this world. It's dark and it's scary—"

"So what?" she snapped. "The world is always dark and scary. But it got a little brighter with you in it, and it got a little less scary, too."

"Less scary?" I raised my voice. "Don't you remember what you had to see? Death, violence, carnage beyond what you ever imagined possible—"

"Yes, I remember. I lived it. Because it was my life too.

And you had no right to take it away from me."

"I had every right. It's my responsibility to protect you."

"Since when!" she spluttered. "Who asked you to?"

"Since forever. Since I let you die the first time."

"The first time?" she frowned.

"Not this lifetime," I elaborated as best I could. "I mean, when I lost you before. I could have saved you."

Rose stared at me. "No, you couldn't have."

I kicked my balcony chair in frustration. "Yes, I could have."

"Did you go back? Did you do the Retracing spell, too?"

"I don't need to," I told her. "I carry the memory with me in every life."

She staggered backwards. "You remember it?"

"Not exactly. I don't know what happened back then, but somewhere in my subconscious, I know that I was to blame for your death. I've always known. How could I forget? How could I ever forgive myself for that?"

She touched the drapes as though she were reaching out to me. The anger began to fade from her eyes.

"Forgive yourself," she said softly. "It was my decision. And I'm going to keep making decisions, with or without you."

I snorted.

She carried on, "You saved my life."

"No, I risked it."

She smiled at me benevolently. "You stopped me from drinking the poison. You gave me the chance to fulfil my prophecy. Sorry, *our* prophecy," she corrected herself. "It was destined for us. If it hadn't been for you, I'd be dead by now, and the line of witches would be too. Why can't we celebrate that?"

I hung my head. "I don't want you in this world," I repeated adamantly.

"You don't want me in your world?" she asked.

I laughed bitterly. "My world doesn't exist without you." I bent down to pick up the two pieces of silver heart. And as I did, she stepped through the drapes, out onto the balcony.

I could see her clearly for the first time, and it was impossible not to stare. Not that I made any attempt to resist.

"That's our heart." The half-hearts were nestled in the palm of my hand. Rose pushed them together. "It's complete."

I swallowed.

She grazed her fingers against my chest, where my real heart pounded in exhilaration.

"I still want your half," she said.

I was crumbling inside. "You can always have my half."

My remark seemed to quieten both of us. For some minutes we stayed in our own thoughts, separate, but also very much together.

Rose smiled sadly at me. "I had to find you, Oscar," she said at last. "There were things I needed to say."

"And now that you've said them?"

"I'll leave."

"No," I murmured. "Don't go."

"I have to. You said it yourself, I don't belong in this

world."

"You belong with me," I blurted out.

I didn't wait for her response. I dropped the fractured heart onto the floor and pulled her into me, kissing her with every ounce of my being. A shower of feathery snowflakes sprinkled over us like beads of confetti. Perhaps I took that to be a sign, or perhaps I was merely tired of insisting I knew best, but from that moment on, everything changed.

"Let me come with you," I said. "Let me stay with you."

She blinked through her brimming tears. "Okay."

I grinned. "I'm running away with you," I declared.

Romantic gesture number fifty-two.

"Where?" she asked.

"Anywhere."

"Millwood?"

"Millwood," I agreed, still grinning. Quite frankly, I couldn't have wished for anywhere else.

She smiled up at me. "Then we should take Caicus with us."

I returned the smile.

"Rose?" I ventured, brushing a snowflake from her cheek. "How did you find me?"

She winked teasingly. "I have my ways."

"How?" I persisted.

She took my hands and held them to her. "You, Oscar Valero, are in my heart. You always have been, and you always will be. And *that* is how I found you."

BOOKS BY THE SAME AUTHOR:

How I Found You
Evanescent
Secrets in Phoenix
The Witches of the Glass Castle
The Witches of the Glass Castle: Uprising

For more information visit: www.gabriellalepore.com
Or follow on Twitter @GabriellaBooks #HowIFoundYou

Thanks for reading!

ACKNOWLEDGMENTS

Huge thanks to Sasha, Greg and Megan, who got out there in sub-zero temperatures to create the perfect Oscar and Rose cover photo. Troopers!

Thanks to the fantastic readers who share and swap! You are amazing and I'm so grateful for your support.

Thanks, as always, to my amazing family and friends: Lepores, Nelsons, Carters, Wynne-Jones/Oystens and the Fabulous Saunders of Whaley Bridge!

Love and thanks to my parents, who've followed every step; To my best squirrel Lorna (you don't), who always shares her food and deviously tricks me into watching way too many episodes of American Horror Story; To Louis, who still holds the record for longest phone call ever.

Special thanks to James, for everything. For fixing kettles and computers, and for thinking things through... because sometimes I don't ☺

Last but definitely not least, thanks to my amazing friend Ben, who believes that together we are unstoppable. I believe it too.

Love,
Gabriella xxx

13304038R00202

Printed in Poland
by Amazon Fulfillment
Poland Sp. z o.o., Wrocław